PRAISE FOR CHICAGO'S DESIGNS

Best…since The Devil in the White City

Peter Green's two central themes, Architecture and Chicago, are linked with magic. His descriptions of Chicago architecture, the city of big shoulders and mob activity are strikingly similar to my own observations as a young architect in Chicago. Green's insights into architectural practice are spot-on. Rich, exciting, fun and a real page turner, this is the best mystery of architecture and Chicago since The Devil in the White City   –Robert O. Little, Former President, Ittner Architects

Fast-moving action, architecture and romance

When a womanizing young architect meets a mobster with a multi-million dollar casino project and a beautiful daughter, what could go wrong? For Patrick MacKenna, "Chicago Joe's" plan to go legit is the career break he's been looking for, and dating the mobster's daughter is icing on the cake. Then Patrick finds himself attracted to a lovely barmaid fresh from Ireland, jeopardizing the deal and maybe even his life…This intriguing glimpse into Patrick's early years brings together fast-moving action, architecture and romance in a satisfying prequel to the Patrick MacKenna mystery/thriller series. --T.W. Fendley, Author of the Zero Time Chronicles

An architect and serious mystery reader

I am an architect and a serious mystery reader. So Mr. Green checked off two important boxes right away…kept it up and educated and entertained me the rest of the way.
—Randall B. Miltenberger, AIA , Miltenberger Architects

An uncanny ability...

Green has an uncanny ability to describe scenes, develop characters, and create suspense

—Nathan Manhart, Member, St. Louis Writers Guild

A terrific read!

Chicago's Designs is…riveting…a gripping whodunit about murder, the mob, sex and love. A terrific read!

—David Margolis, Author of T, The Myth of Dr. Kugelman and The Misadventures of Buddy Jones

ALSO BY PETER H. GREEN

BIOGRAPHY

Ben's War with the U. S. Marines
Radio: One Woman's Family in War and Pieces
(with Alice H. Green)

PATRICK MACKENNA MYSTERIES

Crimes of Design
Fatal Designs

CHICAGO'S DESIGNS

A PATRICK MacKENNA MYSTERY

PETER H. GREEN

GREENSKILLS PRESS

ST. LOUIS

Chicago's Designs, A Patrick MacKenna Mystery
By Peter H. Green

Publisher: Greenskills Press, St. Louis, MO

Copyright ©2019 by Peter H. Green

Cover Painting: Chicago Street Scene, North Side
Oil on hardboard, 32" x 40"
by Ben Green, 1965 ©2019 by Peter H. Green

Interior Book Design: Greenskills Press
Author Photo: Leigh Savage

Address comments and inquiries to:
Greenskills Press, Publisher
An imprint of Greenskills Associates, LLC
P. O. Box 11292, St. Louis, MO 63105
https: greenskills.net

First Edition

This is a work of fiction and is produced from the author's imagination. Any resemblance to specific individuals is purely coincidental. Real persons, places and things mentioned in this novel are used in a fictional manner.

ISBN-978-1-941402-15-3 Trade Paperback

Library of Congress Control Number: Applied for
Visit us on the web at www.authorpetergreen.com

For Alice and Ben Green
avid mystery fans
who taught us to love Chicago

Time this week calls Phillip Marlowe amoral. This is pure nonsense. Assuming that his intelligence is as high as mine (it could hardly be higher), assuming that his chances in life to promote his own interest are as numerous as they must be, why does he work for such pittance? For the answer to that is the whole story, the story that is always being written by indirection and yet is never written completely or even clearly. It is the struggle of fundamentally honest men to make a decent living in a corrupt society. It is an impossible struggle; he can't win. He can be poor and bitter and take it out in wisecracks and casual amours, or he can be corrupt and amiable and rude like a Hollywood producer. Because the bitter fact is that outside of two or three professions which require long years of preparation, there is absolutely no way for a man of this age to acquire a decent affluence in life without to some degree corrupting himself, without accepting that the cold, clear fact that success is always and everywhere a racket.

The stories I wrote are ostensibly mysteries. I did not write the stories behind those stories, because I was not a good enough writer. That does not alter the fact that Marlowe was a more honorable man than you or I. I don't mean Bogart playing Marlowe and I don't mean because I created him. I didn't create him. I've seen dozens like him in all essentials except the few colorful qualities he needed to be in this book. (A few even had those.) They were all poor; they will always be poor. How could they be anything else.

When you have answered that question you can call him a zombie.

—Raymond Chandler, Letter to John Houseman, film producer, circa October, 1949*

*Chandler, *Later Novels and Other Writings*, Library of America, Literary Classics of the United States (New York), 1955

CHICAGO'S DESIGNS
A Patrick MacKenna Mystery

Part I: A Nose for Trouble

One

If Patrick had been born in Chicago he might have known better than to date a gangster's daughter. Local kids learned that stuff in kindergarten. But just twenty-eight, fearless and a newly minted architect, he felt indestructible. Besides, what was not to love about this city's daring crime, beautiful women and breakthrough architecture? In "the city on the make," as writer Nelson Algren called it, he fit right in.

In those happy days before the millennium, global terrorism, destructive climate change and extremist right-wing governments were largely unknown. The greatest public fear back then was that, due to the custom of denoting years with two-digits instead of four, at the turn of the calendar at midnight on December 31, 1999, all the computer systems in the world would crash.

One Tuesday morning in June, Patrick MacKenna climbed to the elevated train platform. A molten sun beneath an angry cloud deck augured a coming blow. It shone cold and bright on his head, sheltered only by a thatch of thick brown hair.

Four-story taxpayer flats lined the cross street. Their street-level storefronts faced walks swarming with workers, vagrants, runners, dope dealers, delivery men and shop girls. Workers scurried, drove and rode bug-like to jobs in cafés, industrial plants, building sites and office cubes — if they were lucky. People awoke to resume routines, prepare children for school or plunge into their tasks. Some mourned loved ones cut down by automatic weapons fire, killed in drive-by shootings while playing on front porches or stolen and sold into the sex trade. Others were awakened by the dull roar of traffic under viaducts, in abandoned lofts, and under cardboard carton roofs on littered sidewalks. The plaint of far off sirens, thumping dumpsters, crunching metal, tinkling glass and grumbling engines sounded a prelude to the day. Through a distant slot beyond, the fiery sky glinted off the great inland sea that anchored the metropolis.

It was a city about as good or bad as any other, full of striving souls, burgeoning life, screaming pain and lonely death. A place rich, vigorous and proud, a city besieged, run down and defeated. "It all depends on where you sit and how you score," Patrick liked to tell Chet, his colleague and best friend. He didn't keep a tally. He didn't care — he couldn't and still face such a day.

A train arrived and he crowded into nearest sliding door. An enormous guy occupied most of the last available seat. Rather than squeeze in next to him and endure his garlic breath all the way downtown, Patrick chose to stand. He gripped a pole and swayed as the car jolted, twisted and turned. He scanned the ads at eye level on curved car cards above the windows. Bold headlines announced driving schools, arthritis cures and career "universities"—not exactly breaking news. He turned his attention to the day ahead. The rail car plunged into its subterranean tunnel, the lights flickered on and he reached his underground destination.

He emerged on the Dearborn Street sidewalk from the stifling, still air of the subway like a scuba diver surfacing for air and eased into the steady stream of pedestrians. Relief with a cooling gust off the lake came when he rounded the corner and headed east, but it blew a cinder into his eye. Further blinded by the sun's sudden glare down the man-made canyon, he stepped out of the flow of walkers behind a light pole, dabbed with a tissue and rolled his eyes up to catch the speck. The offending object gone, he blinked and resumed walking. And yet, glancing upward, he had spotted something oddly out of place. The handsome vertical stone panels concealing cast iron columns between rows of wide windows couldn't distract him from what he'd noticed on the platform. Wasn't the window washer wearing a fedora? He shrugged and figured, it takes all types to run this giant beehive of a town.

But he still would puzzle over it. Patrick had a nose for trouble. He'd made a hobby of visiting crime scenes and enjoyed hunting for clues, trying out alternative scenarios and seeking motives. Even at nine years old, he'd observed a traffic mishap at a street corner near his house and explained his take on how the crash occurred.

He crossed State on the green light with the human throng, cars, buses and taxis screeching to a halt to his left and right. Safe on the opposite walk, he let a stout secretary in high-heeled boots run interference over to Wabash. He dodged a newsstand, elevated train stanchions and wrong-way walkers and plunged into an archway beneath the sign, MacKenna's Irish Pub: Friends You Haven't Met Yet, and descended seven steps to the family business.

"You look like hell, little boss." Dermot glanced up from loading beer bottles into the cooler under the bar. "You get lucky last night?"

"You should talk, Mr. Death-Warmed-Over. Aren't you here kinda early for the night shift?" Two a.m. closing was only the beginning of Dermot's nightly prowl with his unsavory pals.

"Your pa wants me here to stow the beer delivery and help train the new crop of Irish kids. Tomorrow's Ladies' Night. We need all the help we can get."

"You get a look at 'em?" Patrick made it his business to meet the new immigrants Pa brought over from Ireland to work and entertain in the pub. To the delight of patrons, they waited tables, sang and played their authentic Irish music. The pay was low but tips were good. Besides, who'd pass up a chance to come to America and start a new life in the big city? It seemed like a fair bargain to all concerned. He enjoyed meeting these youths from his birth country and loved showing them around their new city.

"Just briefly yesterday. One redhead with freckles is a real beauty. But she ain't stacked like Gloria. I doubt if you'll even notice her."

"Uncle Mike was crazy to hire her for his office," Patrick said. "But you've gotta admit, he sure knows how to pick 'em. Turns out she's perfect for the job, and it has only taken her a year-and-a-half to learn how to type."

"Very funny. You ever get tired of her, you let me know."

"Like she'd even give you the time of day." He glanced at the doors to the kitchen. "My folks here yet?"

"They got here early. She's tending to her corned beef and cabbage. And he's back there somewhere." He pointed a thumb over his shoulder and heaved another case of beer on the bar.

Patrick stiff-armed the "IN" leaf of the leather-padded double swinging doors. His mother issued rapid fire instructions to the cook while she poured a bowl of spices into a huge pot. "Speak o' the devil," she said. "Your father wants a word before you dash off to work."

Seamus MacKenna sat at his desk in his tiny office next to the kitchen, scanning the day's news, his slatted wood chair tilted back on two legs.

"What's up, Pa?"

Seamus glanced up to greet Patrick and held up the front page. "Look at this." The lead story screamed in bold type: NEWSPAPER HEIR MISSING—FOUL PLAY SUSPECTED, By Mona Strong. "Didn't you once date that girl? She was quite a looker, as I recall." He wasn't so old he'd lost his eyesight.

"A few times." They'd had a brief fling a couple of years ago. "It says: 'Walter McDougal Howe, an heir to the newspaper fortune of the Marvell-McDougal family, founders of this newspaper, was reported missing yesterday when he failed to arrive for an appointment at his bank, on a stop in Chicago on his way back home to Washington, D. C.'"

Seamus, a portly man, with bushy brows above warm brown "Black-Irish" eyes — that is, Hispanic, a result of the wreck of the Spanish armada off the Irish coast in 1588— tilted precariously in his chair, over-stressing the oak back legs.

"She was a beauty all right," Patrick mused on, ignoring his father's reading. "But hard as I tried, I couldn't trust her."

It was more serious than that. It wasn't until he'd started taking her out that he'd discovered it. He'd been pleased she'd accepted his invitation. An overachiever and smart, after years of attending tedious City Council meetings, covering lost pets, weddings and funerals, and once, a cow that escaped from a cattle truck and ran loose in the streets for hours, she'd worked her way up the ladder. Now she was involved in the city's mainstream, reporting the day's most important stories. With her gossipy style, her news-hungry paper had promoted her to lead reporter. He liked her stimulating conversation, not to mention the effect her nubile body generated in his fit, young frame. But whenever he discussed his hopes for the future, any tidbit he dropped about a new project he was working on or a crime scene he visited ended up in the paper, often on the front page. Much as she needed to scoop her rivals in the competitive news business, he couldn't convince her that keeping *his* job was as important as how she did hers.

"You ought to read article anyway. It's right up your alley."

"Right, Pa, I'll read it later. This morning I've got to run to a meeting."

"We'll need you here right after work tomorrow night. It's Ladies' Night. You can help the new waiters and the crowds of Happy Hour."

"You think I'd miss meeting them?"

"Doubtful, I'm sure. But you'll have to cut short the social niceties. You'll have yer hands full just to keep the drinks and the food flowin'."

"No problem. You know *me*."

"Don't I, now? That's why a bit o' remindin' never hurts."

"Later, Pa."

◊

In the kitchen, Seamus fumed.

"Cocky young kid. He's not as smart as he thinks."

"Now Seamus," Lily insisted. "do you remember when your father made you quit school, so you could work in his pub?"

"And it made a man of me. I always tried to bring up Patrick right. I made sure he worked hard, helped us in the pub, and acted honestly and responsibly."

"At least we've allowed him to get a good education." In fact, despite her husband's objections, she had scrimped to put away funds for college.

"It turned out lucky for me. He let me work and left the business to me, besides."

"And you won't let your son have a better chance?"

"Sure, and now he's a high-falutin' architect. Ha! That's all we need in this family: a college man who thinks he's better than the rest of us. He'll never work hard enough to beat out his competition in this town. I wonder if he could even run this pub."

"I've been devoting some thought to that, too," Lily said. "When we get ready to retire, Mike's daughter Julie, with her interest in singin' and performin', might have a flair for running the place."

"Huh? Where did that come from? She's still in school, and I'm a long way from thinking about retirement."

"Just saying, Patrick has been a big help to us, but if he's going to make a success in the design field. it doesn't seem likely he'll want to take over here."

"That's my doing. I would always tell him to stick with it. You know—bash on, regardless."

Two

Patrick walked briskly west on Monroe toward his uncle's construction company in the Old Dominion building in the southwest corner of the Loop, designed by his firm over a century earlier. He hoped it would be a new assignment. Uncle Mike said it was a surprise and wouldn't give him a clue. Just yesterday, Jason Halliday had called him into his office and warned that the firm's architectural workload was getting dangerously low. If they couldn't find more work soon, they'd have to lay off some of the hand-picked staff they'd worked so hard to assemble in recent years.

When he was not dodging other pedestrians, Patrick looked up at every opportunity. He passed the Monadnock Block. His uncle had told him on one of their Saturday tours it was the last bearing wall skyscraper. Its walls bulged gracefully outward in a sweeping curve toward the base, thickened to bear the increasing loads added at each floor. Turning on State, he marveled at the Reliance, one of the first iron skeleton buildings. Unlike those cramped, recessed windows of the Monadnock, its glass bay windows and walls of thinnest stone, freed of their structural role, billowed outward like sails on the lake, taking in light and glinting in the morning sun. On their Saturday jaunts, Uncle Mike had explained how a skeleton support structure and Elisha Otis's safety-brake elevators had made it all possible. H. H. Richardson, William Holabird, Martin Roche, John Root and others like them were Uncle Mike's' heroes.

Now they had become his own.

He still wondered, though, about Chicago's architectural pioneers. Weren't they also worried about getting enough work to stay in business? He recalled learning how the master architect Louis Sullivan was sidelined when New York architects horned in and took over the design of the 1893 World's Fair. They decided on a Greek revival theme for the buildings, giving this master architect the design of the Transportation Building as a consolation prize. He ignored their classical revivalism and produced the only example of the new Chicago style in the fair. Also, when Sullivan discovered that his talented young assistant Frank had been designing houses for other clients outside the office—siphoning off potential revenue with his "bootleg" projects—he fired him, causing Frank Lloyd Wright to start his own firm and make architectural history.

Caught in the Monroe Street crosswalk when he lost the green light, Patrick was roused from his musing by honks from motorists. He reached the place where he had glanced up at the scaffold and spotted the dressy window washer earlier this morning. A couple of uniformed officers had lowered the unoccupied platform to the sidewalk. They were rigging crime scene tape and placing cone barriers around the scaffold. Two police cars sat at the curb, blue dome lights flashing. Another patrolman directed traffic around the police cars, while a fourth stood guard at the building entrance, taking names and issuing instructions to those entering and leaving.

"What's going on here?" Patrick asked him.

"Crime scene upstairs. You want to know more, you'll have to ask the sergeant." He nodded toward a plainclothesman talking to two other cops by the decorative brass entry doors.

He approached the detective with the same question.

"We got a situation inside. You go in, you gotta give the officer there your name."

"Funny, as I was walking past here a while ago, I happened to look up at the window washer scaffold and saw a man in a suit and a stylish hat. Too well-dressed for a window washer."

"T'aint funny, McGee," said the Irishman in the suit. "Mind giving me a statement?"

"Sure, no problem." He followed the detective into the building and through an open elevator door. "Name's MacKenna," he said, "Patrick MacKenna, architect."

"Detective Sergeant Matthew O'Malley." The cop stuck out his hand to meet Patrick's. "You work nearby?"

"Not far away. I was just headed over to my uncle's construction office."

At the third floor the detective stepped from the car and led him down the hallway. They turned right along the front of the building, parallel to the street, and faced a door with Fabrizio D. Angionomo, Criminal Attorney, painted on the frosted glass. In the anteroom a half-dozen reporters badgered a cop on guard for details. "Hey Sergeant. you're right on time. Baldwin just arrived. He's in there." The policeman pointed to the inner office.

"Okay, pipe down, boys," the detective told the group. "As soon as the coroner is finished looking around, I'll come back out here and give you a statement."

"I beg your pardon." A female voice rose above the din. "We're not all boys, except my photographer here, and he needs a picture."

Oh, crap. Patrick froze. He knew that voice. He almost hadn't recognized her with her clothes on. But now in front of the herd of hacks stood a familiar figure, her well-formed body barely concealed from his practiced eye by a fire engine red wrapper and a new bobbed hairdo.

"I said I'll let you know," O'Malley repeated. "That includes you, Miss Strong."

She glanced toward Patrick, who stood next to the detective "Oh, it's you," she said. "Looking for architectural clients, Patrick? Too late, again!" The wise-guy reporters erupted in a roar of laughter.

"You know him?" O'Malley asked Mona.

"Oh, yeah. He's always looking for trouble."

O'Malley pushed him through the inner door and closed it behind them. Patrick was grateful for the reprieve. Until he looked around.

Warm, stuffy air in the office, redolent of telltale copper, made it hard for Patrick to breathe. His gorge rose and his eyes watered at the image swimming before him, like a dream scene in a movie. A wiry little man drew curious implements from an open briefcase on a corner of the desk. His quick movements nonetheless made a wide berth around the central figure in the scene.

In the silent room, the lawyer, draped into an ancient wood swivel chair, said nothing. His head lolled back against a bookcase full of law journals. A single red circle dotted the center of his forehead. The back of his skull had exploded on the dusty tomes.

"Looks like Illinois 2nd 1984 will have to be replaced." Patrick said.

"Nah, he won't need it." O'Malley nodded toward the body.

"What's he doing in here?" the mousy functionary raised his prominent snout and squeaked in a sharp nasal tone. "This is a crime scene, O'Malley. You should know better." Even the down-at-heel gumshoe looked uneasy. What had he been thinking when he allowed Patrick to enter?

The flummoxed flatfoot, fresh off his encounter with the occupants of the outer office, struggled to explain. "He's a material witness. I've got to question him."

The ferret-faced medical examiner shrugged. In shirtsleeves and a black vest, he bent his balding head and returned to his task. He dusted the desk for fingerprints with swift-moving rodent-like claws.

"Got anything, Baldwin?"

"Not much. No sign of the murder weapon. Seems like a small service pistol, though."

O'Malley reached for the victim's right pants pocket

"Ah-ah-ah-aaah, no you don't," the medical examiner warned. "My photographer isn't here yet. You can't disturb the scene."

Ferret-face was fussy. The detective withdrew his hand.

"Get his prints, check his ID and make sure he's the guy with his name on the door," O'Malley barked, asserting control of the scene. "Now get busy. We'll be in here." The detective led Patrick through a side door to a vacant adjacent office.

He closed it behind him and took the secretarial chair, motioning Patrick to the only other seat in the room. "The young lady seems to know you pretty well."

"Too well. I'm afraid to spend time with her— it will end up in the paper."

"Yeah. Besides, she seldom gets the story straight." He leaned forward over the desk with his notepad. "So, what did this character look like?"

"Dark suit, burly frame. He wore a fedora. With a red feather in the band. He ran to the next window, in a big hurry. Some window washer! Couldn't figure out what he was doing up there."

"Might have something to do with this." He waved toward the office next door.

"By the way, how did you find out about this?" Patrick tried to sound casual.

"Our tip line. Plenty of good citizens out there are willing to report this stuff—anonymously."

"Sure, who'd want to get mixed up in something like this?"

"You don't seem to mind. Is she right, you always find trouble?"

"Hey, she's the ambulance chaser. I'm curious about crime, kind of a hobby of mine. Just ran into her at a couple of scenes. She seemed too tasty to pass up."

"Can't blame you. I wouldn't kick her out of bed." A faraway look crept into his eyes, which briefly lost their riveting stare. Perhaps he was longing for earlier times, when many fine women would have fought for a chance to meet this hardy young officer of the law.

"I get it—not worth the high maintenance."

"She's trouble—a mine of misinformation

"I'm familiar."

"Case in point," Patrick said, "what did you think of her story on the missing newspaper heir, what's-his-name?"

"Oh, Howe? Too soon to know anything about that. Look, I gotta go back in there and finish our investigation. It's got all the signs of a mob hit." He handed him his card. "You think of anything else, you call me, hear?"

"Will do, Sergeant."

The detective went back into the inner office. Patrick sat for moment memorizing the room and wondering how O'Malley kept his badge. He certainly wasn't the brightest bulb in the set, and he'd seen way too many gangster movies. He would have expected one of Chicago's finest, at least one on the detective force, to make a thorough search of this office for clues.

A sidearm extending from the metal desk held a computer and

keyboard. A double-decked In-Out basket, calendar-desk cover and its occupant's nameplate faced him on the otherwise empty desktop. Careful not to touch it, he read the letter on top of the stack.

```
May 18, Walter McDougal Howe, Page 2

    Regardign the matter of the miss-
    ing stock certificates, as you have
    instructed, I will search avail-
    able corporate and public records
    related to the search and the oth-
    er tasks you have assigned. Sicne
    some of the records date back over
    100 years, this may require sub-
    stantil researcj time.

    My billing rate is $150.00 (one-hun-
    dred-fifty dollars) per hour expnd-
    ed on behaf of these matters. A
    retainer of $1,000 (one-thousand
    dollars) will be requrd to start
    work.

    If the above terms and conditions
    are acceptable, please sign and
    return one copy of this letter
    with your check and we will begin
    work immedaitely.

    Sincerely,


    Fabrizio D. Angionomo

    Attorney at Law


    Accetped by: _____________________

    Date: _______________________________
```

The letter was dated three weeks ago. The nameplate facing him on the desk read: GERTRUDE SIMMS. He wondered why Ms. Simms was not in the office today. The letter looked as if it been typed by Gloria in her early days. What kind of legal secretary would fail to catch such obvious typographical errors? The lawyer must have typed it himself. He cheated on his rule and lifted the top sheet. The front page of the letter was missing. He left by a door to the waiting room, plowed through the paparazzi and retraced his steps along the corridor. Already a half-hour late, he summoned the elevator. A smartly dressed woman arrived from the direction he had come, smiled at him and pressed the Down button.

"It should be here any minute," he said.

"Pretty grim scene in there?" the woman asked.

"Bad enough." He looked away.

"So I heard. The detective stopped by to ask me about it. I told him what I knew—about the commotion coming from his office this morning."

"Detective O'Malley seemed open to my help. Do you by any chance know Ms. Simms, the lawyer's secretary?"

"Why, yes. Gertrude worked for Mr. Angionomo. When he was in court, we used to meet for lunch. I haven't seen her this week, though. She told me she was going on vacation. Then — this happened. So sad." She forced a sympathetic smile.

The elevator arrived and the doors parted. He followed her into the car. "I'm Patrick MacKenna, by the way. Can you tell me how to contact Ms. Simms?"

"I think I have her home number and contact file. Here's my card. Call me after three this afternoon and I'll be glad to give it to you."

He glanced at the card:

Downtown Verdict Reporter, LLC
Angela Atkins, Manager
• Computerized Research
• Settlement Reporting
• New Suit Filings

"I'll do that, Ms. Atkins. Did you know the victim?"

"Yes. I-I can't believe it." Her voice faltered. "Besides, I've lost a client."

"Somehow we carry on." He smiled in sympathy as she stepped out of the elevator. Her elegant business suit accentuated a full bust, small waist and swaying hips. He followed her, enjoying the view of her shapely legs as she walked briskly ahead of him through the double brass doors and out of sight. He turned left and passed the lone remaining police guard. A half-hour late, he dashed in the direction of his uncle's office.

THREE

At MacKenna Construction Enterprises, Patrick stood before Gloria's desk. A low-cut, tailored blouse, a wide belt cinching her tiny waist and a split skirt revealed a shapely figure, a delicious amount of cleavage and gracefully crossed thighs.

"Patrick, you're late—as usual."

"This time I have a really good excuse—you know I can't pass up a murder scene."

"A murder—where?"

"In an office right up the street. I got a look at the stiff on my way over this morning.

"No sh— uh, my goodness! You sure can find trouble."

"I found you, didn't I?" He gestured toward Mike's office, "He in there?"

"He's ready for you."

"Don't lose the place," he cooed, grazing her cheek with his fingertips.

"Later, please." she teased.

"Saturday night we're going to Antonio's, Remember our first date—their divine chicken tetrazzini?"

"Oo-o-h, I simply adore chicken tet!"

He shook his head. Somehow she managed to make this fabulous dish sound like cleaning fluid. But with her abundance of, well, everything else, he could overlook it.

Uncle Mike's office occupied the round corner turret of the building. Through curved glass windows, from his third-floor perch, he had a front row seat for the passing scene—pedestrians, approaching clients and attractive secretaries. This second home was furnished for his comfort and sustenance on long evenings of estimating, bid preparation and crunch times, when big jobs were on the line and they had to meet deadlines.

A huge mahogany desk with carved corner posts provided a generous space where he could lay out plans and sort multipart bid proposals. By pulling up side chairs, he could also hold board meetings, staff briefings and consultations with multiple subcontractors. An eight-foot brown leather sofa lined the wall to the left of the corner entrance, where he could nap, read or cavort, as the need arose. A long bookcase, plan rack and tilted drafting table occupied the right-hand wall, for doing takeoffs from plans, storing his engineering reference books and job specifications.

"Hey, Uncle Mike, got something for us? We really need a new project this time."

Mike looked up from studying a contract, beaming. "Patrick, it's the opportunity of a lifetime!" His eyes twinkled merrily in his ample face. He looked, as Aunt Rose was fond of saying, like the cat that swallowed the canary.

"No kidding?" Bringing a new project into the office was a big deal for any young architect.

"Absolutely. It seems all those long Italian family dinners I sat through, late nights at the bar and days at the racetrack paid off. Not to mention giving his daughter a good job.."

"You mean… the client is Joe Bohannon?" A chill ran down his spine. Bohannon's unsavory reputation might clash with Halliday & Robb's distinguished, hundred-year legacy of historic buildings.

"Joe wants me to build his new casino, hotel and resort out in the rural town of Rockville, about 45 miles northwest of the city. Oh, by the way, he's happy to have you as its architect."

"But… Joe is an underboss of the Chicago Outfit."

"True, he plays a little rough. But be careful how you put it when you tell your boss. We can't afford to have any naysayers on this team."

"But…but what if he quits the project or refuses to pay? Will he threaten us—or send out the boys to break our legs with baseball bats?"

"I've known him for years. He doesn't threaten and doesn't get tough. He makes such good business deals for his colleagues, they comply willingly."

"I see." Rather than follow his conservative pubkeeper father's advice, Patrick was naturally more inclined to see things Mike's way. Still, Patrick wondered, what if they killed someone?

"I've known him for years. He had to fight his way up, it's true. But he won't on this job. He needs us—our expertise and our respectability. You know the old saying around Chicago politics: 'Get on, get honest, get honor.' He's hoping to do this and retire from the mob."

Patrick's firm needed this work. He'd lusted for such an opportunity. Besides, any architect would jump at the chance to design this dream project. But he was scared—at its size and difficulty, at his client's reputation and at his boss's reaction. What if Jason Halliday balked? He swallowed his misgivings.

"Assuming we proceed, what's the next step?"

"Hell, there's no question of stopping now. You go out and see him tomorrow — he holds court in the back of his bar in Bucktown every day from ten until noon. This is his first project, so we'll have to educate him a bit. Your usual approach will be fine. Tell him what the steps are in the design process. Listen well, so you know what's involved."

He still wasn't convinced.

"How do I talk to someone as powerful as this guy? I know the man to say hello, from dating his daughter, but I don't know how to approach him with a business deal."

"I've done all the selling. Just do what you do best, explain how you go about preparing a design. Then promise him another meeting to present a building program—types of spaces, with proposed floor areas for each, number of buildings, phasing, all the outdoor site features, the works."

"Then what?"

"You and I will develop it together over the next week or so, and we'll meet him at the site. We'll get his take on it, see how he reacts and give him a chance to correct our concept of the project. Then we can give him an idea of what each part costs and find out how he wants to phase it."

"I don't know if I can—" His gut kept coming up with objections.

"Look" Mike continued, as if he hadn't heard Patrick, "here are four Bulls tickets for next Saturday afternoon. You and Gloria can take Joe and his wife to see the game." He took his wallet from his pants pocket and handed him a couple of hundred-dollar bills. "Buy them lunch. This should cover it. Treat 'em like royalty—it always helps you get over the rough spots, especially when it comes time to collect the money."

"That would be great! But…but don't *you* want to take them to the game?" Patrick stared at the money and the costly tickets facing him on the desk, less than pleased. He feared entertaining this powerful man by himself. What could they talk about? How do you make light chit-chat with a gangster?

"Your cousin Julie has a lead singing part in the junior high school production of Oklahoma. Rose and I don't dare miss it. Anyway, you're the architect. You've got to take charge, get to know him better and become his friend."

"If you say so." He was eager to get back to his office and report his success to Jason Halliday. He hoped this would allay his conservative boss's concerns about finding new work. But first, he knew Gloria would demand some special attention.

On his way out, Patrick placed his arm on Gloria's. "Hey, how would you like to bring your parents with us to the basketball game on Saturday afternoon? Bulls against the Toronto Raptors."

"Another business obligation? You're impossible." Gloria sighed in frustration "Ever since high school, I've admired you. But honestly, when are we going to go out dancing and have some real fun?" She'd objected before to his staid habits—quiet nights at home reading, designing or listening to longhair music. The few social events they had attended together were deadly. "You know how I crave bright lights, fast dancing, rock music and wild parties."

"Oh, we'll do plenty of that. But this is important. I've got to know your father better. And I hardly know your mom at all."

"I guess so, but don't forget the other stuff."

"Trust me, I know. But I have to do my work. So, you're on for Saturday?"

"Fine. I'll see you then." She turned and resumed typing a letter.

On the walk back to his office, Patrick recalled her disaster at last year's Architects Association Christmas party. She planned to make a hit among his colleagues in a pale blue off-the-shoulder, puffed sleeve princess dress, beribboned and ruffled at the hem, with a wide floppy hat, topped by a long curling feather. It had been cold enough navigating to the party from their street parking space through a snow bank — perhaps her Southern Belle style was not ideally suited to Chicago's winter. On arrival she was comfortable enough with the men, including Patrick, who wore identical tuxedos with black ties from Oscar de la Rental. Men had it so easy— just dress like every other guy. Next to the women, however, in formal gowns by Versace, Armani and Herrera, she looked like Little Bo-Peep. The only shoulder that made an impression in the room that evening was the cold one the snooty architects' wives and girlfriends had turned toward her. What was wrong with her? Was she destined forever to be dressed wrong, to play catch-up, to stand out in a crowd? She'd told him all she really wanted was to fit in.

Patrick hoped she loved him enough to learn how to dress and act among his peers and their ladies. He was comforted by the fact that his ship was about to set sail. In the meantime, though, he felt he had one foot on the pier and the other on the boat's deck, and the gap over open water was widening. He'd never been good at acrobatics, especially not the splits.

Four

Patrick threaded through the crowded Loop sidewalks to the offices of Halliday & Robb, Architects-Engineers, a firm founded in the glory days of Chicago architecture. He entered the street level doors, bypassed the elevator and climbed the stairs to the second floor, fully occupied by the venerable architectural firm.

He entered the lobby, a boxy enclosure—four walls in yellowed white plaster, with an ancient stamped tin ceiling. They displayed a few black-and-white framed photos of the firm's classic office buildings and a cut-out logo of the company's name, which Jason Halliday's son had made in wood shop class. The reception area was illuminated by a couple of surface-mounted fluorescent lights, no doubt GE's original model. Potted mother-in-law's-tongue plants, a brown wood secretarial desk and two orange-padded, cane-backed stainless steel Breuer chairs provided the room's only spot of color.

Yolanda looked up from her keyboard.

"Nice of you to drop by today, Patrick. You're up so early."

"Unlike you, I went to bed early last night." Their office banter postponed his entry into the maelstrom. Besides, it provided a chance to admire her trim figure. It was wrapped today in a raspberry-colored A-line dress with a swag that modestly accented her pert breasts. She wore her long blonde hair in a discreet bun, European-style. She returned his gaze with eyes as blue, cool and deep as the Baltic.

"Chet's looking for you," she said and turned to her computer. "Be good."

"I am good. Speak for yourself, Patrick."

He passed behind a free-standing rectangular wall and through an opening that separated the reception space from the work areas. The office hummed with the chatter of people arriving. He crossed the drafting room, a sea of sloped, wooden drafting desks. The executive offices lined the Lake Street side of the space. At the newer design department in the northeast corner of the building, he hung up his jacket in his large cubicle.

Outside the windows, an elevated train squealed around the northeast corner of the Loop, the circuitous trestle which gave the downtown district its name. Its racket, fumes of overheated brake linings and the smell of burning grease poured in a few open windows, adding to the stale odor of the huge loft's stagnant air. One of the last downtown buildings without a modern air-conditioning system, this architectural firm's quarters reminded Patrick of the proverbial doctor whose patients got well but whose own children were always sick.

In the aisle between the cubicles Dolores Patuklas, executive secretary, told her colleagues her latest tale of woe. It seemed her beautiful new, red Mustang convertible, which she had carefully eased into the downtown parking garage up the block yesterday morning, had been broken into while she worked.

"Somebody stole my bucket seats!"

She had bubbled enthusiastically for the past two weeks about sporty new car, her proud new possession now a reason to curse. "Last night I couldn't even drive the damned thing. I had to call my brother for a ride home."

"Sorry to hear that." Patrick shook his head. Everything happened to Dolores.

"Do you know what the dealer wants for new bucket seats? It was so expensive to insure this baby, I had to accept a-thousand-dollar deductible to swing it." Dolores, now approaching forty, had long ago lost the fight against secretarial spread, and her bloom of youth had faded. Her dilemma, in its way, was beyond sad. Why did he secretly think it was funny?

He shared the dolors of Dolores, who had no place to plant her bucket, with Chet Neuzing as he passed his nearby cube. Chet's perpetually raised brows, wide-open blue eyes and a shock of curly hair standing straight up on his head gave him a permanent look of merry incredulity. This was handy, since it displayed his constant wonderment at his friend's take on his job, his women and the world in general.

"Give her a break, Patrick. If it was your new car, you'd react the same way."

He'd been lucky to team up with Chet. He was as essential to Patrick, he had to admit, as the steering wheel and seats in Dolores's car—the governor on his juggernaut, his reality check. Patrick and Chet, total opposites in so many ways, had hit it off right away. He was tall, good-looking and an instant hit with the girls. Chet was shorter, fatter and shy with women. He married young to a motherly type, one of those the goodhearted "practical girls"— whose friends all say, "You'll love meeting her. She's got a great personality." The kind Patrick passed up for the flashy ones.

Chet's face turned serious. "Have you got any idea what we can work on next week?"

"I'm pretty sure we've got a big new project. I'll know more in a few days."

"Wow, great! I've been wondering how to keep all these people busy."

Patrick grabbed the revised floor plan for the Star-Dispatch building expansion and headed across the office to attend to matters at hand.

He walked briskly across the drafting room to the office of Herb Slagel, Chief Structural Engineer. He passed Old Hal's drafting station, its green drape still covering his drawing board and his drafting lamp off, just as he had left them. When Patrick worked here during two summers, Hal would don his green eyeshade and work apron every day, as he must have from time immemorial. He'd been helpful to Patrick in getting his drafting table organized, so he wouldn't knock everything on the floor when he moved his parallel bar to draw a line. Every day at noon sharp, and again at 5:00 p.m., people could set their watches by his punctual march up the aisle to the exit. Last week, he failed to go to lunch, and they had found him, stone cold dead, slumped on his already shrouded desk at 12:05 p.m.

The chief structural engineer sat in his cubicle, calculating on a quadrille pad. Patrick waited until he jotted down the answer and interrupted him.

"Herb, here are the revisions I told you about for the Star-News building."

"Again? Come on, we just made all those changes you wanted."

"Can't be helped, client's orders. Archie Scott wants an overhang on the new top floor on the river side, so they'll have a clear view from the conference room, plus a couple of nice balconies at the corners,"

"I don't know." Slagel scratched his balding head. "I'm not sure it will be safe." A member of the old school, a very old one, Herb didn't believe in cantilevers. The new design had wide overhangs beyond the support columns. "Calculating those cantilevers takes a lot of work,"

"Then get one of your young engineers to do it," Patrick snapped. "And make sure it gets done right away. We're issuing the change order on Friday."

"You're a hard man, Patrick," Slagle grumbled. "Jason Halliday is concerned this job is running way over budget already."

"I'll deal with Jason. You're the structural engineer. Make it happen." He spoke with new confidence, now that he had news of the casino project to report to his boss.

He passed Martin Jackson's desk. The fortyish chief draftsmen, their highest-paid African American employee, also had considerable responsibility. He sported wide suspenders, a bow tie and a goatee, He spent hours on the interoffice phone with the receptionist Yolanda, the only cute girl in the office. Since they were both married to other people, this was how they carried on their relationship, with questionable benefit to the firm. He kept a roll of bills hidden in a locked drawer of his desk. After work, Patrick had spotted him peeling off enough for a cozy after-hours dinner, while they told their spouses they had to work late.

But he had to cut Marty some slack. When Patrick had been a cub draftsman during his summers at the firm, he would pull out rolls of old drawings, beautifully inscribed with ink on starched translucent linen, of some of the firm's historic office buildings. He showed him huge sheets, sometimes six feet high, with elevations drawn to scale, of twenty-story structures with three-part Chicago windows, white terra cotta cladding and exquisite cornice details, and regaled him with stories of the firm's former glory. He couldn't argue with Marty's appreciation for beauty, especially feminine beauty—a man after his own heart. He figured Yolanda must be quite a tasty dessert for Marty to savor after their intimate dinners.

Apart from his aesthetic interests, Marty had introduced him to Helga, a German immigrant, project architect for Federal Office Building 10-B, to be built alongside the Capitol Mall in Washington, D.C. She strode to her drafting station every day with a forward-leaning executive tilt to her solid frame, her graying brown hair drawn back in a neat bun. Every day she reviewed tall stacks of drawings. Although they were drawn at the small scale of one-eighth inch per foot, a bath towel-sized drawing could only show one quarter of the block long floor. This meant, for the ten-story structure, there were forty sheets of architectural floor plans and another forty sheets for each trade—structural, plumbing, mechanical and electrical. The floor plans alone totaled two hundred sheets, not even counting the basement. The full set included even more sheets: elevation drawings of the front, sides and rear of the building, and many more—wall sections, assembly details, reflected ceiling plans, door schedules, listing every one of the hundreds of doors in the building, and schedules of room finishes for each surface of every room: walls, floor and ceiling. To accomplish this, she and her assistants supervised an army of junior architects, engineers and draftsmen.

"How can you stand doing all this work, Helga?" he asked her one day.

"I luff the challench of beek buildings," she said in her Teutonic accent. Her glee at the Herculean task glowed in her clear blue eyes. "Really big."

Patrick spent weeks of his first summer at the firm working on a change some bureaucrat in Washington had ordered for this building. The architects had laid out the several office floors to locate executive and managers' offices adjacent to the core by the elevator banks, possibly to save them walking time. Their offices had glass walls, so they could oversee the other workers and look be-yond them to the many windows on the exterior. The other work-ers would see directly out of the exterior window walls. It was a bit unconventional, but it allowed everyone in the building to have a view of the outside. But the top bureaucrats in Washington would have none of it. They insisted the layout be changed back to a more conventional plan, with the executives and managers claiming the choice spaces beside the windows for their offices and leaving all the junior workers in windowless interior space.

To accomplish this design change, Patrick had to move parti-tions and air ducts on each architectural and mechanical floor plan (80 sheets total) for the small cubicles from their original location near the core to their new places along the building's perimeter. Ev-ery time an air duct passed through the fire-resistant corridor wall, the code required that a fire damper be installed, which would close off each duct from the spread of smoke when a fire was de-tected. Supervising this arduous task was a disgruntled draftsman named Tom Buttafumo, who rode Patrick hard every day.

"You forgot the fire damper here," he said as he pointed to a place on the drawing, "and here and here." Patrick soon learned how to spot every one of them and got good at catching these omissions. Tom finally ran out of things to criticize, but he found even more detailed faults in his drafting. One day after three weeks of this harping, Marty came by his desk while he and Tom were poring over a drawing. "How's our boy doing? he asked the junior technician.

"Terrible, as usual. This work is full of mistakes," Buttafumo said. "Takes me half a day to correct them." He stormed away, no doubt confident he had ruined Patrick's reputation with Marty.

"That's unfair," Patrick protested. "I've gotten quite good at this work. Here's a sheet I just finished."

Marty took off his distance glasses and examined the drawing. "Looks good to me," Marty concluded, "It's about lunch time. Why don't you take a break while I review your work on the whole set?" Patrick complied.

He worried the chief draftsman would find more errors—if so, Buttafumo would be right and he would sink in Marty's estima-tion as well. He walked to the nearest greasy spoon and bolted a so-called hamburger—it tasted more like cardboard than food and went down about as smoothly. He gulped down his Coke and tried to kill time walking among the anonymous crowd until the lunch hour was over.

Back at his drafting desk the chief had completed his review. "This set is almost perfect," he said. "Don't you worry. I'll take care of Tom."

Patrick was allowed over the following weeks to finish the job by himself, without any further interference from this resentful employee.

He recovered on the next assignment. He was asked to check a list of every door, called a door schedule, which showed the size, material, style and special features for each of the many types of doors to be ordered for the project. After Patrick set his mind to mastering the task, he asked, what if? He checked the style of doors specified for the toilet rooms and gleefully informed Marty of his findings.

"All the doors for the ladies' rooms are specified to have clear glass in them. I know this is designed to let in more light, but don't you suppose it would be nice to use frosted glass instead?"

Marty cracked up at this one. He told everyone in the office about Patrick's discovery. Even Jason Halliday heard the story and told him, "Boy, Patrick, if they had built this according to our door schedule, we sure would've had egg on our faces."

Buttafumo's usefulness to the firm fell into dispute. By the end of the summer, when the office building was done, if the staff had no job big enough to replace it, he would be the among the first to be laid off.

Patrick's ship, however, had come in. Like the Admiral of the Queen's navy in Gilbert & Sullivan's operetta, who got his first promotion when he carefully "polished up the handle of the big brass door," Patrick had his first break as an apprentice architect, distinguishing him from the crowd. After that, he was on his way.

So went a typical morning in the life of an architect. Interruptions, office conflicts, design problems and unhappy, demanding clients — you name it. Not exactly atypical either. All this for a roller coaster work load — feast or famine — and a modest income for most workers in this field, at best. Why Patrick, or anyone else for that matter, stuck with it, he was at a loss to explain. You only have fun during that small percentage of your time when you're designing — in the zone, your imagination free to invent a place as it might be, if you had enough money in the budget. And at every step you risk a lawsuit, angry clients or worse. Building failures, cost overruns or injuries to clients, workmen, or yourself. You don't get rich, you don't have much fun and you could even end up broke, hurt or dead.

Every other month you wonder if there isn't some easier way to make a living. Then your phone rings, someone shows up at the door and there stands a new face with a new problem, a new unmet need and a little bit of money. "Come in Mr. Snaggletooth. What can I help you with?"

Just like today, when Uncle Mike called him in and offered him the opportunity of a lifetime.

FIVE

Patrick rolled over in bed and resumed his pleasurable dream.

He and his fellow satyrs had romped all night through flowered fields with buxom beauties clad only in diaphanous veils. They now danced, facing each other in two rings, the males circling right and the females circling left. When the music stopped this time, he faced the most beauteous of the bevy, who welcomed him with outstretched arms. He grasped her hourglass waist and pulled her silkiness to him. She enfolded him in her arms and crushed her smooth softness into his broad, muscled chest, as the hillside beneath them turned to cushioned silk. They coupled, rolled and struggled until he was blinded by a flash of brilliant sunlight and exploded in an eruption of pleasure.

"Oh, my love. Again, again." Gloria's moans broke the silence.

A sun-ray beamed through a crack in the blind. He awoke with the glorious nymph in his arms.

That was the best—ever!" Gloria sighed.

"Mm-m-m." he muttered, with feeling. His dream faded.

Stroking her smooth curves proved his dream was real. Her breathing slowed as he watched her breasts rise and fall, at last subsiding into sculpted serenity. The hillock of her hips beneath the satin sheet transitioned into a ridge of long, luxurious limbs. Satisfied, they both slept again.

Patrick rose, got dressed and puttered at the stove in the cozy apartment. When Gloria next opened her eyes, the aroma of strong coffee and broiling bacon roused her. Sweeping the top sheet, Roman style, into a wrap, she came alive like a latter-day Pygmalion, tripped teasingly across the room and disappeared into the mists of the shower.

Emerging again, dressed, her hair wrapped in a towel turban, she sat at the small round table where lay the morning Clarion. A bold headline screamed: LAWYER SHOT IN DOWNTOWN OFFICE. She read it aloud. " 'By Mona Strong. Police found the body of attorney Fabrizio D. Angionomo in his downtown office Tuesday, the apparent victim of a determined shooter, Police detective Matthew O'Malley told this reporter.'

"My, my, what next?" she said.

"Looks like Mona's at it again."

"Didn't you date that woman at one time?"

"Where did you hear that?" Spatula in hand, Patrick turned and stared at her.

"Oh, word gets around. Your reputation, anyway."

With this encouragement, Patrick ventured the truth. "Oh, I went out with her a couple of times. A passing fancy—nothing serious."

"Is that what I am, too?"

"Oh Gloria, no! Never." Patrick set down his spatula, turned off the gas and put his arms on her shoulders.

Especially now, since her influential father had become such an important person in his life.

Patrick placed a plate of scrambled eggs, a short stack of pancakes and bacon before Gloria, and another one at his place, and sat down. "Try it and tell me what you think."

She took a bite and replied thoughtfully. "Delicious! You can cook, too."

"It's a matter of survival." He paused and said, "Speaking of that, why would someone kill that attorney?"

"Why are you worrying about that?"

"Because I saw a letter in his secretary's out-basket. He represented someone named Howe, a descendant of the Marvell-McDougal family, founders of the Clarion. They were very rich, and I imagine he's living off his share of the family fortune."

"So why is this important?"

Patrick stared blankly out the window, as he recited what he knew about the family, more for his own review than for Gloria's benefit. "I'm doing a project for their competitors, the Star-News, to add a new executive floor to their building alongside the Chicago River. There's been a huge newspaper rivalry in this town for years, and he might still be a stockholder in the competing Clarion."

"Who knows? Usually there's a specific reason for it. Old enemies, or maybe he was in debt. You know, follow the money."

"How did you get so clever at playing detective?"

"Playing? Hardly. My parents were always one step ahead of the sheriff. Either that, or there would be hell to pay."

"Were?" he said. "Has something changed in recent years."

"Oh Patrick, you have no idea." She turned to face him, tears forming in her eyes. "My parents did everything they could to teach me how to do the right thing. But when something went wrong, at school or even playing outside in my neighborhood, everyone blamed me."

Patrick reddened. He had always avoided this topic with Gloria, since he didn't know how much she knew or how much he ought to intrude in very private, possibly secret matters. The less he knew, the better.

"Because of my family's reputation," she went on, "I've never felt clean, or innocent, even though I was."

"Must have been rough."

"Further down in the article it says—holy shit!— 'Detective O'Malley indicated that this case bears all the earmarks of a mob killing.' Despite what I said, I hope my father has never heard of him."

"Remember, Mona is the most unreliable reporter in town," Patrick said. "And that O'Malley, who showed me the crime scene, strikes me as pretty sloppy in his work."

"Now can you see why I can't stand to read the papers? I'm terrified my family will be disgraced—again." Her eyes filled with tears. "You have no idea what I've been through with them." She began to sniffle again.

"Sad," He meant it.

"I've lived it—and now I can't live it down."

"So, when you read about something like this in the paper, do you have to wonder whether your father's involved?"

"These days, he's just a smart businessman. He never talks business around the house, but when pressed he says, 'You don't kill or beat up people who won't do it your way. You show them why it's in their own best interest to do so. Most of the time, they will do it, through leadership, not force.' I admire him and love him more than anything. There's no way he would be involved in anything like this."

"Well, I hope not, anyway."

Gloria's eyes widened, and she glared at him.

"See, Patrick, you don't believe me. You're no different from the rest of them." She turned away from him and covered her eyes.

Patrick put his arms on her shoulders and kissed her on the cheek. "Oh no, Gloria I do trust you, and I love you. I would never hold anything like that against you."

At his encouragement she wiped her eyes.

"Why are they adding to the Star-News building?" She changed the subject.

"The Canadian who owned the newspaper was forced by financial pressures to sell it. Because of the paper's long-standing tradition of defending the common people, Archibald Barnes Scott, great-grandson of the retail king, has put together an investor group to buy back the paper and expand it, to carry on its great tradition."

An opposing paper, Chicago Clarion, he explained, in the tall tower just up the river, was owned by another famous newspaper family, James Marvell and his descendants, the McDougals. Joseph McDougal Peters ran the paper from an arch-conservative point of view. Col. Randolph McDougal, the Clarion's longtime editor, had a bitter rivalry with the Star-News. He claimed to represent the people, but mostly represented the moneyed interests. "The two papers have been rivals for over a century."

"Money talks, all right, doesn't it?"

"I listen carefully."

"So why are you working for their rival?"

"They need an architect right now, and through Uncle Mike, I met Archie."

"I wish I could change my name."

"You will, someday."

"If someone will have me. I can dream, anyway." She smiled hopefully at Patrick. "I'm happy you'll be working on my father's big project—a real, legitimate real estate deal. It could be such a wonderful opportunity—not just for my future, but for both of us."

"Right, but first, let's see if we can get it built."

Nonetheless, Patrick reflected on the murder case. In the face of this disturbing development, what were the chances of realizing Gloria's hopes—and building his dream project? What the hell was going on?

SIX

At 10 a.m. on Wednesday, dressed in his newest suit and silk tie, Patrick fidgeted and smoothed his hair as reflected in the glass front of the Joe's Little Place in the Bucktown District of the North Side. Inside, he asked a rough-looking bartender who was stocking his back bar, "Hey, buddy, where can I find Joe Bohannon?"

"Back in his office," the bruiser said to the mirror. He pointed a muscular arm with a rolled-up sleeve toward the rear.

Patrick passed a couple of morose early drinkers, facing the bottles and neon signs lining the long bar mirror. Past the end of the bar behind two rows of empty four-tops, two men leaned toward each other in a booth further along the pine-paneled wall, conversing in low tones. On the opposite side, two middle-aged women gossiped over their morning coffee. A spirited couple devoured a large breakfast near the center aisle. He knocked on a door marked Private in the rear wall.

"Yeah, come in," came a gruff voice.

Bohannon stood. "It's you Patrick! Sorry about this dump. Soon as we fix up the old farmhouse out on my casino property—we'll have a much more elegant place for a meeting."

Joe wore an Oxford blue shirt with white stripes, contrasting white collar and a purple necktie. The jacket of his pinstriped navy blue suit hung on a bentwood coat tree in a corner behind the polished mahogany desk. He broke into a wide smile, his dark brown eyes crinkled beneath the shadow of a black beard the razor couldn't erase.

The wall behind his desk was adorned with family photos, especially Gloria's, from her childhood to the present. He motioned toward a large oval table at the opposite end of the room.

"Patrick, this is my dream. After clawing my way up in this life, and fighting to stay here, I would love to have something to show for it and to leave behind for Gloria. Who knows, maybe she will marry someday and share it." He looked significantly into Patrick's eyes. "And you know, I care more about Gloria than anyone in the world."

"Wonderful girl." No pressure here. He took a seat and accepted a cup of black coffee Joe offered.

"Tell me how you got the idea for this project," Patrick began.

"I bought this property years ago in the hopes I might retire on it someday. That's what I plan to do, although not quite in the way I imagined."

He motioned to a property plat pinned to the pine-paneled wall. It bore the seal of a land surveyor. It showed a curving gravel road leading to a farmhouse located next to a lake. The site area was designated as 149.27 acres. Most of the site showed dashed lines, like large cumulus clouds, outlining wooded areas. All this survey showed was property boundaries and main features, with no indication of hills and valleys. Along the left side of the drawing was the shoreline of the Rock River.

"It's a beautiful piece of ground," Patrick said, flabbergasted by the prospect of such a big project, on the one hand, and the obligations that might come with it, on the other. "Does the property have rolling terrain?"

"Oh yeah," Bohannon said. "How would they show that on a drawing?"

"For a big property like this, we start with available topographic maps, which show the contours of the land. They're prepared from existing aerial stereo photographs. These can be bought at modest cost for most areas around Chicago. Then we walk the property with you, to choose where to put the buildings. Once that's decided, we can choose a smaller portion of the site where we'll place the buildings. Next, we'll have a land survey firm prepare a topographic map showing the actual contours in more detail."

"So far, so good. Then what?"

"Why do you want to build here?"

"I'm tired, Patrick. Tired of being a big bad man, with more money than I know what to do with. I made lots of dough. I've got a beautiful blond wife. She's got a fortune in rocks, more in furs, more than she'll ever wear. I sent my daughter to an exclusive private school—Stephens College in Missouri—she took her horse there, for cryin' out loud! I got a butler, a maid, a cook and a chauffeur, not including the goons that follow me around most days. It's 'yessir,' 'nosir,' everyplace I go. The best of everything—the finest food, drinks, the works. I've got a place in Florida, with a yacht and a crew. I got a Caddy, a Beemer, a Lincoln Navigator and a Camaro for Gloria. Wouldn't you like all that?"

Patrick remained silent a moment and thought it over. "Not really, Joe. A good job, a good woman and lots of fun are all I need—and I never want to be bored."

"No worries, Patrick. I've had all that, and more. Now I want to turn it over to someone young and smart and enjoy what I've got"

"In your business, can you do all that and stay alive?"

"It has been done. I'm not calling it retirement. It will be a new business, legitimate for a change, just like all the other straight companies we've started with our cash—delivery services, restaurants, insurance companies, and so on—that obey the law, pay taxes and win awards for good service.

"I've been strugglin' all my life," Joe went on, "fightin' for a few bucks here and there, scramblin' with the rackets, and I've had it with the hookeries and the massageries. It's like Sodom and Glocca Morra."

Patrick smiled at Joe's creative use of language.

"I want to run a classy, profitable game in the country, by the peaceful river, the lake and the hills."

"Let's see how we can make that happen." He put on a brave front, but he feared he lacked the guts to pull it off. He hoped his uncle could show the way.

"First, I want a fabulous riverside casino, something like the luxurious layouts the Indian tribes build in Oklahoma and other states. It should have big hotel, with a high-rise tower and some little one-story chalets overlooking the lake. All around the casino I want restaurants. The biggest one should also be a nightclub with tables on raised areas overlooking the performance stage. We'll have celebrity acts coming through here from all over the country."

"Do you have approval of the Illinois Gaming Commission? They watch this stuff pretty closely, you know." In fact, Patrick realized, one of their main objectives was to keep out criminal elements.

"Not a problem. I talked with Representative Ferguson, who spoke to the governor last week. They want to do this for us. The law requires part of the casino to be located on a riverboat. We're perfectly situated on the Rock River. Then we can connect it to a building on land. That's where I'm counting on your ingenuity to make it all fit the law. It's practically a done deal."

"Hey, that's great!" Patrick squirmed. He didn't know what "practically" meant, what Joe would have to do to get that sign-off, and he didn't want to want to know. It was Illinois, after all.

"What's the next step in a project like this, Patrick?"

"It starts like this," Patrick said, recalling his uncle's advice. "I'll take all the information you give me here today, do some research on other casino projects, restaurants and hotels and prepare a written building program, which identifies all the spaces in the casino, hotel and restaurant buildings, It will list a detailed breakdown of floor areas required for each of these functions, outdoor amenities such as walks, drives, gardens, pools, patios and anything else you might like, such as putting greens, and the land areas required for each element of the complex."

"I may not want all those things at first. Certainly, the casino should come before everything else. And we won't know the answers until you've told me what all this is going to cost."

"Right. That's why I want to put a big menu of choices on the table. Then, we can meet again —Mike will come along, so he can react to your questions about cost — and you can set some priorities, such as which building comes first, and which spaces, such as hotel rooms, lobbies and restaurants, ought to be developed at the same time as the casino. Then we can begin to get a feel for a budget and phasing plan."

"Hmm, there's a lot to this. You and Mike will have to guide me along here, so we can figure out how to pull all this off."

"Yes, I'll call you in a week or so and we'll set a date for our next meeting. It would be best to meet you out at the project site. You can show us where you'd like to locate these buildings and how you would prefer the project to look. At that point, I'll bring a copy of our contract form and the typical design cost for each phase of our work, so we can talk about how you'd like to schedule the work."

"You mean, you want money for this?" He grinned.

"No worries. We'll try to take small steps, so we can allow time for you to be sure of your gaming license, line up your investors and financing and run some revenue projections. This way you can ensure you've got a feasible project before we start incurring any big design costs. Once we have the scope of work nailed down, we'll present a design contract to get our part of the work done."

"It's all on me, isn't it? So many decisions to make. But, dammit, your cost estimates had better be right."

"You're calling the shots, Mr. Bohannon. Mike and I are here to point the way."

"Call me Joe. Sounds like a plan. Here, take a copy of the survey and find out about all that topo stuff."

"Will do. We can get together in a couple of weeks." Patrick rolled up the drawing and stood up. "I can't wait to see this property. Now that I know where it is, I think I'll drive out there right now."

"Really? Hell, I got nothin' urgent on the schedule till four this afternoon. I'll get Marge to make us some sandwiches and take you out there. What do you want? I'm getting the corned beef on rye."

"Hey, that sounds delicious, with a dill pickle and some chips?"

"You got it."

SEVEN

A few minutes later Patrick and his new best friend Joe picked up their bag lunches and two bottles of beer. They left by the back door of the bar, climbed into Bohannon's dark red Cadillac Seville with grey leather seats and headed out the Dan Ryan Expressway for Interstate 90 and the tiny village of Rockville.

"Set up the beers, Patrick. Let's relax." Joe obviously wasn't concerned about the law prohibiting open containers.

"You're driving." Patrick reached in the bag, twisted the caps off the beers and set one in each cup holder. He placed the take-out box with two sandwiches, dill pickles, a tray of chips and napkins on the console. When the car reached cruising speed in light traffic, Joe took half of his sandwich in one hand, nodded toward Patrick to help himself and kept his other hand on the wheel.

"How did you manage to start your own operation?" Patrick asked.

"This isn't the 1930s anymore. Al Capone is long gone. We're not loan sharks or pimps. We're businessmen. We have services our competitors need. If we make it profitable, they'll join us willingly. There's no need to force them. If they've got a problem, they come to me and I'll solve it. If I can't, we'll use a little pressure as a last resort—but it almost never happens."

Patrick was shocked he would open up on this subject, and he really didn't want to know. But his curiosity got the better of him.

"How did they choose you?"

"I think because I was good at business, reliable, dependable. I found ways to make lots of money, never failing to send the Outfit their share."

"But, why would you quit now, when everything is going so well?"

"I've been very lucky. I had wealth, a happy team that everyone wanted to be part of. But it involves a huge amount of work and responsibility. It consumes all my time and energy. It's time to turn it over to the younger generation."

"What about the crimes you read about in the papers?"

"That's not us—not me, not the big boss. In fact, we're still tryin' to figure out who's doing it. Violence is bad business. There's no need to force them, and there are no exceptions to the rule. But we've had problems lately. Out of town operations are tryin' to move in. That's another reason I want to hang it up.

"The way I look at this project," Joe continued, "is a retirement program for me and a legacy for Gloria, and someday, her beautiful family. I'm not gettin' any younger. It's harder to get out of bed in the morning and it's harder to walk with my embargo—you know, stiff legs and joints. I don't see as well as I used to, and I don't have that old pep anymore."

"Must be hard." Patrick resisted a chuckle at Joe's choice of words. Still young and able, he had trouble relating to the problems of aging, but he still could sympathize.

They passed through a short row of shops, a bar and a café on Main Street, which made up the town center of Rockville, and into open country again. Bohannon pulled into a gravel road and the site of his new project. The gently rolling acreage overlooked the Rock River on one side and, in the middle, a pristine lake sparkling in the morning sun. Chicago Joe Bohannon stood on the shore, gestured with both arms, and shared his vision for a casino boat on an inlet from the river, extending into a huge casino building at its center.

"Beside the lake, we'll have a luxury hotel, chalets, a gourmet restaurant and several bars scattered in the casino and on sunlit patios next to an Olympic-size swimming pool."

"Fabulous," Patrick said. "What if we set the high-rise hotel next to the river, overlooking both the river and the lake?"

"Great idea!"

Patrick drooled with anticipation at being assigned this project, an architect's dream, so early in his career.

"How will you design and organize the complex?" Joe asked him.

"I have some ideas of how to start. The building program will include the main casino space, cashier's cages, counting room, electronic monitoring room and offices; two or three themed restaurants, with their dining areas kitchens, dry storage, refrigerated coolers, freezers, restrooms, and the hotel, including lobbies, front desk, number and sizes of the offices, indoor and outdoor swimming pools, workout room, meeting and conference rooms, exhibit hall and staff areas. Then there are the outdoor spaces— pool, cabanas, patios and gardens."

"There's a lot to think about, isn't there?"

"For sure. When I get back to the office. I'll start planning immediately. I'll get with Mike this week about his part of the work and then I'll send you a contract to get us started."

When they had almost arrived back in the city, Patrick realized this was last chance to make his move. It felt awkward. He hesitated, tried his voice and blurted it out.

"Um, er …Mr. Bohannon — Joe— Gloria and I would like you and your wife to join us at the Chicago Bulls game on Saturday afternoon. The tipoff is at two We can eat at the Bulls Club and then enjoy the game."

"Delighted!" Joe boomed. "We'll look forward to that."

"We'll pick you up at your house around noon."

He took his leave from Chicago Joe and climbed back into his car, bubbling with ideas, eager to begin his design. But by the time he got back downtown for his triumphal return, the hour was late. Jason had left, along with most of the others. It was the chance of a lifetime: he had to make it work. Not only eager to get started, he also couldn't wait until next morning to tell Jason Halliday about the big new project he would be bringing into the office.

The racket from an El train rounding the corner of the Loop reminded him it was time to go home. But the silence in the usually busy space set him thinking.

Chicago Joe seemed friendly enough—a regular guy, willing to learn and work with him. He was nervous that Joe wanted to pass him the torch. He said he wanted his legacy project to be free of organized crime.

But beyond the normal jitters of a young architect tackling such a big project, why was he so uneasy? Had he bitten off too much? What if Bohannon had killed people? What if they wouldn't pay? What if Joe wasn't happy with his work, the cost, the finished job? What if Gloria wanted more from him than he could give?

What had he done?

But he had no time to fret any further. He was overdue to begin work. His parents were expecting him for the big night at the pub.

EIGHT

Patrick walked down Wabash to MacKenna's Irish Pub. He changed into his waiter's shirt, bow tie and dark slacks and busied himself setting tables for the dinner rush. It was Ladies' Night, with a bunch of new help. All bets were off on the staff's ability to make it through the evening.

Seamus MacKenna ran an immigrant shuttle, a regular Irish connection. Every spring, he brought over a fresh crop of Ireland's freshest faces, with authentic Irish brogues. These included red haired, green-eyed, brown-eyed or blue-eyed youths. Occasionally they were tall and dark, "Black-Irish," like his father, Uncle Mike and Patrick. They waited tables, tended bar, sang and played—guitar, flute, tin whistle, fiddle, goatskin drum, harp, hammered dulcimer, bass— each one energetic and talented. They signed on, eager to come to America, the land of new Irish legends. Visitors staying at nearby hotels and locals from all over Chicagoland flocked to hear them sing the songs and tell the old tales. Tonight, two new acts, featuring the latest crop of arrivals, were to debut.

His father hauled a case of Paddy from the liquor storage room through the kitchen. Patrick set some bottles on the back bar and the rest on shelves below.

The crowd began pouring in. Soon young office workers, tourists and local regulars lined the bar three deep. Later, when the first act of the night's entertainment appeared, Patrick, his father, and his mother lingered in the shadows and watched expectantly. A strapping young man with thick dark hair stepped up to the platform along the front wall that served as a stage, his guitar slung over his shoulders. He was accompanied by a shorter, fatter red-headed youth with freckles, who hefted a string bass into the spotlight. The tall lad grabbed the microphone.

"Good evenin', my American friends. I'm Sean, and this is me brother Eamon." He pronounced the names *Shawn* and *Yar-men*. We'd like to bring you a few Irish ballads as they're sung in County Cork."

Lily squeezed her husband's hand. "They're from my home county."

He launched into a rhythmic rendition of Molly Malone: "In Dublin's fair city/ Where the girls are so pretty…" The bass rocked to the rollicking meter and the song picked up momentum, Sean's crisp baritone cut the air like a knife. At the end the crowd greeted them with enthusiastic applause.

"And now," said Sean, we'd like to introduce, for her premier performance in the States, one o' the most talented singers among those celebrated pretties of Ireland, Miss Kitty O'Connor." She was greeted with admiring words and polite applause.

Petite, with flaming red hair, highlighted with a coppery glow, and green eyes, in a lace-collared, full-skirted green Irish dress, Kitty O'Connor stepped into the lights in front of the mic.

Patrick felt as if he'd been punched. He gaped, breathless. Her form was perfect, and her smile innocent and sublime. Sean began a ballad with a driving three-quarter time, accented by Eamon's deep voice and an insistent rhythm plucked on the bass.

> There's one fair county in Ireland
> With mem'ries so glorious and grand,
> Where nature has lavished her bounties
> In the orchards of Erin's green land.

Up close she looked even more striking than she appeared from across the room. But what left him spellbound were her eyes — a combination of innocence and catlike eagerness to pounce.

To Patrick, her beauty was surpassed only when she parted her lips to sing. Kitty held the mic stand with her fingertips. Despite her diminutive size, in a strong but sweet soprano, she closed her eyes and began the refrain:

> It's my own Irish home,
> Far across the foam,
> And though I've oft-times left her
> In foreign lands to roam,
> No matter where I wander,
> Be it near or far,
> My heart is at home in old Ireland
> In the County of Armagh.

She relaxed her stance and resumed with the next verse:

> I love her cathedrals and cities,
> Once founded by Patrick so true.
> And she bears in the heart of her bosom
> The ashes of Brian Boru.

In the second chorus, Sean and Eamon added their crisp baritone and bass voices in a glorious crescendo of three-part harmony.

By the end of the song, Lily MacKenna shed tears. The audience, now packed densely around the bar and in front of the stage, broke into applause and cheers. Patrick stared, spellbound and speechless. She connected him with his roots, his people. He could hardly believe his own eyes and ears at this miraculous being who had appeared before him.

He found himself in front of her, hesitated and finally spoke. "Kitty, I liked your song."

"Thank you kindly, sir."

"My name is Patrick."

"I know. I noticed you right off. I'm much obliged to your father for bringin' me over. I hope to save money to send to me family?" Her voice rose at the end of each phrase, adding a tentative note to every line.

"Do you have brothers and sisters?"

"Yes, eleven of them?"

"Oh my. You'll have to save lots of money. How do you like America?"

"I miss my mother so. Some days I feel so lost in this big town, I wish I'd never set out."

"It's a grand place," he said, lapsing into his father's vernacular. Gathering his courage, he said at last, "Chicago might please you more if I could show you around a bit."

"How lovely."

Then he panicked. Surely her handsome, virile singing partner had already claimed her. "But what about Sean? You sing so beautifully with him."

"Oh, he's a nice boy? We met on the boat. He taught me the rest of the words to that song and rehearsed it with me?"

"Don't you love him?"

"Love? Ha! Look at me mum and pa. That's what love'll get ya—twelve children."

"But that's what women want, isn't it?"

"I want to see somethin' o' the world. I don't fancy that I'll ever marry."

He weakened, tempted to break a long-held vow, which he renewed every Monday morning. He craved self-control. He would never take drugs, drink too much or fall in love. When he'd seen Gloria for the first time since high school at his uncle's office, she was irresistible. Despite a warning from Chet and the alarm bells going off in his head, one thing had led to another.

He would have to double that resolve when it came to Kitty. He didn't know what to make of her. But she seemed too complex for a relationship anyway, not predictable like the American girls he'd come to know. He tried to make it sound offhand. "Well, at least let me show you around."

"That would be very fine, indeed."

Aha, a connection at last. "Maybe next Sunday, then, when the pub is closed."

NINE

Thursday morning, a panicked phone call greeted him as soon as he got to his desk. "Patrick, we've got a problem." Uncle Mike sounded quite upset. "My damned crane just fell in the river!"

"Oh, no! Is it where I think it is?"

"You guessed it—at the Star-News project. Meet me over there as soon as you can!"

The project site was only a fifteen-minute walk from Patrick's office. When he arrived, Detective Sergeant O'Malley was looking for eyewitnesses, while a patrolman was interviewing one of them and taking notes.

"The crane on the bank was lifting a bundle of steel beams from the end of that barge. It must have lost its balance," a well-dressed black woman with a shopping bag explained to the patrolman.

Patrick approached.

"Not you again!" O'Malley exclaimed. "Mona Strong was right— you always show up when there's trouble."

"Hi Sergeant," Patrick said. "I'm the project architect for the Star-News expansion. My uncle, the general contractor, is on his way over."

Mike MacKenna hopped out of a cab and joined the pair, out of breath.

"Frankly, Mr. MacKenna, I don't know why they sent me over here. Looks straightforward to me. The crane operator picked up too much load."

"That's what it looks like, but not with Dan Steen in charge," Mike said. "He's our best crane operator, and he's well trained. He knows exactly how much load this rig can lift."

"Let's ask him," the detective said.

Mike MacKenna looked around for his crane operator.

"Oh, crap!" O'Malley exclaimed, "Did he fall in?"

"Not likely. He's trained to jump clear if this ever happens. He would have landed right where we're standing. Even if he did, he's a strong swimmer."

Patrick gazed at the water. The boom of the crane was sticking out toward the middle of the river, obstructing water traffic, with its main mass submerged directly below them.

Mike shook his head in disbelief. "Dan's been with the company for thirty years. He's scheduled to retire next month." He turned to O'Malley. "Sergeant, we've got to find Dan Steen. Will you send out an all-points bulletin for him? Dan doesn't make mistakes like this. He could be the victim of foul play."

O'Malley instructed the patrolman and addressed his partner, "Jonas, secure this barge. Nobody gets on or off."

"We've got to find Dan," Mike muttered.

"Might be too late. He could be ten miles away by now. Call it in," O'Malley ordered the cop.

"Right away, Sergeant." The detective followed the cop to his car as he reached for his radio.

Patrick agreed with his uncle about foul play, but Mike and the detective were not making sense. They were sending his men off on a wild goose chase.

The patrolman finished interviewing the woman with the shopping bag and took his post at the gangplank to the steel barge. The woman said to Patrick. "I forgot to tell the officer, I heard a loud noise just as the crane swung those beams away from of the barge."

"Really," Patrick said, "A gunshot?"

"It sounded like it—what I hear every night in our neighborhood."

"Mike," Patrick said, "what if Steen were shot and fell in the water—and is still in there?"

The realization dawned on his uncle. "Oh crap, I'd better send for a diver."

"Right," Patrick said. "And while you're at it, you'd better call in a salvage boat to get your equipment out of the channel."

TEN

Back at the office, Patrick found Tom Buttafumo, the troublesome draftsman, waiting for him at his desk.

"Late again, Patrick?"

"Business. What's on your mind, Buttafumo? I've got a lot to do this morning, and I need to get to it." He stared at the skinny, hawkish face of this man, who had never attracted much attention for his own design work. In fact, he was the one who harassed Patrick during his first summer at the firm. He was known around the office as troublemaker and a fuck-up. Helga nailed it when she said he suffered from *schadenfreude*. He took pleasure in the misfortune or failure of others.

"Thought I'd give you a friendly warning that Halliday's on the warpath this morning about time and cost overruns on our jobs. I doubt if he'll be pleased you were late again."

"That's it?" Patrick replied, incredulous. "Jason and I are tight. Besides, this news will cheer him up big time."

"Oh, what's that?" Buttafumo's ears perked up. He was always ready to pounce on any morsel of new information Patrick was willing to share.

"I've landed a new development project—casino, hotel, bunch of restaurants, pool, patio the works. Out in Rockville." He unrolled the survey plat, which had a little location map in one corner.

Buttafumo glued his eyes to the tiny map. "I grew up near

Rockville. I used to make deliveries all over the county for a construction company." He drew himself up and sneered. "So you're going into the casino business," he muttered under his breath. "Crap, I hate this job already."

"Cool it, Tom," Patrick said. "They're going to build them anyway, whether we're involved or not. Might as well get our share of the booty." There wasn't much he could say to cheer up this soured employee. "With any luck, you'll be assigned to the team—at least you can claim a bit of the glory."

"Big whoop." Buttafumo stalked away.

Patrick carried the drawing it into Jason Halliday's office.

"How did your meeting go yesterday?" He looked up from editing a contract.

"Great!" He spread out the plat of the 149-acre site and held it up. "Do you believe this? We get to program, plan and design this whole resort complex — casino, hotel, restaurants and all the recreation amenities." Then, in a quieter tone, he said, "The client is Joe Bohannon, a loyal friend and long-time customer of my uncle, Mike MacKenna."

Halliday stood and helped Patrick support one edge of the large sheet. "My goodness, it couldn't have come at a better time. What's your take on Joe Bohannon? "

"He says he's trying to retire from the rackets. I think he wants to build a monument to his career — have something to show for all his struggles."

Halliday released the drawing and sat again. He leaned back thoughtfully in his saddle leather executive chair. "We'll have to proceed carefully, educate him along the way. Clients who have never built anything this big seldom have any idea of the time, effort and money it takes to pull off their dream."

"Jason, we discussed that. As a matter of fact, he even admitted how much he's got to learn, and he's willing to listen."

"Has he applied for a gaming license?"

"He says he's got a deal with Representative Ferguson."

"Ferguson? He's the crookedest representative in the House."

For Illinois, that was saying something.

"I would just as soon take his word for it," Jason said. "If there's any slip-up, it won't be our fault."

"He's got big plans for a resort complex.," Patrick went on. "I'll show you my notes as soon as I get the memo written."

"It also takes a deep-seated motive to keep a client from getting discouraged in the long haul, with all the hoops he's got to jump through to pull it off."

"Oh, he's committed. He's doing it for his daughter, Gloria. He wants to create something beautiful for her and leave her with a tangible legacy when he passes on.

"Your girlfriend?" Halliday grimaced. "That doesn't make things any easier. Knowing your track record with women, you dump her and we'll be out a lot of money."

"No, it's not like that. I love that girl."

"This is a risky client to begin with. With mob connections, even if they're in the past, we don't know how Bohannon will behave as an architectural client. If we try to collect our fees, he may get nasty."

Patrick cast his eyes down. "Gee, Jason, after your recent talk about how much we needed new work, I thought you'd be thrilled that I brought a big project into the office."

Halliday walked around his desk and put a hand on Patrick's shoulder. "Don't get me wrong. I probably should've congratulated you first."

"I'm bursting with ideas for designing it. I want to phase it carefully, with the casino first, so he starts making revenue right away, and he can pay our bills."

"I'm very happy you took the initiative and have gotten our firm selected. We'll just have to proceed very carefully. I'll work closely with you on this contract, so we get paid enough in advance to cover each phase of the work. If he ever fails to pay a bill, we won't be out so much money."

"Thanks, I'll need the help. My uncle Mike MacKenna will be watching the costs and guiding us as well. I'll keep you informed about everything that's going on. By the way, I'd like to select my own team from our crew in the office."

"No problem." Halliday sighed. "I've gotten us into this situation by not lining up enough work to support our staff. I'm committed to your success. Go get 'em, tiger!"

On this cheerful note, Patrick left the office, put the drawing back on his desk and sought out his fellow architect and best friend in his glass-enclosed cubicle. "Chet, big news. Got time for lunch?"

"Where to?" Chet stood up, stretched and donned his sport jacket.

"Were celebrating. Let's go to the Wild West Café."

They walked south on Wabash, a couple of blocks past MacKenna's pub to the restaurant, for which the firm had recently completed the interior design..

The maître d' brightened when he saw Patrick and his colleague. He welcomed them and showed them to their customary booth under a lower perimeter ceiling in the front corner of the quiet, softly lighted space. He and Chet sat on a banquette facing the other diners. Two dozen tables occupied the center of the room, beneath a higher ceiling than that over the booths, of textured acoustical tile, lit softly the from all sides with cove lighting. Framed watercolors and oils—depicting herds of buffalo, deer and tribesmen on horses, racing across the prairie grass, each with its own brass-shaded light—graced the horizontal walnut shiplap paneling of the walls. Tan tablecloths, dark-stained wood, leather chairs and thick beige carpeting completed the hushed effect of casual luxury.

"Comes now, for de forst time in dis cawntry," Chet intoned in a mock middle-European accent, "da crate harch-ee-tect, Pet-rick Mick-Kenna, mit his meck-nificent rest-o-rant design."

"Chet, what am I gonna do with you?" He gazed in wonder at his friend and colleague. Heavyset, inquisitive and easy-going, he loved to play with words and kid around with foreign accents.

Carl, the dark-jacketed waiter, approached. "Good day, Mr. MacKenna. What will you and your friend have today?"

They ordered the bison burger special with a glass of their house red wine.

"Excellent choice, sir." Carl collected their walnut-framed lunch menus.

"Now that you've been open six months, how are you doing?" Patrick asked the waiter.

"Business has been wonderful. The people love your decor." He bowed and backed away from the table.

"Too good for 'em," Chet said. "Dey don't de-serve it!"

Patrick shook his head. Chet was irrepressible. He might as well let him ramble on.

Chet was level-headed, the "let's get real," practical one. He was one of the few who could understand what Patrick's rough sketches meant. He could read his mind and interpret his ideas into concrete, steel, bricks and mortar and glass. From that he could create a set of final design drawings, and then working drawings, sort of an instruction manual any contractor worth his salt could read, buy the materials for and build. He also served as regulator on Patrick's volatile moods. When he panicked over a discontented client, Chet would say, "Now, Paddy, how will this really affect the project? Are they going to fire us over our choice of a louver style?" When Patrick had a brilliant design idea that would nonetheless exceed the project budget, he'd say, "Forget the architectural award—just design a building." Each made up for what the other lacked.

"So, Paddy, tell me your good tidings."

"Thanks to Uncle Mike, I've brought in a project for a change."

"Again? What is it this time?" Chet loved to rib him about all the trouble Patrick created for the staff.

Patrick described the new casino and resort project in Rockville.

"Oh, I get it. This project has everything—political, legal *and* the usual construction problems. When do we start?"

"Right away, and you're the man for the job. As Project Manager I'm officially designating you Project Architect."

"Excellent choice, sir, as they say around here."

Jason Halliday liked the way Chet could keep control of costs on his projects and additional work the clients requested. The computer in his brain kept a running tab of all job expenditures. Chet made clients his friends. If their projects ran over budget, he could convince them that opening their wallets to pay for it was a worthwhile investment. He was partner material. They had even talked about someday forming their own firm.

"There's only one thing that bothers me, Chet. The new client is Joe Bohannon. He's rumored to be an underboss for the Chicago Outfit, heading up the old Irish North Side gang."

"Oh, right. Now we add romantic problems. You're literally in bed with his daughter!"

"Chet, do you have to be so crude about it? We've been dating seriously for a long time. It's the mob I want to know about."

"Yeah, my New Jersey buddies knew all about them. In fact, a friend of mine had a cousin Louie who worked out of that laundry, the basis for the fictional Tony Soprano hangout."

"So what do you know about them?" Patrick asked. "Can we do this?"

"My old neighborhood in New Jersey—everyone out there pronounces it Joisey—was mostly Italian."

"But your folks weren't, right?"

"My dad was from an old German family—he pronounced our name Noi-zing, like Joisey, although most other folks say Noo-zing, like snoozing. They were brought up to work hard. Pop drove a cab at night. Ma worked in a dress factory in the daytime — they were quite a spiffy couple in their day. But we didn't see them much because they worked their asses off for Sis and me. The Italian families on our street took pity and had us in for breakfasts, lunches, dinners, and sometimes whole weekends. They practically adopted me and gave me an Italian nickname they *could* pronounce, Nunzio.

"Every Italian family I knew either had a relative, or knew somebody who had a relative, in the Mafia. They were kind, caring people, except when it came to 'business' in the mob. They cherished their families and would never bother another member's woman."

"It's the 'business' part I'm worried about. What if they don't like what we do and try to break our legs? And how in hell can he *retire* from the Outfit?"

"Look, If what Chicago Joe says is true, he *can* retire from the mob and live to tell about it. It's been done before—some guy named Franzese did it. He lectures about it all over the country to this day."

"Is it really a thing of the past?"

"Yes and no. In the fifties and through the late sixties they still held to their code of silence and honor among each other and the five crime families. Only when the New York Association began to crumble under the ever-tightening noose of the FBI heat and the RICO law, they lost their lucrative trucking, slot machine and petty gambling rackets. Until then they were too proud to commit crimes that victimized people. But under all this heat, rival bosses rose up who had no compunction about pursuing victim crimes, including prostitution, the drug trade and the combination of these two vices in human trafficking.

"Along came the Internet and a multi billion-dollar pornography industry," Chet continued, "which fit right in with the victim crime picture. When politicians smelled money, the mob even lost control of gambling. Today it has been legalized in more and more states. So, the victim crimes, which used to be small change to the old mobsters, are now the big thing among today's gangsters. The smartest of the old bosses, like Joe Bohannon, run these rackets alongside legitimate businesses, like moving companies, legal casinos and big restaurants and hotels. Since they only use their muscle as a last resort, they're very hard for the law and the politicians to find and root out."

"You think we can pull this off?"

"Hey, not only can we do this—we can have a lot of fun along the way."

"But, what about Gloria?"Patrick asked.

"Remember, what I said about honoring each other's women? If you treat Gloria right, they'll leave you alone."

"And if something goes wrong?"

"Hey, I can help you deal with it. But I'm not a miracle worker."

Patrick sat silent for a long time, pondering his situation. Finally, he said, "Well, in that case, your first official duty is to assign someone to begin developing a base drawing for my conceptual site plan. To do that, you'll have to order a stereo-photo-generated contour drawing. I'll give you the plat on my desk."

"I'll put Buttafumo on it right away." Chet drew a sigh of relief.

"Are you sure? That guy has a bad attitude."

"Don't worry, Tom and I get along just fine. We have an understanding. He gets too far out of line, and I remind him how we met—after he'd been out of a job for a year. He doesn't want to go through that again."

Their bison burgers came. They sipped their wine and savored the tangy low-fat meat of these once-threatened range animals.

Carl returned. "Is your luncheon satisfactory?"

"Everything is great," Chet said. "Hey, can you send over that new waiter there, to ask us the same question?" he whispered in Carl's ear. He nodded and went over to his new colleague. To Patrick, Chet said, "Now let's have a little fun."

When the waiter came over and asked how they enjoyed their meal, Chet looked at Patrick. "Well, Frankie, whaddaya tink o' de joint? Da Boss man wants to know."

"Not too shabby," Patrick fell in with the gag. "But I dunno, Fingers, what if Mistah Tony don't like it. Maybe not enough class."

"No problem for da Boss."

"Right, he'll send out the boys to shape it up."

"You're a riot, Frankie."

"Is there a-anything else I c-c-can bring you, sir?" The waiter fidgeted, his eyes darting warily around the room, as he waited for an answer.

"Hey, I know," Chet said to the new waiter. "Get me some more o' them fries."

"Yes sir, coming right up," He raced toward the kitchen.

"See, Patrick?" You work for these guys, you get respect,"

"I don't know. I just feel so jumpy around Bohannon. Like I'm sinking in quicksand—no solid ground under my feet."

"Did you talk to him like a friend?"

"I tried to. Chicago Joe opened up to me about how he came up in the ranks. His comments were so vague and confusing."

"I'm not surprised. They talk around things in a special language. In case they're overheard or recorded, what they say is so vague it can't be used against them in the courts."

"Man, that's scary stuff." Patrick shivered to think of it. "But Joe said, since the 70s it's been more civilized, more like a business, with violence used only after all other possibilities have been exhausted, as a last resort."

"Sounds about right—like Joe was being straight with you."

"But what if they ask us to do things we can't do, for our professional ethics?"

"That only happens if you cross 'em. Trust me, I know what buttons to push to keep 'em happy."

"I sure hope so." He'd worked too hard to get his architectural license. It would only take one proven involvement in a felony to lose it.

ELEVEN

Saturday afternoon, Patrick picked up Gloria at her place, met Joe and Candy at their house and took them all to the United Center on West Madison. They found their seats in the front row of the second level, not far from center court.

"Hey, these seats are great!" Joe waved toward the brilliantly lit basketball court directly below them. "We come here for the Black Hawks games. This is an even better view than at court side, below."

"Uncle Mike is no dummy." The price on the tickets, only half the cost of the prime seats Joe pointed to, was shocking enough. "He'd be here, except his daughter's starring in her school play."

"Family comes first," Joe said, "no doubt about it."

"Anybody hungry?" Everyone nodded. Following Mike's previous instructions, Patrick led them to the club on the same level and they ordered lunch.

Seated in handsome, leather-cushioned chairs at glittering chrome and glass tables, with a panoramic view of the basketball court, Gloria and her mother ordered United Center salads, while Patrick selected Joe's suggestion, their special club sandwich. The waitress brought beer for Joe and Patrick and iced tea for the women.

"Joe," Patrick said, following his uncle's script, "what's it like to run such a huge organization as yours — dealing with all those beautiful women, muscular guys and big responsibilities?"

"It ain't all milk and honeys. You might think it's glamorous, but most of the time I 've had to deal with the problems nobody else could solve — turf wars, going out to buy Tampax in the middle of the night, even umpiring cat fights."

At the mention of feminine supplies, Gloria made a face, and her mother half-turned her back to her husband and began chattering with her about a new gold lamé sheath she planned to wear to the Fireman's Ball.

"No kidding?" Patrick, encouraged by his success in getting Joe talking, pressed on. "So what is your biggest challenge in holding it all together?"

"You've got to keep your eyes on the prize, Patrick. If you're a step ahead of your team—knowing what their best move would be, even before they see it, showing them how to close a deal and letting them know you put them first—you make them strong. They'll go to the mat for you, and their success becomes yours. But today…" His voice trailed off and he shook his head.

"Something has changed?" Patrick asked.

"Crap, today everybody's in a hurry — they want shortcuts. To get ahead, to make your mark, to get rich — you name it. Discipline has gone to hell. You can't have that in any business. Take you, for example —"

"Me?"

The food arrived, and conversation lulled for a moment. Joe took a bite, sipped his beer and resumed his point.

"Patrick, think about it." He pointed his index and little finger at him. "You studied what you were supposed to. You learned it. You passed the state test. Now you can draw blueprints—a real artifact."

"Architect," Patrick corrected. He couldn't avoid a grin at Joe's free-wheeling language. "But they're white prints now, not blue any more.

"Our profession has its own problems," Patrick continued, "Everybody thinks he can do my job, as if it's only as easy as arranging furniture or deciding whether to use brick or stone. That's important, but it's only part of the story. Not too many folks understand how many things we have to worry about just to put up a building. We have to comply with the building codes, make sure the structure is strong enough to stand up, provide ways for people to get out in a hurry in a fire. There are a thousand details, and the list is endless. But a client who understands that, somebody like you, is a valuable partner on a project—that's worth a lot."

"Patrick's got big plans for us, too," Gloria, who had paid attention when Patrick started to speak, was now back in the conversation. "I'm looking forward to—"

"Someday, that will happen, I'm sure," Patrick said, cutting her off. "First, though, I've got to earn my keep by doing a good job on this project."

"Now, Gloria," Joe counseled her in a stern tone, "you get just about everything you want from me. It's time to listen to the men for a change. Patrick ought to keep his eye on the ball, if you know what I mean, and design our casino and resort. In the meantime, don't be a destruction. Remember, you stand to be the biggest winner in the casino."

They were done eating, Patrick plunked down both hundred-dollar bills to cover the check, told the astonished waitress to keep the change and headed back toward their seats.

"Thank you, son, that was very good indeed." He put his arm on Patrick's shoulder as they walked from the table.

Joe's paternalism made him nervous, but he didn't want to nix the future son-in-law angle. "Our pleasure, Joe—mine and Uncle Mike's."

"As I told you from the start, I don't want to do this forever. Gloria has a good head for business. I look forward to you two taking over someday."

He eased out of the embrace. He took Joe's vow to quit the mob at face value. But the feds would surely catch up with him. Joe was grooming him to assume his operations, in case he ever had to go away, or retired early. Patrick liked being an architect. After his hard struggle he had no relish for changing careers. He feared he wasn't cut out for this. His gorge rose, and he tasted his turkey sandwich again, as his stomach threatened to reject it.

When they returned to their seats, four men in dark suits and sunglasses walked down the steps to the balcony rail, just to see Joe.

"Hi, boys."

"Great seats, Boss," the tallest said.

"We can thank Patrick for that, Arnie," Joe offered, by way of introduction.

"Just wondered if you'd make a friendly wager. Here's a sawbuck says Toronto's gonna win by six points." He held out a ten-dollar bill.

"Hey, you're on. How about you, Bulldog?" Arnie asked the muscular dude,

"I'm in." Bulldog leaned closer, grinning. "Don't let the cops know people are betting on this game."

"Hell, they should worry that we will find out!" Joe replied.

The "boys" laughed heartily at Bohannon's wisecrack. Patrick nervously joined in.

"Get outta here," Joe said. "Don't you know how to behave at a game?"

Arnie, the loudmouthed one said, "Oh, sure, Boss. We know what to do."

As the others climbed back up the risers, Bohannon snagged Arnie by the sleeve. "Who's your new friend? He looks familiar, but the other guy is a mystery to me."

"Dugan? He just blew in from Detroit. Says he wants out of that fast crowd. The other one came with him."

"I don't like it. But with your crew, at least we can keep an eye on them."

The game was close. Every time the Bulls scored, the Raptors answered, and the lead see-sawed back and forth. At five seconds to halftime Chicago was tied with a tough Toronto team. The Bulls forward sank a Hail Mary shot from half court to take a three-point lead just at the buzzer. Wild cheering after the score drowned out all other noises. Patrick noticed a crowd gathering on the ground level in the far corner of the hall. The clamor died down to a shocked hush. After a long delay, a man was carried out on a stretcher. Although not announced over the loudspeakers, word buzzed around the hall that a man had fallen from the upper deck to his death.

"That poor man! How could that happen?" Gloria cast her father a questioning look.

Joe calmly regarded his daughter. "My dear, it's just one of those things." He shrugged.

TWELVE

On Sunday morning, Patrick picked Kitty up at the apartment where she was currently staying with other new staffers. He drove her south along the lakefront to Jackson Park. He hadn't been to the Museum of Science and Industry since he was twelve years old. Arriving in front of the museum, he stopped the car to marvel at the domed classical revival temple. Curiously, no one was climbing the stone steps leading to massive Ionic columns, where he and his father had entered for many years.

"This was the Palace of Fine Arts from the 1893 Columbian Exposition," he said. "It was originally put up to last only for one summer in a material which was not stone, but a mixture of plaster, cement, and jute fiber called staff."

"It looks more solid than that, as if it had always been there," Kitty said.

"They rebuilt it in the late 1920s with permanent materials, replacing all the exterior plaster with limestone." He explained that it was founded due to the efforts of Chicago's Commercial Club and Julius Rosenwald, a wealthy industrialist with a vision for a science museum. "He wanted it to be like the Deutsches Museum in Munich, which had interactive, hands-on exhibits. He put a total of five million dollars of his own money into it, probably close to twenty times that amount in today's dollars."

Instead of the surface lot where they had parked for years, he was now directed to an underground parking ramp and charged twenty-two dollars for the privilege. From the garage they entered a reception space on the lower level. Patrick had to buy tickets.

This was far different from his childhood experience of the place. In those days distant echoes of the machine exhibits and a murmur of human activity bounced off high ceilings and hard stone and metal wall surfaces in a calm, dignified neoclassical interior. He and his father, among the few Sunday morning visitors, had rattled around in the vast spaces, learning, like the discoverers themselves, about the secrets of science. When they entered for the first time since his youth, instead of the hushed murmur of exhibit halls, his senses were assaulted by throngs of people lining up at cash registers, the ringing of commerce, bawling babies in strollers and people clamoring for tickets. The volunteer at the counter assured him the basic pass would include all his old favorite exhibits.

They worked their way up to the main level, among a swarm of other visitors, to a domed space near the center of the rambling galleries. Beyond a large portal, a gambrel roof and the white-washed front of a barn stood behind a fenced farmyard. Patrick spotted a familiar sight and pointed through a gap in the crowd. "Look, there's the farm!"

The sound of a mooing cow came from inside the barn. "Pa and I visited this exhibit many times." At the barnyard fence, a new brood of baby chicks just hatched in the incubator picked at a trough of seed.

"Aww, there's one just breaking out of its shell, poking its little head up." Kitty pointed. "There's a white one among all the yellow babies. She looks really lonely. They won't let her get near the feed."

"I'll fix that!" Patrick clapped his hands loudly several times. The chicks scattered away from the trough. The lonely white chick saw her opportunity and helped herself, pecking to her heart's content.

"My hero." Kitty said with a grin. She held his arm and leaned her head against his shoulder, then straightened. "What's this?"

To the left of the barnyard, he recalled, the blades of a red farm reaper had once revolved before a small patch of wheat stalks depicted in the background by a huge black-and-white photograph of a field of wheat. Now they faced a tall green combine, fitted with all sorts of attachments to thresh, bind and prepare the grain for processing.

"They used to have an original McCormick reaper here. International Harvester, the company that grew from McCormick's original workshop, sponsors this exhibit, so we city folks can learn about Illinois agriculture."

"It's simpler back in Ireland. I could just walk to a neighbor's farm and buy a basket of eggs and a sack of the farmer's milled flour. That's when I first fell in love with baby chicks."

Patrick motioned to a door where a placard announced the name of a movie, *The Romance of the Reaper*. "I used to sit in here with my father to watch the very same film." They took seats in the small theater.

"When did your father come to America?" Kitty asked.

"First, my Uncle Mike came here over twenty years ago and started working in construction. His boss took a great shine to him. Soon afterward, the old man got ready to retire and sold the business to Uncle Mike. He found a nice downtown restaurant and bar for sale and sent for my parents. They settled here in Chicago to start our pub, where they still operate today."

"Your uncle's a builder. Is that why you're an architect?

"He took me around town to see all the great buildings—all the skyscrapers downtown and the houses by Frank Lloyd Wright in Oak Park, where we live now. Then he took me to his jobs, and I worked for him during the summers. I knew from the start I wanted to design buildings here.

"Enough about me," he said. "Why did you decide to come to America?"

"I can't face living as my parents have, with the drudgery and boredom they endure just to get by and keep their twelve children fed."

"Can't blame you there. I feel the same way about my family's business."

"When I heard about your father's offer, I used my singing ability to be part of the group. It was the chance of a lifetime!"

They watched the grainy black and white film, which dramatized the struggles of Cyrus McCormick to invent and perfect his mechanical reaper. In those days it was pulled by a team of horses.

"Reminds me of the way we once did things in Ireland," she

whispered.

"The switch from hand reaping to the mechanical method was the first of many inventions to revolutionize farming," he said, "and the beginning of modern agriculture."

From the farm and movie theater, they wandered into the Transportation Hall. The biplanes that always hung above in the vast three-story space now had a new companion. The fuselage of a Boeing 727 hovered above them. On an upper balcony, visitors lined up to walk inside the cabin.

"I heard on the news that the museum director accepted the offer of a retired plane from United Airlines. He figured a majority of the population had never flown on an aircraft and wanted to show them what it was like inside. Visitors can even sit in the pilot seats in the cockpit."

He recalled the publicity when this aircraft had made its last flight from O'Hare to Meigs Field on the downtown lakefront, ending in a dramatic short-runway landing in a crosswind. From there it was towed on a barge to Indiana, modified by removal of the wings and stored. A year later it was towed again by barge to the lakefront. By knocking out walls, they created a way to lift the huge aircraft inside the Transportation Hall.

The large model railroad Patrick recalled from his youth originally occupied the entire floor of the high-ceilinged space. The exhibits featured towns with real streetlights, factories, stores, houses and schools. Passenger trains with glowing windows and long freight trains raced across the fields, through valleys, hills and across bridges over rivers. But it was too high above the ground for small children to see. His father always had to pull a bench over to for him to stand on, so he could see the trains.

In the recent redesign, exhibit designers had been permitted to give their imaginations free reign. With new competitors for space on the floor level, they carved the original railroad layout into irregular polygons and reassembled them in a free-form arrangement, which meandered into the adjacent exhibit hall. The new layout had large indentations, where visitors could walk right up to a rail yard, a town or, in fact, the Chicago River, where it abutted the streets and towers of downtown Chicago. The once-static model exploded with city's economic vitality, sprouting towers, riverboats, low industrial buildings—in fact a complete, up-to-date replica of Chicago's most densely constructed district. While the model was still at its original height, steps were available in many locations, so the children could climb up, look in and see railroads, the city and countryside in magnificent detail.

"Oh, my goodness," exclaimed Kitty, as she examined the sprawling exhibit, "this is the hive we live in! Is there no place left for repose of the body and mind?"

Just as the city had taken over the countryside, the train model, had spread its cancerous claws into the adjacent hall.

Patrick, put on the defensive, explained. "That's why architect Daniel Burnham envisioned a system of parks and preserves the lakefront — so the open, green space could develop right along with the offices, public buildings, factories and homes."

"It looks as if the buildings are winning."

He agreed with Kitty. His job required him to cast his lot with the builders. Although they destroyed some natural life in the process, they supported human activity—creating jobs, supporting businesses for the workers, contractors and owners, and constructing singular works of urban beauty. This was all around them in the architectural wonders of Chicago.

In the model before them, Patrick pointed out the major landmarks. The old Palmolive building, with its Lindbergh beacon, had once been one of the tallest structures. It was now topped by the X-braced multi use John Hancock building, and Big Stan, the Standard Oil tower with its twin antennae and the multi-shafted hundred-story Willis Tower, originally the Sears building. "See the tallest one? I'll take you up there sometime, and we can get an even better view of this whole scene from the top floor."

Kitty spotted a directional sign. "There's not really a coal mine in this building is there?"

"You'll see." He led her into another hall full of machines. At the center a large steel framework reached toward the ceiling of the tall space. Behind a safety fence, wheels driven by a large motor rotated, paying out a cable strung from a drum to a pulley at the top of the structure. The machinery periodically started and stopped with a whirring sound, activating the cables.

Patrick and Kitty climbed to a platform part way up the structure and waited with other visitors until a wire caged car reached their level. A coal miner in striped overalls and a matching peaked cap slid open a door to the elevator cage and invited them in. When the car was full, he closed the door again and operated the controls. They felt the car move downward. The walls beside them, visible through the wire mesh, started to rise. The speed of their descent appeared to increase, and they had the impression they were sinking hundreds of feet below the surface of the earth. After a minute or so the car stopped, and the miner opened the cage doors again. They emerged into a black-walled tunnel, presumably rough-hewn from a solid seam of irregular, shiny lumps of coal.

At a widened place along the dimly lit tunnel, a miner stood with a large orange machine. He flicked a switch, and a loud whine accompanied the rotating of the horizontal bit as it penetrated the wall of coal. He spoke rapidly, his voice rising loudly over the noise. But he spoke so fast, all the words ran together. When he turned off the drill, Kitty looked perplexed. "I didn't understand a word he said."

"This machine lets miners plant sticks of dynamite in the seam, so they can break off lumps of coal."

"Oh. Why didn't he say so?"

The group moved through a narrow passage to another room carved out of the coal, illuminated with a standing floodlight. This time a short, fat miner identically dressed in corded blue overalls and cap tended a larger machine with a big horizontal chainsaw cutting a slot in the wall. He explained that this one was for cutting horizontal slices out of coal out of the wall, which they could break into lumps of smaller size and load into rail cars.

When they reached the end of this passage, a three-car train pulled out of another tunnel and came to a stop in front of the crowd. The engineer ushered them aboard. They sat on wooden seats in the narrow cars, surrounded by a wire cage and lit only by a dim bulb in the ceiling of each car. When all were seated, the miner took the seat of a donkey engine at the head of the train and drove it into a dark tunnel, steel wheels clanking, bumping and rattling as they forged ahead, the car's dome light blinking on and off. At one point the lights of the train went completely dark and yet the motion with the rumbling, clacking and grinding continued. In addition, it sounded as if the train's sides were scraping against narrowing tunnel walls. Kitty clutched Patrick's arm with both hands and squealed, as did several others on the train. At last the lights in the car blinked on again and they rolled to a stop outside the tunnel. They alighted onto a smooth concrete floor.

The last room of the tour held a dozen narrow, backless wood benches arranged to face a large lab table at the front of the room. Another tall and thin man in miner's garb took charge. He had an ugly scar from a gash on the side of his face.

"Now we come to the most important part. I'm Miner Mc-Gurk and I'm going to tell you about mine safety. The greatest hazard in a mine is the accumulation of deadly coal gas, which can not only suffocate the men, but also explode. This is a Davy lamp, invented by Sir Humphrey Davy in 1815, to protect coal miners. We use these lamps to warn us of the presence of gas in the mine. He brought us a long way from the use of canaries." He grinned at his own joke.

"He's different from the others." Kitty whispered in his ear. "He speaks so I can understand him."

"He doesn't seem like a coal miner to me," Patrick said. "His speech is too citified, and I wonder how he got that scar."

Patrick had seen this demonstration so many times, he had become a critic of the presentation. McGurk described the testing of the lamp with unusual glee. He placed a good lamp into the test cabinet and pumped gas into the chamber. Seen through the glass front of the cabinet, the lamp glowed a little brighter. Then he showed them a lamp with a hole in the protective screen around the flame and placed it in the enclosure.

"Sit tight," Patrick warned Kitty. When the miner pumped coal gas into the test chamber, a loud explosion burst through a paper seal at the top of the cabinet with a whoosh of flame against the ceiling in a cloud of smoke. Kitty squealed and jumped up in her seat.

Miner McGurk cackled with eerie glee. "The safety lamp can prevent this from happening in the mine!" He took a perverse delight in the experiment.

When the demonstration was finished, they stood and filed out of the rows through doors at the front of the room. Kitty kept her seat.

"What are we waiting for?" Patrick asked.

He's the only miner I could understand on the whole tour. And his eyes are so dark and deep, it's as if he sees far beyond us."

"So? This presentation is the same no matter who gives it. I've heard it dozens of times. Let's go." He stood and waited for Kitty.

On the way to the door, Kitty stopped at the front lab table, where the miner was resetting his test cabinet for the next group, replacing the paper lid and cleaning the glass. Like his parents she had a distinctively Irish, forthright quality of greeting strangers on the street and asking how they were.

"Miner McGurk, are you from England?"

He turned toward her and chuckled. "Actually Detroit. Why?"

"You remind me of someone I once knew — he was a coal miner. You're not a real one, though. I can tell."

"No, just a museum guide — for the present"

"I ask because the man I knew got a scar like yours in a mining accident."

"No, I never was a miner." He offered no explanation for the scar. "But I *am* looking for another job." He cast a plaintive look toward Patrick. "I'm so sick of this, I babble this speech in my sleep."

"Kitty, let's move on." Patrick was impatient to leave.

"What kind of work did you do in Detroit?" she persisted.

"I was sort of an executive assistant," he said, "and I know how to fix all kinds of machinery. Do you know of anything available?"

"Where did you say you're from, Miner McGurk?" Patrick would never get out of this conversation unless he ended it himself.

"Detroit. But my name is Nicholas—Nick, for short. I'm new in town—with no connections here."

"What kind of work are you looking for?"

"I want to invest in Chicago real estate."

"And you're working *here*?"

"Long story. Do you know anyone who can help me?"

In fact, he did. He had clients with projects ready to go but no front-end money to get them started.

"Could be—I can ask around." Patrick handed him his card. "Call me next week and I'll see." Released at last, he guided Kitty through the exit doors.

"Look," Kitty said, "we're still in the museum."

"As a child, until I caught on to the trick, I was always baffled. Our long elevator ride only took us to the basement. I expected we'd have to return from deep underground."

Through a doorway nearby was another of his old favorite exhibits—Colleen Moore's Fairy Castle. Between 1928 and 1935, he explained, the wealthy Hollywood silent film star and heroine of Tom Mix westerns, spent a half-million dollars to create her nine-foot-square, twelve-foot-tall doll house

"This is no doubt the world's largest doll-house," Patrick said. "It was donated to the museum in 1949 and became a permanent exhibit."

"Wouldn't you love to live in a place like this, Patrick?"

"If I were a king and had plenty of servants to take care of it. Even this scale model has cost the museum a lot over the years to renovate and repair."

"Ooh, look in that huge living room, a tiny grand piano!" She stepped into the lowest walkway, right next to the glassed-in exhibit.

"As many times as I've been here, I always see something new." He pointed out heart-shaped chair backs made from diamond brooches, grandfather clocks with functioning works, crystal chandeliers, miniature bearskin rugs. "She bought fine silks and damasks for wall covering and upholstery in the castle's décor."

On the way back to her apartment, Kitty raved. "What an interesting place. I could spend days there."

"What was your fascination with that McGurk character?" Patrick said. "I thought I would never tear you away from him."

"My uncle Ian worked in a mine in Newcastle. When he visited he told us scary stories. Blue Cap was a benevolent spirit who haunted the coal mines. He was mostly invisible, but sometimes he appeared as a light blue flame. He loaded coal all day, just like the human workers. He expected his wages. The men calculated his pay and left it for him in a corner of the mine."

"Was he a good spirit?"

"Oh, yes. My uncle said Blue Cap would tap out warnings when the roof of a tunnel was weak and about to collapse. He helped many men escape in time and saved their lives."

"Right. What's that got to do with McGurk?"

"He was too bright for what he was doing at the museum."

"So what?"

"With his blue-striped cap and intelligent eyes, I had a good feeling about him. He might be in touch with Blue Cap. And when he produced that light blue flame for the safe lamp—I knew he would bring us good luck. I hope you can help him get a better job."

"You and your Wee Folk." Like his mother, Kitty brought baggage with her from the old country—Irish superstitions. She believed in leprechauns.

"Don't discount the Little People. They steal babies and brides or do good deeds—full of mischief and merry pranks. It's folly to ignore a spirit—such as this Nicholas."

"I won't argue with that, but I doubt if my few contacts can help him."

"You'll be glad you did."

He was unconvinced

"Thank you so much, Patrick," Kitty said, once they were back in the car, driving home. "This has been a grand day. Could we do it again?"

"Of course, a lot of fun," he echoed, preoccupied. His head buzzed with contradictions and new problems. As with any new visitor to Chicago, he'd wanted to take Kitty around and show off his city, but something was different about this time.

Kitty's take on Chicago was so different from his, so distant from his American-bred point of view, it was refreshing but deeply puzzling. Ireland had given her a regard for nature and life itself. The young women he knew were so plastic—acquiring beauty through manufactured goods, makeup, designer clothes, fiber-filled bras, rubberized underwear, nose rings, tattoos and even plastic surgery. He didn't know what to make of this creature—so fresh, spontaneous and natural. Moreover, she challenged his conventional views and made him think.

His interest in Kitty was different from his ordinary solicitude and lust for the newly arrived Irish girls. He not only wanted to see her again, he needed to. He wanted more of her — a lot more.

He also had an unsettling feeling about allowing this McGurk character to intrude into his life. Who was he, really? His efforts to be open, with Kitty and with this unsavory stranger, made him question his easy-going, trusting nature. This situation was racing out of his control.

Thirteen

That night, Patrick drove west on the Eisenhower Expressway to Oak Park. He cruised down the handsome tree-lined streets, where he'd spent many weekends during his youth tracking down Frank Lloyd Wright houses and getting his parents to arrange visits to their interiors. He passed Wright's home and studio, recalling the building's long history of renovations and expansions to accommodate a growing family and an expanding architectural business.

When he pulled up in front of the family homestead, a sprawling home with peaked roofs and many windows, he spotted Mike and Rose's car in the driveway. This Sunday's family dinner was to be larger than usual. He walked around to his car trunk and removed a wood captain's chair he'd bought at an antique store. For months he'd intended to restore it in their basement wood shop.

Lily MacKenna met him at the door. "We have enough chairs," she teased. "You don't have to bring your own."

"Well, *I* don't. I can only invite two guests at a time to my apartment."

"You didn't bring Gloria," she said. "You know she's welcome at our family table."

"She couldn't make it tonight," Patrick said, and looked away. He hadn't invited her. Tonight he didn't feel comfortable with her at his family table. He changed the subject. "What's that wonderful cooking I smell?"

"I made a rib roast," she said proudly, "and I'm about to make the Yorkshire pudding."

"Yum," Patrick said, "your specialty." He carried the chair down to his basement workshop, where he liked to while away winter afternoons, thinking and solving problems while he was occupied with repairing, re-gluing and refinishing furniture. It was a soothing pastime, a pleasant escape from his hectic pace.

Dinner conversation turned to the disappearance of Walter McDougal Howe, descendant of the Clarion's founding family.

"How are these newspaper families related?" Patrick asked.

"It's complicated," Mike said. "According to Chicago lore, there have long been two competing newspaper dynasties in this town — the Marvell-McDougals and the Barnes family. This was back in the days of the great city builders of the late nineteenth century. These included such men as Joseph Leiter, a client willing to sponsor innovative design for his warehouses.; William Rainey Harper, who founded the University of Chicago, and Phillip Armour, the meat-packing tycoon. He founded the Armour technical training institute, which became the Illinois Institute of Technology, where I studied engineering. Jacob Marvell's clan founded the Clarion. The newspaper claimed to represent the people but really represented the conservative, moneyed business interests. Andrew Barnes, the mercantile genius, staked a chunk of his substantial fortune to create the Chicago Star, which later acquired the News, with a competing philosophy of journalism. He tried to represent all the people, including workers, and looked out for their interests. While the Clarion has moderated its tone in recent years, the two rival newspapers still advocate opposite political views."

"But the murder victim didn't work for the newspaper. Why him?" Patrick asked.

"Ever since the 1880s, these rivals have competed fiercely, sometimes resorting, with the help of the mob, to violent acts against dealers and distributors of each other's newspapers."

"Really?" exclaimed Patrick. "They still seem to compete just as fiercely today."

"You gotta watch them reporters," Seamus warned. "I don't trust 'em a bit. And some are even worse. Take Mona Strong—"

"You take her, Pa. I don't want anything to do with her." Patrick chuckled.

"Did you see her story in today's Clarion about the crane accident?'

"No, I went to the museum with Kitty. Didn't even have a chance to look at it."

Seamus handed him the front section. Patrick shook his head in disbelief and read the story aloud.

CRANE FALLS IN RIVER – ONE DEAD
Construction halted, river traffic blocked

By Mona Strong

A 95-foot crane fell into the Chicago River last Thursday morning, killing its operator, halting construction, and delaying river traffic for six hours. The ill-starred Chicago Star-News was forced to shut down its building expansion project Friday, while divers worked to retrieve the body of its operator, Daniel Steen, 65, and a salvage crew worked to remove the 60-ton construction crane from the river bed. Steen was a long-time employee of MacKenna Construction Enterprises

This crane tragedy set back the latest attempt to revive the failing journal, long supported and headed by relatives of the mercantile tycoon, Andrew Barnes. Archibald Barnes Scott purchased the newspaper last year after resignation of its former publisher, a Canadian ownership group, when they lost a lawsuit, judged guilty of mismanagement.

This tragedy is the latest in a string of difficulties plaguing the troubled newspaper in recent years. These included a bankruptcy of the previous owner and the wreck and sinking of the freighter that had delivered bulk paper to the Star-News, the SS Edmund Fitzgerald, on Lake Superior on November 10, 1975, subject of the song often heard on the radio, by Gordon Lightfoot, commemorating the disaster.

"What a muckraker!" Patrick exclaimed. "She has to drag *that* up after all these years. It wasn't the newspaper's fault the ship got caught in the perfect storm. The newspaper's only loss was a delay in the shipment of newsprint."

"After bankruptcy of the Canadian news chain that took over the Star," Mike said. "Archibald 'Archie' Scott, a fifth grandson of its original investor, formed a new investment group. He's now trying aggressively to expand the newspaper, carry on their liberal tradition and restore it to its former influence."

"Thanks to you, Uncle Mike, I met Archie Scott," Patrick noted, for the benefit of his parents. "After you won the job, you got us hired to design his building expansion.".

"Exactly, but after this latest incident with the crane, I'm concerned that someone is trying hard to make sure it doesn't happen."

"Do you have an autopsy report yet on Dan Steen?"

"We should have it this week. So far it doesn't look good. A wharf surveillance camera shows a video of someone approaching the cab of the crane. Here's the Star-News take on the story."

He drew out a folded copy of last Saturday's Chicago Star-News and read it aloud.

CRANE COLLAPSES: CAUSE UNKNOWN*One Dead; River Traffic Blocked for Hours*

by Margaret Larson, Staff Reporter

An eyewitness to the crane accident at Chicago Star-News headquarters, currently undergoing an expansion project, heard a loud noise resembling a gunshot, just as the crane operator swung a load of steel beams over the river toward the wharf, she told police Friday. "The boom of the crane lurched," said Mrs. Luella Robbins-Jones, "and the load of beams, the crane and its operator plunged toward the river." Due to the difficulty of retrieving the body from the riverbed, the cause of death of the operator Daniel J. Steen is as yet unknown. An autopsy report was delayed but will be made available later in the week. The witness, of Prairie Avenue on Chicago's near South Side, signed a police report confirming her observations at the scene of the accident.

Mr. Steen, union machine operator, had a forty-year career, twenty years of which were spent at MacKenna Construction Enterprises. He was planning to retire next month. He is survived by his wife Marjorie and three grown children.

This reporter observed the accident from a third-floor window near her desk in the newsroom of the Star-News. As the crane's boom toppled, it dragged the cab, machinery housing and operator of the 60-ton crane into the water. The boom of the crane lay partially submerged, obstructing the river channel. It was removed by a salvage tug later that afternoon.

When asked how this accident will affect construction progress for Star-News expanded facilities, publisher Archibald Barnes Scott said, "We are greatly saddened by the untimely death of Mr. Steen. We offer our deepest sympathy to his family. We are anxiously awaiting a determination by police of causes of the accident and a solution to what appears to be a heinous crime. Michael MacKenna, president of the construction company, has assured us another crane will be in place by Monday morning, and work will proceed as planned. Any reports to the contrary are false. We look forward to a renewed and strengthened Chicago Star-News and many years of leadership and faithful reporting of all the news important to Chicagoans."

"Poor Dan," Mike shook his head in dismay. "He almost got to enjoy his retirement." We'll contribute to the fund to help his family, but it seems such a senseless loss. And if it's murder—"

"If you accept that these murders are somehow related to an old newspaper feud," Patrick said, "why would they still be feuding after all these years?"

"Why not?" Seamus said. "They're still competin' to sell papers."

"For once I agree with you, Seamus," Mike admitted. "And particularly now, when the Star-News is run by a descendant of its original crusading family."

"Why so violent? I still don't get it," Patrick said. "Doesn't that run against the grain of both newspapers? If they're ethical journalists they'll stand up for justice and let nothing get in the way of reporting the truth."

"There's your key phrase right there," Seamus said. "Put another way, they might resort to anything to convince the people what they believe is true — and let no one stand in the way."

"In the heat of politics," Mike concluded. "both then and now, some publishers — not all, mind you — will do anything to sell papers."

"So how do you tell the good guys from the bad?" Patrick asked.

"A good rule of thumb," Mike said, "which we learned in the Watergate scandal. is, 'Follow the money.'"

Fourteen

Day by day, the harsh winds of winter yielded to breezes bearing the passions of the South to Chicago's wind-chilled streets and homes. Like the light new green of honey locust fronds lining the city streets and boulevards, the sap rose in Kitty's youthful limbs and filled her with a feeling of overflowing goodwill, which she yearned to share with another. Between serving the guests and clearing tables, she sang those sweet ballads of longing for the old country, loved ones across the sea and her joy in the wonders of her new world.

One Friday night Kitty sought out Patrick at the pub as he waited the tables. After the band's second set, she found him at the staff table in the kitchen.

"Patrick, I must get out of the city. There's so much paving and masonry around me, I'm afraid I'll forget the names of the flowers. Is there any chance we could take a ride, somewhere in the country?"

After a pause, he said, "I suppose there's the botanic garden, the zoo—"

"Isn't there anywhere that's not a public garden?"

"Hmm…What if I showed you the site for our new resort project?" Patrick said, "I want another look at it. We could walk the site and sketch. You might enjoy getting out in nature."

"What a wonderful idea!"

"I'll pack a picnic lunch. We can explore the site, and I'll bring a sketchpad to jot down my ideas."

"How grand! I can write letters. I owe so many to my parents and friends."

At 10 a.m. Sunday Patrick picked Kitty up at her shared flat on the Near North Side. He took the Dan Ryan Expressway to Interstate 90 and reached cruising speed.

"I need to see this site without the client, with no distractions—to feel the spirit of the place."

"It will be good to see some hills and greenery for a change," Kitty said.

"What about discovering Chicago and all the sights of the big city?"

"Bright lights, music and excitement are fine. But this girl from Ireland was beginning to think she'd never see grass and trees again."

"I understand. How am I doing so far as a tour guide?"

"No complaints."

"Nothing missing?"

"I miss Ma and Pa and my brothers and sisters. But I have employment in an interesting locale, a place to live and friends, what more could I wish for?"

"Some girls want so much more. They want love, marriage, babies, houses, cars, furniture and standing in their community."

"So far in my life, I feel no need for all that. Men like to start all that up by taking their pleasure and causing no end of pain, work and trouble for womenfolk. I have seen plenty of it."

"No worries, I have no unmet needs in that regard.

"Don't brag, Patrick. I'm not even curious."

"Have you ever been in love?"

"That's a very personal question, Patrick." She wondered what he was fishing for. She wasn't going say how she felt about him. His ego was inflated enough already. She wouldn't give him the satisfaction. Her protective older brother, Jerry, had graphically explained what to expect and what to avoid, and her best girlfriends had made it abundantly clear what she was missing. She wouldn't reveal her own experience with men, slight that it was. Michel, that beautiful boy she'd met at the Hotel California during her marvelous week in Paris, had given her pleasure. But it was too random and rushed for real fulfillment.

She did have a juicy tidbit to give him, though. "Since you're so blunt about it, no, not really." I have had my tussles with the local lads in Cork, but I wasn't interested and resisted. And I once entered my parents' bedroom on a Saturday afternoon to put away the clean clothes and caught them in the whole ghastly act."

"My God, you saw your parents doing it?" Patrick could not contain his laughter. "And in the broad daylight. No wonder you have so many brothers and sisters!"

Kitty joined him in his laughter. "Precisely. Now can you see why I feel no urgency in the matter?"

"Precisely, as you say."

"In that case," Kitty said, "let's be friends and merely enjoy ourselves."

"Thank goodness we've put that subject to bed."

On that note, they both roared mirthfully. Patrick extended his right hand across to her, and Kitty shook it.

In Rockville he pulled into the gravel entry road of the 149-acre property and drove to the center of the site.

"Ah, the gently rolling hills," Kitty said. "This is glorious."

The wind blew the pale, yellow grass into waves. A pristine lake sparkled in the midday sun. The road led past an old stone farmhouse crowning the hill. Primrose hugged a path leading to the front door, where a few pale, yellow jonquils struggled to open. The field was framed by deep woods, stripped to bare trunks. They branched into a delicate filigree of twigs, clipped as if by a giant eraser, to an artist's silhouette of a precise skyline contour. Against a sky of deep cobalt, a hazy wash of pale yellow-green hinted at the first signs of spring.

She imagined the wheels turning in his brain in his process of creating buildings suited to the lay of the land. He was making finished places for people to work and play. She'd had such hopes for her older brother Jeremiah, whose brilliant imagination, songs and stories illuminated her life. Whether or not his dreams were realistic was less important than his ability to spin visions and see possibilities. When he'd met his sad fate— drowned in a storm when his fishing dinghy was swept out to sea—her vision of the future had dimmed. She had resolved to leave for America, put those grim memories behind her and move on to a new life.

Patrick parked and grabbed the picnic basket. They hiked to the center of the wide bridge of land between the lake and the Rock River and stood still to listen. The silence of the gently rolling, awakening landscape on a warm spring day was broken only by grass and leaves swishing in a balmy breeze, gulls' mews and the cawing of crows. Beyond, a distant outboard motor buzzed on the river.

If she could encourage Patrick in his seemingly impossible dreams, it might fill the hollow place in her breast left by her loss and dashed hopes for Jerry's future. She might at least help Patrick avoid traps and pitfalls, as she'd always helped Jeremiah. If she could do so, it would be a welcome balm to her injured heart.

He returned to their spot, opened the basket and drew out a bottle of wine and some sandwiches he'd made, He set them on the beach towel, to Kitty's delight.

"Oh, what a lovely picnic!"

"I've brought a bottle of Beaujolais Villages, from the first crop of the current year. This is one wine you can drink without aging." He opened it with a corkscrew from the basket and poured each of them a plastic cupful. "Let's toast to your arrival in America and many interesting adventures."

Kitty lifted her cup. "To your health and to new adventures."

She sat on the beach towel and pulled her writing folder from her new, American-size handbag. She began a long letter to her parents, brothers and sisters about all her adventures and new friends in America.

Fifteen

Patrick walked down to the lake shore. The terrain began as a high bank and further along eased into a sloping beach. Behind it he discovered a skiff covered with a tarp, staked down against the wind and rain. Where the beach frontage transitioned into the high bank, he imagined a row of private chalets, each with its own dock and a lakefront view. He knelt and probed the depth with part of a dead tree branch he found lying on the ground. It was deep enough for individual boat docks at each cottage. Satisfied with his findings, he returned to their picnic spot.

The sun ducked in and out of a few cumulus clouds and warmed them from the morning's cooler temperatures. Patrick sketched on a drawing pad he'd placed in his provisions sack as Kitty resumed writing.

They worked contented for a couple of hours. Kitty wrote another letter, to her closest friend back home. Patrick sketched a conceptual view of the recreation patio with the high-rise hotel on the left and a restaurant and casino on the right, against a ground of trees in the distance. In another sketch he envisioned a lakeside resort with a vast casino at its center, next to an inlet from the river, where the obligatory casino riverboat would be permanently moored. A fast food buffet, a gourmet restaurant and several bars would be grouped around the courtyard and open to the casino. A centerpiece of the sunlit patio would be an Olympic-size swimming pool, surrounded by a kids' pool, hot tubs, a sauna and private cabanas.

He explained the site layout to Kitty.

"Will there be more?"

"Eventually, we'll build a river marina here, so people cruising up and down the Rock River can stop to visit the site. See that inlet over there? We'll put the main casino on the water, as the law requires, extend it on the land side and connect all our restaurants and hotel rooms to it. We'll also put a breakwater at the head of the inlet to create a marina. Visiting boats can come from anywhere on the Mississippi and then come up the Rock River to this site, and from all over Northern Illinois and the neighboring states of Iowa and Wisconsin."

"America is such a big place, compared to little Ireland."

"It's hard to imagine how big it is, even for me," Patrick admitted. "Over by the lake, we'll have moorings and a dock for sailboats and fishing craft, and then some chalets on the lake with their own water access."

"This should be a fine place to stay, indeed." Kitty zid.

Patrick wondered how, or even if, it could all be done.

"Can you imagine my good luck at being assigned this project, an architect's dream, so early in my career?"

"Be careful what you wish for, Patrick. You may get more than you expected."

"What could you possibly be saying in that long letter?" Patrick asked.

"Oh, impressions of Chicago, the people's flat, Midwestern accents, the comfortable American food—greasy, meaty and salty—and the crush of walkers downtown, rushing here and there with such haste and purpose. The friends I've made, the sights I've seen, the bigness of everything—streets, skyscrapers, parks, the lake, architectural monuments and crowds."

Patrick jotted down some visual impressions and notes on a sketch pad, totally absorbed in his work, unaware of the passing time and oblivious of a freshening wind blowing in from the northwest, as the temperature dropped. Patrick stood and stretched. "What do you say, should we think about heading back home?"

"Oh yes, look at the time. They'll be waiting dinner for me." A cloud bank blocked out the sun. Kitty looked up, shivered and stood. The broad, unsullied landscape took on a greyish cast. She surveyed the extent of her view, where the entry road disappeared into a stand of trees,

"Look, Patrick, we're not alone." She pointed to two figures, moving around the dark shape of a sedan parked behind the first few tree trunks along the entry road.

"I see. They're about a quarter of a mile away. But I really don't want to have to explain to strangers what we're doing out here. This project, so far, is a well-kept secret, as any client's new project is, until it is announced to the public." Furthermore, he didn't want anyone who knew his client Joe Bohannon to see him with Kitty.

They stowed the basket and bulky parcels in his car. Instead of retracing his route into the site, he pulled the car forward toward the next wooded valley and concealed it beside a thicket past a curve, where he was quite sure it would be out of their sight.

"Let's see what they're up to. At least Joe will appreciate knowing what people are doing out here on his property." He led her on a shortcut through the woods to the shore of the lake with a view of the point on the road where they had spotted the black sedan.

The sun was gone, and the landscape took on a dim. colorless aspect. The surface of the lake, glassy when they arrived, now roughened. Small breakers lapped the shore. The clouds had advanced across the entire northwestern sky and the day's pleasant temperature had dropped. Now, with a wind chill, it felt like 40. Kitty put on her Macintosh raincoat. Patrick had dressed lightly. His pastel cotton sweater did little to break the wind, and he shivered. They chewed on a few remaining cookies, ate the apples he had packed in their lunch and crouched behind a bush, sheltered from gusts and out of sight, peering out to see what these men were up to.

The two men stood beside the raised trunk of their sedan and appeared to be unloading something. Perhaps at the end of the week, Patrick explained, they had hoped to get out and do some fishing. A change in the weather seldom discouraged dedicated fishermen and sometimes caused the fish to bite, he mentioned, especially now that the sun was setting. Kitty agreed. Their view of the men became so dim they could barely make out their forms against the backdrop of bare, black trees.

"Looks they're carrying something toward the boat," Kitty offered. "Maybe their fishing poles and tackle boxes."

In the growing twilight, the two headed for the shore and lifted the covering from the rowboat. They put in their gear, dragged the boat toward the shore and pushed off.

"Those characters are a bit odd, don't you think?" Kitty said.

"Hard to tell. They don't exactly look like fishermen, but maybe they hope to catch fish with the change in the light and the weather."

"We should go, I'm really getting chilly."

"Okay," Patrick said. "They won't see us leave."

Patrick waited until they rowed out toward the center of the lake. He started his car, turned off the automatic headlights and proceeded as slowly and quietly as possible in the growing darkness down the road toward the main highway. As he drove into the far woods and passed the parked sedan, he stopped, alighted and checked the doors to see if he could find any registration information or identification for the owners inside. But since they were locked, he paused long enough to turn on his keychain flashlight and jotted down the license number of the car.

"At the very least," he said, "Joe would surely like to know who was fishing on his property." In the weak beam of his light something glinted on the ground. He leaned over and picked it up—a ballpoint pen with a spun aluminum barrel. He stuffed it in his pocket and climbed back in the car to head home.

On the way back toward her apartment, Kitty thanked Patrick for planning such a refreshing day and their delightful time together. But what a curious ending. Patrick remained silent. They had wished for a day in the country. He wondered what unexpected trouble they had acquired in the bargain

Sixteen

Monday morning Patrick decided to drive to work. He parked in the Star-News lot by the Chicago River for a scheduled project meeting with Archie Scott, his architectural client and publisher of the newspaper. The river had been cleared for traffic, a new rental crane was in place and construction had resumed, with private armed guards posted around the construction site. He was ushered immediately into the publisher's office.

Scott looked up from the story he was editing, set down his red pen and stood to shake hands. The fifty-five-year-old publisher looked trim and fit in shirtsleeves, a red sweater vest and a matching bow tie. His crew cut receded above his brow and showed greying sideburns. Sea-grey eyes behind round steel frames regarded him intensely.

"Arch, I don't know where to start. Construction is proceeding again, but I was with Mike last night and he's pretty broken up about the accident."

"Patrick, I can't tell you how upset we are about the loss of Dan Steen. I talked with Mike when he was over here Friday. He's blaming himself for it. Thanks to the eyewitness, Ms. Robbins-Jones, and our alert reporter, who happened to be looking out the window at that moment, we're convinced there has been foul play. I've got Margaret digging into the archives right now to see what else we can learn about last week's victim from the lawyer's office, where the other murder occurred."

"She wrote an excellent story. Once again, the Clarion and Mona Strong need to be reminded what journalism really is."

Scott sighed. "I think we do a better job of reporting, but we don't have anything like the Clarion's ad revenue."

"I'd like to meet her and see how she's proceeding with that research."

"Here, let me let me see if she's there." He pressed buttons on his phone "Hey, Margaret, This is Arch. Can you come in here a minute? There's someone here I'd like you to meet." He hung up. "She's on her way."

Patrick unrolled a set of prints on the publisher's desk, facing him.

"Is this the latest?" Arch asked.

"Right," Patrick said. "It's the new floor plan for the top floor, showing the balcony, the new executive offices, the editorial department, newsroom and employee lounge." He unrolled the other sheet. "And here's how it affects the elevation facing the river. You can see how it puts a nice horizontal cap on the structure, which extends beyond the original building volume on the long, horizontal side."

"That's beautiful, Patrick. We'll have an architectural landmark here. I can hardly wait to move up there, so we can expand the sports department on this floor."

A thirtyish woman with bobbed hair knocked on the frame of the open door.

"Come in, Margaret. This is Patrick MacKenna, architect for our building expansion."

"Nice to meet you, Mr. MacKenna. We can sure use the extra newsroom space above."

"That was a fine story you wrote for Saturday's paper, Ms. Larson."

"I'm not done yet. Our helpful archivist produced several stories about William Barnes Scott, a nephew of Andrew Barnes IV, who died in 1985. This Barnes descendant took over the newspaper in the 1950s and he's the one who sold to a Canadian firm."

"Did you know him, Arch?" Patrick asked.

"We only saw him at weddings and funerals. Uncle Andrew he ran in a different crowd, on the East Coast. Although we'd all been favored with a part of the Andrew Barnes fortune, I always figured a lot was expected of me that I had to live up to. I look back to our grandfather Andrew III, who ran Barnes Enterprises. My goal is to carry on his work in the liberal tradition."

"Do you really think Dan Steen was murdered?" Patrick asked the reporter.

"All I can tell you," Margaret continued, "is that I was there when Detective O'Malley and the medical examiner retrieved the body. From what they said, and the bullet wound they found, it sounded like murder to me. They can fill in the gory details."

"As for poor Dan Steen, we'll all know more when the autopsy report comes back later in the week. But I can tell you this, he was the best crane operator in Uncle Mike's company, and he'd be damned careful not to drop a load of steel in the river."

"I'm not going to let go of this one," she said. "Come on back to my desk and I'll show you what I've got so far."

"Do you want us to proceed with the new plan, Arch?"

"Yes, go ahead, Patrick. And for your uncle's sake, I sure hope that crane was well insured."

Margaret guided him past a sea of desks to her own area and showed him a chair opposite hers. She turned her computer screen sideways, so they both could see.

"Look, Ms. Larson, I just want basic research on this, plus anything you can find on the newspaper's enemies."

"Call me Margaret, please."

"Of course, Margaret." Beneath the tailored, navy blue business suit she had a fine, trim figure.

"You're probably aware of this newspaper's reputation for defending the underdog and standing up against crime and corruption," she continued. "Since you mention enemies, in my search of the archives, I ran across an original series the Star did in the fifties on mob influence in the press. In addition to representing business interests and hiring thugs to destroy newsstands and intimidate distributors, the Chicago Clarion was shown at one point to be protecting the Syndicate. She brought up an old Star headline on the screen: CLARION SUPPORTS ACCARDO CANDIDATE FOR MAYOR. The story went on to describe behind-the-scenes connections of their rival newspaper to a candidate backed by Chicago's longest-tenured mob boss at mid-century.

"That was a courageous stand. But what's that got to do with this case?"

"I've been wondering about motives for this murder of someone from a newspaper family, and this latest attack on the newspaper itself. "

"It makes me concerned for the people here at the paper. That reporter put his life on the line."

Margaret shuddered. "If we worried about things like that, we couldn't come to work every day. But it's true: gang influence is not dead in Chicago. These crimes may be connected."

"Really? You read about it from time to time—there was even a TV show about it—*The Sopranos*. I don't know how much I can believe of their portrayal as harmless."

"Don't kid yourself. Since the Al Capone days, they've infiltrated legitimate businesses—laundries, taxi companies, juke boxes, trade unions and delivery companies, to name a few—but they still use threats and strong-arm tactics to get their way. They have a code of silence, never to reveal one's mob membership and never to testify against a blood brother. And even if the feds have broken up the crime families, new ones are forming all the time. Nowadays they're involved with even nastier crimes—the lucrative drug trade, pornography. prostitution and human trafficking. Their methods keep honest citizens so terrified, they're afraid to report gang activity."

"I'd heard rumors, but I had no idea they were still that active."

"I'll keep you posted if I find anything else." She stood and offered her hand to Patrick.

He took it, gave her a business card and said, "Thanks, Margaret. Let me know what you find."

He left the building confused. Was the crane mishap really an accident? He also wondered whether the death of a newspaper heir might be related and whether organized crime was involved.

SEVENTEEN

When Patrick arrived back at the office, Detective Sergeant O'Malley was waiting for him in the reception room. To keep curious eyes from observing the scene, he hustled him off to the small conference room, where they took seats across one corner of the table "What can I do for you today, detective?"

"I hate to bother you with this little detail, Patrick, but I have to follow up on every lead."

"Not a problem, Sergeant. What is it?"

"I've been asked about some activity at Joe Bohannon's property in Rockville."

"Interesting," Patrick said. "Isn't that a bit out of your jurisdiction?"

"Very true, but we were called in by a colleague at the FBI."

"Why the FBI? "

"They got a report from the local sheriff, who was notified of some unusual activity at Bohannon's property over the weekend. Since we watch Bohannon's activities closely, we have them notify us on any unexpected movements."

"We have a project on Joe Bohannon's property, true, but it's a casino, hotel and resort. As with all our clients' projects, we try to keep it confidential until they get ready to announce it in public."

"Any chance you were out there Sunday, fishing, perhaps."

"I was, but certainly not fishing. I wanted to walk the site get the feel of it and make some sketches to test out where the buildings should be located."

"Can you prove that's what you were doing?"

"Yes, in fact I was with a young immigrant from Ireland, one of the new waitresses at my father's pub, showing her a bit of America. I can show you the sketches. What's this all about, anyway?" It was more than O'Malley deserved to know, and he still wanted to end this line of questioning.

"Mind you, the law would not normally concern itself with Mr. Bohannon's land. Unless, of course, we suspected illegal activity."

"And you do?"

"I'm sure you're aware of Joe Bohannon's connections."

"I know he owns some restaurants, night clubs and other small businesses. I just met him recently. He seems like a fairly straightforward guy." Patrick didn't offer more.

"He's direct, all right, especially when he wants something. He's got a long history as a mob underboss. We're just waiting for him to step out of line. Anyway," the detective continued, "this situation seemed worth a closer look. Two strangers were seen on the property at dusk."

"We did notice a couple of men uncover the boat, load up a bunch of gear and move it out into the lake."

"What kind of gear?" O'Malley leaned back in his chair.

"From where we hid, it was hard to tell."

"You hid?"

"Yeah, at the edge of the woods. I wanted to do Joe a favor and see what these trespassers were doing on his property. I didn't want to raise any questions about what we were doing there. It was Joe's business and not theirs. The property is posted, and Joe said only he can authorize people to go out there"

"How considerate of you. So, what did you do?" O'Malley said in a sarcastic tone.

"We had been out there most of the afternoon, picnicking, writing and sketching. When we were preparing to leave at about sunset, we noticed a black sedan pull up and park in the woods near the boat ramp. I concealed my car beyond the hill, so we could observe unnoticed from the other side of the bay. We saw them take something out of the trunk of the car. I assumed it was fishing gear. It was getting dark and I could see less and less as time went on. The wind was coming up and the air turned cooler. I thought they were hoping the fish would bite under the changing conditions. After they launched the boat and headed out on the lake, we drove off. I guess we all agree there were fishermen on the lake. So?"

"It seems that some friends of the owner arrived at twilight, hoping to get in an hour's good fishing, but the boat was already gone. You sure what they loaded into that boat was fishing gear?"

"Detective, we were a quarter mile away on the other side of the lake. It was getting dark. We could barely make out the fishermen going around back of their car to the trunk.

"That's all you saw?"

"On the way out, on the road to the main highway, I stopped by their car and got out. I tried to look inside for any ID or registration, but the car doors were locked. I did write down the license plate number on the car." He reached in his wallet and pulled out one of his business cards, which had the number scribbled on the back. He handed it to O'Malley."

"Oho, that's a lucky break. Thanks." He took the card and studied the number. "Did they see you drive away?"

"I hope not. I killed the lights on the car and drove quietly so as not to attract their attention. Did these other fishermen see anything suspicious?"

"It was almost dark, but they spotted the boat in a deep part of the lake." O'Malley said, "saw these two guys lift something very long and bulky over the side and watched as it sank. Without the boat, they gave up on fishing that day, got the hell out of there and went straight to the sheriff. Were there other witnesses on Sunday?"

"You can ask Kitty O'Connor, who was with me, but I would hate like hell to get an innocent young girl involved with police. She works at my father's downtown pub."

"We may not have to." O'Malley wrote down the name anyway. "We've got plenty to work on for now, to find out who those birds were. If it was a body, we'll have to have a heart-to-heart with Joe. In the meantime, MacKenna, you be damned careful whenever you're around him."

"Right. Oh, by the way, Sergeant, I found this where the car was parked." He reached in his shirt pocket and set a rolled handkerchief on the table, which contained a ball point pen with a spun aluminum finish. "I have no idea what this means."

The detective examined it for a long time. He used his own mechanical pencil to poke away the wrapping, roll it over and examine it. Some blue text was imprinted along the length of the barrel:

PETSMART, SILVER SPRING, MD

EVERYTHING FOR YOUR PET

He took a plastic evidence bag from his pocket, poked the pen into it and labeled it with time, location and date. "Good work, MacKenna," he said, as he replaced the bag in his jacket pocket. "This may help us identify the body."

"Happy to help, Sergeant. Any time."

When the detective left, Patrick returned to work in his cubicle.

Chet Neuzing popped his head around the partition. "Hey, Patrick, have you seen—?"

Tom Buttafumo appeared outside Patrick's office.

"Oh, there you are, Tom. Since you're working on the site plan, I need you to go over to the surveyor's office and pick up the stereo contour drawing. It's ready, but they can't deliver it until tomorrow. We need to get going now." Buttafumo, always eager for any excuse to get out the door, headed for the coat rack and the elevator.

"What did O'Malley want?" Chet asked. "You were in there quite a while."

"Looks like those fishermen I saw out there Sunday weren't fishing."

"Oh yeah?"

"Kitty and I thought they loaded their fishing tackle in the rowboat. Some real fishermen who came along after we left saw them dumping something long and large in the center of the lake. He's concerned it could've been a body."

"Oh brother! I thought Bohannon was retiring from the Outfit."

"That's what Uncle Mike told me, Chet. Maybe some of his boys didn't get the word. This project is beginning to worry me. To think I took Kitty out there."

"Now don't worry about it. I'll let you know if things begin to look dangerous," Chet reassured him and left the room.

Patrick worried anyway.

◊

Later, when Tom Buttafumo returned with the contour drawing for the meadow where Patrick planned to place the principal buildings of the site, he taped it to his drawing board, overlaid a large, sheet of translucent mylar preprinted with the Halliday & Robb logo and began to slide it around for the best placement of the site plan.

Chet Neuzing stopped by his drafting table to check the layout.

"I've placed the contour map right in the middle," Buttafumo said

"I'd move it to the left an inch or two, so we have plenty of room on the right for our notes and the location map. Where, exactly, is this site, anyway?"

Buttafumo pointed on the corner of the survey drawing to the location map. "I know where that is. It's on the Rock River, near Rockford. I used to make deliveries out in that county, in Rockville."

"Make Patrick and me copies of this location map. I'd like to check it out next weekend."

◊

It was already 4:15 p.m. and Patrick prepared to leave.

He opened the locked lower right drawer of his desk and placed the Glock 9-mm pistol his Uncle Mike had given him in the file pocket on the lid of his attaché case and set it on the side chair next to his desk. He wanted to have it with him wherever he went.

Jason Halliday stopped by. "Patrick, will you please come into my office? Right now." Halliday's urgent tone signaled it wasn't a question.

Rattled by the sudden demand and the harsh tone in Halliday's voice, Patrick turned immediately and followed Jason into his office.

◊

Buttafumo laid a copy of the location map on Chet's desk. He folded the extra one he'd made and stuck it in his pocket. He wanted to see this one for himself. Since it was almost the office quitting time, he donned his dress topcoat. Before he left, however he stopped to place the third copy in Patrick's cubicle, which was vacant. Its occupant was away from his desk, apparently in a meeting somewhere. He took his time leaving, to see what he could learn. The desk was clear of clutter and his drawing board held only a print of the site layout he'd been working with this afternoon. He saw the open attaché case perched on a side chair. The document folder in the lid bulged and gaped open. In hopes of finding some memo revealing what was really going on around here, he spread the accordion pleats wider with his hand and peered in. To his shock, he discovered the Glock 9-mm pistol. He put on his left glove, removed it, secured the snap on the document folio and checked the magazine. It held nine bullets, a full clip. "He oughta be more careful," he muttered. He made sure the safety was on and stuck it in the pocket of his topcoat. He took the elevator to the street and headed for his car, in a cheap space on the roof of the City of Chicago parking garage two blocks away.

◊

When Patrick entered Jason's office, Halliday stood before his desk and took up his monthly labor reports.

"This month's time sheets show you have three people working on the Bohannon resort project, and your charges amount to $8,523.78," Jason began. "What exactly are we to do about this? Can we bill anything?"

"Look, Jason, give me some slack. Joe hasn't even seen all this work we've been preparing." For all his great qualities, Jason could be a stuffed shirt at times. "We'll meet with him next week." Look at the walls of my space. They're plastered with color sketches of the future casino-resort. "Once he sees these, we should be able to get the contract signed and an initial payment to cover it."

"He should be impressed. But I'm still concerned. Do I need to remind you of this firm's distinguished and honorable reputation? He's getting into us very deep. Casinos are lucrative, but the architect deserves to be well-paid, too. Otherwise, the risk to the firm's reputation by dealing with these greedy, rough people will not be worthwhile."

"Jason, trust me. Mike and I have this under control."

"And Detective O'Malley showed up first thing this morning.

What was that about?"

"When Kitty and I were out there on Sunday, sketching and figuring out how to use the site, we spotted a couple of fishermen on the lake. According to the local sheriff, after we left some real fishermen with permission to use his boat showed up and found it gone. The skiff was already in use, so they had to take a rain check. Turns out it's not likely the first two guys were fishermen. I had no information that could help them."

"That's a relief. Could be, with all this responsibility, I worry too much."

"Gee, you were so anxious about having enough work. Now you just have to give us a chance to do it. You and I can work together to write a good contract that will cover our costs."

"Don't get me wrong. Patrick. I'm delighted you took the initiative and landed the job. I'm concerned, that's all. I just hope this client's shabby reputation doesn't drag us down with him. And you're dating his daughter."

"Hey, we've been together for months now. That must count for something."

"I'll admit, that's a record for you. Three weeks is more typical. What happens when you're done with her?"

"Aw, Jason, that's a low blow. I've never mistreated Gloria. Uncle Mike is solid with this guy, and Chet is from New Jersey and knows how to talk to these folks. Not to worry."

Halliday turned and put his arm around Patrick's shoulder. I guess I'm just worrying out loud. Those sketches you've been working on are beautiful. I'm sure they will impress him. Hopefully we'll have nothing to worry about."

At 5:45 p.m. Patrick grabbed his latest sketches. tossed a few unread office memos in his briefcase, closed it and put on his jacket. As he drove back to his apartment, he rehashed the tumultuous events of the last few days. *No pressure*, he muttered to himself, as he sweated, just thinking about it. But he should be able to keep Gloria happy, design a terrific project for Joe Bohannon and lead a very pleasant life indeed. And yet, as he drove home, he daydreamed about Kitty.

Eighteen

Stuck in traffic on the Dan Ryan Expressway, Buttafumo stewed about the abuse and disrespect he suffered at the office. He mumbled out loud to himself: "Since I'm working on this site, why didn't Neuzing send me out here to the site officially, on office time? Why do I bother buying a nice coat and wearing a tie? All they send me out for is to run errands, carry around their architectural models or get coffee, getting my expensive clothes dirty and torn. And that Neuzing, he's always giving me commands, never says "please," and seldom asks my opinion about how things should be done. MacKenna, now, he's a case. I used to be his boss. Now he hardly ever talks to me, makes me deal with Chet.

"Dammit, he thinks he so smart. I'll fix him!" he said. Someone observing him talk to himself in the car might have assumed he was on one of those new speaker phones, but he couldn't afford one of those, either, or he'd call them all and give them what for. Surrounded by bored, irritated drivers creeping along at seventeen miles an hour, he wondered what they thought of him. Maybe they figured this skinny guy in a once-green rust bucket Chevy, ranting to himself, was crazy. Maybe he was. Some days he wondered if he could hold it all together.

When he got to Rockville, he thought he remembered seeing the entry road to this place along one of his delivery routes. He knew he had missed it when he came to a bridge across the Rock River. He pulled to the side of the road and walked down the embankment to the river's edge. He withdrew the Glock in his gloved hand and took a pot shot at a duck. The gun kicked hard and he missed. He swept the ejected brass into the water with one foot.

He retraced his route, found the gravel entry road and pulled into the site. A police car with a boat trailer was parked at the shore. In the fading twilight, he spotted the boat it belonged to, inching across the center of the lake. One man rowed, while the other held a rope which trailed in the water. It took him a few minutes to realize the cops were dragging the bottom of the lake. The officer standing at the stern of the dinghy spotted Buttafumo. His partner shipped the oars, while he reeled in his drag line, fired up the outboard and sped toward the dock. Frozen where he stood by the policeman's gaze, he waited until they docked the boat, killed the motor and approached.

"This is private property. What are you doing out here?"

"I'm inspecting this site for my boss. We're architects, planning a project for the owner." Buttafumo pulled out his property map, which showed the title block with the firm's name on it. "

"You been out here before?" The other officer asked.

"No, this is my first inspection visit. But my boss, Patrick MacKenna, has been out here a couple of times. He sent me out to have a look at it, so I can do my work better." Well, he should have, anyway, Buttafumo figured. How was he supposed to draw a decent site plan without knowing the lay of the land? He asked the cop, "What are you looking for?"

The junior policeman said, "A couple of fishermen were out here and they saw—"

"Police business," snapped the first officer, interrupting his assistant, "strictly confidential."

The police took his name and information and resumed their work. The boat sped back to the center where their search had left off.

In the dim twilight, Buttafumo slipped on his gloves and carefully placed Patrick's gun in the bushes lining the dock.

Nineteen

Early in the following week, Joe Bohannon called Patrick at his office. "What the hell is all this paper I got from you in the mail?"

"It's our contract, guaranteeing that we get the work done and that you will pay us monthly as our work progresses," Patrick said.

"You don't trust us? Of course, we'll pay you!" Bohannon retorted.

"Okay. If there's no problem, just sign it and send us our check for five-thousand dollars and we'll begin work." Even though ten-thousand would have been preferable to cover their preliminary costs to date, he had convinced Halliday to cut the figure in half to avoid alarming Bohannon.

"Crap, I don't know about this."

"It's pretty standard stuff, Mr. Bohannon. All of our clients sign it."

"I don't know, Patrick. These amounts—the total cost of your work—think of the carpet that would buy in the casino!"

That hurt his feelings. Was all his team's years of education and experience less valuable for the project than a few rolls of carpet? Some days Patrick wondered why he hadn't just decided to sell insurance, earn a nice retirement and live off residuals.

"I'll tell you what, Joe. Why don't we have that meeting we've been planning? Then Mike and I can show you what we envision for the project and explain what's involved in each phase. But first,

Mike and I will need to get together,"

"Seems like I ought to know how much this project is going to cost before I start signing contracts."

"You'll have our preliminary estimate soon, another very close estimate before construction begins, and an even clearer idea of costs before we start. Normally, we start work, spend a lot of time with you and make several drawings before we know what size buildings you want and how much they'll cost. The further along our design, the more accurate Mike can make his cost estimate. This will help you determine if the project is feasible."

"Theas-ible." He repeated the unfamiliar word as he'd heard it. "Of course, it's gotta be theasible."

"What if we get together later this week? I'll check with Mike to see when we could arrange it."

"Let me know. You guys better have something good."

He called his uncle, checked the date and confirmed the meeting with Bohannon.

"But you and I need to put our heads together first," his uncle cautioned. "I need to see your building program for all the different phases of the project and a sketch site plan, so we can get a general idea of the size and scope of this project. Let's not go into this with a bunch of hidden surprises for Joe."

Patrick agreed to work on it with Mike after lunch.

Detective Sergeant O'Malley called Patrick and said he was coming over at ten o'clock.

"One of your employees, Thomas Buttafumo, says you've been out to that Bohannon property several times," O'Malley said.

"Yeah, we're designing a project for Joe Bohannon out there. How come you were talking to our employee?"

"We found him at Bohannon's property late Friday afternoon."

"What? How?"

"I'll explain when I get there." The detective hung up.

It was already 9:45 a.m. Resigned to getting nothing done this morning, Patrick slammed down his pen again and headed conference room. O'Malley was beginning to get on his nerves. Despite his slouchy, retired staff sergeant look, he had a rep around town as a bulldog. He could get hold of your leg and hang on until he got a piece of red meat. He wished the detective would just go away.

Patrick didn't have time to speculate on who might have done what throughout the City of Chicago. Nonetheless, O'Malley didn't leave him much choice—he had to talk to him.

Patrick picked up the phone. "Buttafumo. Get in here!" Momentarily, the draftsman's gangling frame appeared at the entrance to his cubicle.

"What were you doing out at the job site last Friday?"

"Huh? How'd you—" He stopped to rephrase. He shuffled his feet. His dark brown eyes shifted around the room.

"Sit down."

He sat in the guest chair next to the desk. His eyes wandered to the color sketches of the project filling the wall.

"I just had a call from the police."

"So?" His jaw was set, his facial expression sullen, heightened by a day-old growth of beard.

"The FBI called them after they found you trespassing on Joe Bohannon's site in Rockville last Friday afternoon."

"Why do you care? You never talk to me anyway."

"I'm talking to you now. Spill it."

"It's pretty hard to draw a site plan without seeing the property."

"Yeah, so you went. What were they doing there?"

"I don't know. Two cops were out in the lake. They saw me, came back to the shore and asked me the same thing."

"Well? Did they use that rowboat that's tied down out there?"

"Naw, they brought their own police outboard, with its own trailer. Pretty slick."

"And they wouldn't say what they were doing?"

"Hey, I asked but they wouldn't tell me. Said it was none of my business."

"In the future, you are to clear all site visits with me in advance."

"Yeah, right."

"That's all," Patrick said, "but stay close. I may have more questions for you."

Buttafumo left the room.

He hoped Chet knew what he was doing, putting this malcontent on the team.

When O'Malley arrived, they again sat in the same small conference room.

"Detective O'Malley, back so soon?"

"It could be worse. I could've asked you to come to Downtown Headquarters. It's crawling with bedbugs." O'Malley reached behind his back and scratched.

"No fooling?"

"They're everywhere—they creep out of the carpet, the bookshelves. They even ooze out of the cracks in the old wooden desks."

"Can't you complain to somebody about that?"

"Nobody wants to. You don't make waves. I think somebody filed an anonymous complaint with the State of Illinois. Maybe the gov will complain to the mayor and he'll even send out an exterminator." He raised his arms in a gesture of futility. "Or maybe not."

The detective squirmed violently, and a tiny, black speckfell off O'Malley's shirt and landed on the green pile carpet. Patrick watched it disappear into the fiber. "They'd better," he said, "before the whole town is infested." He made a note to have the office sprayed,

"What's up, Sergeant?"

"We got a tip from those fishermen we talked about last time. What you couldn't see in the twilight before you left. They loaded a body into that rowboat and dumped it in the middle of the lake. We dragged it last week and, sure enough, it's now identified as that of a distant cousin of the Clarion's editor, Col. McDougal, chief competitor of the Star-News. "We were speculating on the circumstances. What if someone at the Star-News wanted to get even for the crane accident?" he said, as if to remind him.

"They couldn't. They wouldn't," Patrick protested. "You're trying to make this sound like the newspaper gangs of the old days."

"We don't know anything about that, just the facts." He sounded a lot like Sergeant Joe Friday in TV's Dragnet re-runs.

"Why are you telling me this, Sergeant? Sounds like a police matter."

"Too many coincidences, MacKenna. Buttafumo said he was out there inspecting the site. He says you've been out there several times. The body was identified as that of the missing Walter McDougal Howe, whose family's newspaper competes with the Star-

News. There was that crane incident at the Star-News project. You keep turning up like a bad penny."

"An old Irish expression, as I recall."

"Then, to top it off, a Glock 9-millimeter service pistol turns up at the site. It's registered to you. It had only one set of prints on it—yours.

"At the site? It can't be. I keep it locked in my office, until Friday afternoon. I became concerned about all this and put it in my attaché case to take with me. Wait, I'll show you." He dashed out to his office and returned with the case, open, just as he set it every day on a side chair next to his desk, just as he'd set it when he arrived this morning to remove the C-notes to give to Jason Halliday.

"I put it in this file pocket, right here in the lid…" He reached into the accordion-pleated pocket. "Holy crap—it's…it's gone!"

"At first, we thought it was beside the point, as far as you're concerned. The victim's skull was badly bruised when he landed on the deck below the balcony. The guards at the stadium carried the body out to the dock. While they waited for the van to take it away, police questioned the guards in an adjacent office."

"What was the cause of death?"

"The guards and stadium medics assumed he died on impact. By the time the police van arrived and the interviews were done, the body was gone. Bystanders reported that four men in black suits collected the body and hauled it away in a funeral home hearse."

"What about Buttafumo? He must have planted my gun on the site. But how could he have known what he was looking for? Was he stupid enough to think I would have clobbered the guy with the butt of the pistol?" Patrick swore silently. He wasn't too bright either, to have suggested this possibility to the detective. "Had it been fired?"

"It smelled like it. And the magazine was one bullet short of a full clip. The gun is yours. We've turned it over to forensics for analysis."

"No evidence, so, what's the beef?"

"We'll have to wait for the coroner's report. There was a lot of mud on the body. No telling how he died."

Crap. What was the next piece of bad news this gumshoe was going to lay on him?

"And by the way, I don't know what Joe Bohannon has on you,

but you've got to be crazy when you work for the likes of him. He's got a rap sheet as long as your arm."

"He's retiring, or so he says."

"Ha! Most guys don't retire from the Outfit. They work until they drop or get whacked."

Patrick's stomach turned and he felt light-headed.

He reached for the phone and punched in Chet's number. "Chet, can you send Tom Buttafumo in here, please?"

Two minutes later, Chet rushed in, breathless. "He's gone! Along with his drafting tools, electrical eraser, his topcoat and his assigned computer."

"I'll be damned! I guess this means we have to start looking for a new technician."

'The biggest problem around here," Chet said, "will be replacing the computer."

"That's all I've got, Patrick." O'Malley stood, removed his suit jacket and turned away from him. "One more thing. Could you scratch my back?"

Patrick complied. "How's that?"

"A little to the left. Aah, perfect."

Patrick returned to his cube and stared blankly at an El train screeching around the corner of the Loop.

Dolores Patuklas walked by. "What could possibly be so interesting out there?"

"That train," he said. "It expresses me."

"I know exactly what you mean."

Patrick's eyes raced desperately around his cubicle. He had gotten himself into a box, all right, and he might be hauled out in one before he was through. He was running out of options. But if he scratched O'Malley's back, maybe the detective would scratch his.

TWENTY

Sunday morning Patrick knocked on the door of a suburban Winnetka home, where Kitty had been invited to stay by a well-established family. He parked in the driveway and walked up a winding path past rosebushes and carefully tended planters sprouting pansies and jonquils just bursting into bloom and rang the bell. The door swung open. A tall, well-groomed man with a healthy winter tan, clad in sweater and slacks, greeted him with hard blue eyes in a withering stare.

"Yes?"

"Sir, I'm Patrick MacKenna. I've come to pick up Kitty."

"Kitty, your friend is here," the man called over his shoulder. "Ross Hunter," he said extending a hand. He opened the door wider.

Patrick shook it. He smiled broadly when Kitty appeared, radiant. She wore a simple turquoise sweater and a matching skirt, which set off her long, blazing red locks. "Ready to go?" he said.

"Where are we going?" Kitty tilted her head inquiringly.

"Yes, where *are* you going?" Mr. Hunter said

"I thought we'd go to the Art Institute, take in the Impressionists and then maybe have lunch in McKinlock Court."

"Look, Mr. MacKenna," he said stiffly. "I promised Kitty's parents I would take good care of her while she stays with us. I want to make sure you do the same. Drive carefully, and make sure nothing happens to her."

Patrick hardly knew how to respond. He had answered the man directly, without guile. He felt a bit put upon and uncomfortable at the same time. "Why, I've been driving for several years without a traffic ticket, and I admire Kitty very much. I'll make sure nothing happens to hurt her."

"Well, just don't make any mistakes." He looked knowingly at Patrick.

"Ah, don't you worry about a thing, Mr. Hunter," Kitty chimed in. "I've come all this way from Ireland, and I can take care o' myself."

Patrick hustled her out the door and ushered her into his Honda.

"A bit of a heavy, isn't he?"

"No need to worry. The Hunters are very refined people, and very kind. I believe their sort feel responsible for taking good care of me."

He headed south along Lake Michigan on Sheridan Road, the scenic route downtown. They wound through the undulating terrain of wooded moraines, from which tiled roofs, and sometimes an entire estate, peeked through the trees. "On your left is the Bach House by Frank Lloyd Wright." Patrick said, like a tour bus driver.

"I've heard of him. Didn't he design lots of houses in Chicago?"

"I can show you plenty of those," he said, "especially near our family home in Oak Park."

Around another bend, on the lake side of the road, appeared a large three-story mansion, fronted by a classical pedimented porch, with six white Ionic columns and broad steps. He pointed with pride to the imposing estate "That one belongs to our new client for the hotel, restaurant and casino project."

"Oh my! Kitty marveled at the mansion before her eyes. "Do you suppose he would give us a tour?"

"Uh—I don't think so. I've only been inside the place a couple of times myself. I didn't get beyond the study." He squirmed over this one. A tour of Gloria's family home would be out of the question, fraught with awkward questions from Joe and Candy, even without their daughter present.

They followed the lakefront to Chicago's city limits, past the

Edgewater Beach Hotel, Belmont Harbor and the Yacht Club. In an azure sky with fair weather cumulus clouds, the brilliant sun cast ultramarine shadows on a choppy sea, dotted with sails in a swirl of myriad blues, white and golden sand.

"Ooh, boats bobbing in the harbor! This reminds me of home. We could look out to sea from the point at Cross Haven." Along Lake Shore Drive honey locusts lined the multi-lane roadway, framing a row of high-rise apartment towers.

"Do people swim in the lake?"

"Most certainly, but it's a bit chilly for that today. In fact, we don't really go to the beach until late June. Even then, the water's cold."

"Would you take me sometime? As children, we loved to romp on the strand."

"Of course." When they reached the magnificent mile of North Michigan Avenue, he pointed out the Drake hotel, the old water tower, the Clarion tower and the Wrigley building. They crossed the Chicago River and passed the Prudential building on North Michigan Avenue. In a row of lower buildings facing Grant Park, he pointed out Louis Sullivan's facade for the handsome Gage building. He drove down a ramp and into the eerie green illumination of the vast parking garage beneath the park. Climbing to the street level on foot, they walked south until they came to the steps of the Art Institute, between the lions guarding the portico. Kitty ran toward the nearest one, climbed up next to the pedestal, kissed his leg and squealed, "He's really sweet!".

"He's loyal, anyway."

Inside he led her to the museum's large collection of Impressionists. Their eyes feasted on the works of Manet, Corot, Pissarro, Monet and Seurat. "See how much these painters were influenced by the camera? They captured flying flags, drifts of smoke, just as the shutter freezes an instant in time—"

"Hello there, Patrick." A voice from behind interrupted him.

Patrick turned to the voice. "Oh hi, Russell." He greeted Russell Mannheim, a project architect from his firm, and his wife. "And who is this lovely young lady?"

"This is Kitty O'Connor. She works at my father's place. I'm showing her around the city."

"My pleasure, indeed." He winked at his wife. "I've always said

Patrick has a good eye."

"Oh, yes," Kitty said, "He loves this art collection: it's beautiful." She either was dodging the compliment or had missed the point.

At lunchtime they climbed to the top of a Renaissance-style double stairway to the upper level and passed through an archway. They marched through a series of galleries that seemed to extend for several blocks. "This is Gunsaulus Hall," Patrick explained. "This promenade bridges over the wide Illinois Central rail yard beneath and connects the Art Institute with its Annex building, on the far side of the tracks in Grant Park." Almost to the other end they arrived at the McKinlock Court museum café, a handsome, colonnaded space, once an open courtyard, but now enclosed by a glass roof, where they sat amid potted palms and taller trees. The sun filtered intermittently through the clouds of the springtime sky, amid the pleasant splash of a central fountain and the scent of lilies.

"Tell me more about your family, Kitty."

"We're a rowdy bunch. It's never quiet around the house. Did I mention we live on two stories above the family pub? It's located at Cross Haven, overlooking the sea just outside of Cork."

"Right, pub keepers as well," he said. "Thanks to the clientele, we get a good education on life."

"Happily, the younger children are put to bed on the third floor by the time the customers get boisterous down below. In the early evening, they talk more quietly, so I can read or finish my schoolwork at the kitchen table one floor above without too much disturbance."

"You must have a riotous time."

"Don't I know it, now? On Sunday night the pubs are supposed to be closed — they're very strict about it these days in Ireland, you know. On this particular Sunday, my father invited a couple of very good customers and their relatives visiting from America to come up and sit in our kitchen. He started serving them beer and bitter. They put their money on the kitchen table. There were about eight of us sitting around. Father was nervous. Even though this was just a social occasion, everyone knew we were crossing the line. We had my fourteen-year-old sister Eiliesh on the lookout, my younger sister Sinead posted by the window at the landing and ten-year-old Mary watching from the bottom of the stair below."

"What happened?"

"We were having a grand time. Their cousins came from Chicago, in fact, two college boys, the tall one quite handsome and the shorter one very talented. He serenaded me with folk songs on his ukulele. The older folks were laughing and making bets on whether I would fall in love with the foreign stranger."

"I can see myself in that scene."

"Just then, Mary and Sinead burst into the room, while Eiliesh called out from the hall. 'The Guards! They're almost up to the door.'

"'Hide the money!' Mother warned Father."

"Oh my God!" Patrick said. "Then what?"

"Two officers came in and walked around the kitchen, very serious, writing down everyone's names and addresses, including those in America of our visitors. Father said, 'We were just havin' friends in for little drink and a visit.' 'Sure, and you were,' said the one in charge. 'Just behave yourself and don't let this happen again. We're watchin' you.' He pointed to my father. After they left, Ma was upset. But Pa and the rest of them had a good laugh and a story to tell."

Their salads and sandwiches arrived.

"In this very building," he said, "downstairs at the Junior School, I used to take Saturday classes in drawing and painting during my high school years."

"I learned some of that from the sisters in the convent. Have you ever been to Europe?" Kitty asked.

"One time I spent almost a year in Paris, working for six months in an architectural office."

"My goodness! Where did you stay?"

"My job was in a suburban location, Neuilly-sur-Seine, just a half hour Metro ride from the Latin Quarter. I decided to stay in the heart of the city for my sightseeing. I had a huge trunk, which I didn't want to carry to the upper floors, When I found a hotel with an elevator, the Hotel California on the rue des Ecoles, it filled the bill."

"We stayed there, too, for the same reason—to save the bus driver's back. Do you speak French?"

"French people praised my pronunciation, although it's a devilishly difficult language to understand, especially as rapidly as Parisians speak."

"I know. I spent a summer studying with the Religious of the Sacred Heart. I studied French with the sisters at St. Catherine's College in Armagh. In fact, it was through them I got an offer to stay with the Hunters. At the end of the course we celebrated with a trip to Paris. It's so hard to speak in the idiom."

"For sure."

"Do you recall, this was a very old hotel, with a shared tub and shower room on each floor?"

"Right. You had to call a maid to get the bath ready. I felt like Inspector Clouseau, in the Pink Panther film," Patrick said. "I remember in one movie," Patrick said, "He said with a French accent, 'I want to rent a rheum,' which could mean, 'I want to catch a cold!'"

"You should have heard my phone calls to the front desk," Kitty continued. "It went something like this:"

«*Allo. Je voudrais prendre un bain.*»

"You said, 'I would like to seize a bathroom.'?" Patrick translated, and chuckled.

« *Quoi? Ah, vous voulez vous baigner?*» the concierge replied, meaning, "What? Oh, you want to bathe yourself?"

« *Oui, exactement.*»

"Yes, precisely," he translated.

« *Certainement, Mademoiselle., La bonne arrive tout de suite!*»

"Of course, Miss," he interpreted. "The maid is arriving presently."

"Then she brings towels, unlocks the room and knocks on your door to say everything is ready."

Now both Kitty and Patrick laughed until the tears came.

"You speak French quite well," she said.

"So they say, although your version is much more amusing." Patrick stood and held out his hand for hers. "Ready for the next gallery?"

"Show the way," Kitty said. They rose to leave and entered a narrow aisle between tables. Headed toward them, the hostess led a woman and her daughter, who stopped and blocked their way.

He faced Gloria and her mother. "Hello, Patrick," Gloria said. "And who is this?" Her icy tone froze him to the spot.

"Why, hello, Gloria! And Mrs. Bohannon. Uh…er…this is Kitty…O'Connor," he stammered. "She works at my father's pub. She's just come over from Ireland. I was showing her the sights of Chicago."

"Pleased ta meet ya, I'm shu-ah," her mother chimed in. "Whaddaya know? Patrick's got a different goil every day! I'm Candy Barr Bohannon. I take in cul-cha he-ah, ever since I met my husband in the course of business affairs."

"Intercourse business affairs?" Patrick verbalized what he was thinking before he could catch himself.

"To be shu-ah," she replied.

Luckily, the subtle dig went over her pretty head, coiffed in a blonde wave, Marilyn Monroe style. He immediately regretted his gaffe and feared Kitty and Gloria would catch it. He wondered if Candy's maiden name had really been Barr. He'd better not go there, since he had indeed gone to the girly shows on visits downtown with his high school pals. That name sounded just right to be advertised on a strip-show marquee.

She bulged out of a short sheath dress with a deep-cut neckline and high-heeled boots. Such a getup would make even her much younger, much slimmer daughter look cheap. She'd told him her premarital career was as a dancer. No doubt the lap and table varieties had formed part of her extensive repertoire, in addition to appearances on stage and video screen.

"Welcome to Americer, Miss O'Conna," she simpered to Kitty. "I'm shu-ah Patrick will guide ya well. He soitainly seems to know his way about town." She turned abruptly away. "Come, Gloria, we mustn't delay Patrick's tu-ah with his little bah-maid."

Patrick stiffened at the awkwardness of the whole encounter. Besides, he didn't appreciate her putting Kitty down by calling her a barmaid.

"Who *are* those people?" Kitty said to Patrick, when they were safely out of range.

"Relatives of a client," Patrick muttered, red-faced. "In business in this city, you meet all kinds."

"That girl—if you'll pardon the nautical expression—I don't like the cut of her jib. And her mother—she'd make a good figurehead for the boat!"

"Right, right," he mumbled, staring intently ahead.

Afterward they made their way back to the highway and cruised toward the house in Winnetka.

When he saw the relieved and welcoming smiles on the Hunters' faces, he understood their attitude. Ross Hunter wanted to be assured of Patrick's sincere interest and his honorable intentions. After spending a joyful day with her, he realized how rare, delicate and unspoiled she was. No wonder Mr. Hunter had such deep concern for her well-being.

TWENTY-ONE

Patrick arrived early at the Old Dominion Building for the progress meeting with Joe Bohannon. He found Mike MacKenna at his big desk in the round corner office, involved in a long phone conversation with his old friend and lumber dealer, Ed Frank, checking quantities on a large order. That work complete, as they reminisced about old times, his own thoughts drifted to how his uncle had introduced him to the construction industry.

On a subzero Christmas day when he was twelve years old, Mike took him and his father to one of one of his jobs, one of the City of Chicago's first public parking garages. They drove though the vacant downtown streets on the holiday to the construction site on Lake Street, where a concrete structure with flat slab floor construction was coming out of the ground. On the previous day they had poured concrete and Mike was concerned. They had to keep the structure warm to prevent the concrete from freezing. The structure was completed up to the fourth story, enclosed in tarpaulins, and the interior kept warm with a salamander-shaped heater in each column bay.

Mike had hired a watchman to keep the heaters going. If any one of them went out and any part of the fresh concrete should freeze, they would have to chop it out and pour it over again.

They climbed construction ladders to the highest built slab. Under the tent-like structure, his uncle found a salamander smoking—it had been allowed to run out of fuel and burn out. Uncle Mike searched for the watchman who was supposed to be on duty.

"Because of the holiday," he said, "we're paying that sonofabitch triple overtime, a dollar a minute, and he's not even here!" He combed Lake Street, checking every bar, while Patrick and his father stood shivering next to a heater to stay warm. A half-hour later he returned. "I finally found the lazy bastard. Fired him on the spot!"

They had to wait around longer until a replacement watchman arrived. In the meantime, his uncle explained exactly how the structure was built. Patrick admired the way Uncle Mike took control and ran things. He resolved then and there to join the building industry. The best lesson he learned that day, though, was to wear wool socks in the frigid Chicago winters.

Mike finally wrapped up his phone call. "Gotta go, Ed. They're arriving for my meeting." He stood and greeted Patrick.

"Hi, Mike."

"Looks like you've got some pretty big ideas." He pointed to the large presentation case Patrick had toted with him into the room. "What have you got for Joe?"

"Everything he wants and more." Patrick opened his flat portfolio and took out the plans he'd worked out so far for the casino and resort. He had each sketch taped to stiff foam board. He set up his collapsible easel and placed the stack of display boards on it. One top he showed a site layout sketch and a list of buildings.

"In addition to the casino, he wants restaurants, offices and a 200-room high-rise hotel with twenty lakeside chalets, as well as docks, a marina and lush landscaping. The complex totals about 300,000 square feet of building space plus major outdoor patios a swimming pool and sauna and outdoor bars.

"My God, Patrick, you're talking at least a forty million-dollar project!"

"That's what he says he wants."

"We'll have to break this down into phases," Mike said, "so Joe doesn't have a heart attack when he finds out the cost."

"Wait, I'm not done." Patrick began removing display boards from the stack to show each one—rough color sketches with exterior views of the complex from the water, the patio bar and swimming pool, and interiors of the casino and the hotel lobby.

"Wow! He'll be impressed. Our best strategy with Joe would be to get him excited about your big ideas. But we won't know about detailed costs until next time, after you and Joe can firm up the plans."

"I'm still uneasy about working for someone with connections to the mob."

"Patrick, that was all in the past. Today he runs a dozen legitimate businesses. He's been a good client for me, and this is *your* chance of a lifetime."

Patrick looked up to Uncle Mike. While his father lived by a strict work ethic and was disciplined in finances, Mike took a broader view.

"Look, don't worry about a shortage of funds—if the purpose is good, money will be found." Uncle Mike wasn't afraid of tackling the big jobs, including those others considered too risky. He could see beyond obstacles — physical, bureaucratic, ideological or political. If he was convinced something should be done, it could be done. He'd find a way.

Mike had taken Patrick in when he was just beginning to think about his career. He had shown him everything he knew about construction—handling personnel, winning new business, estimating and bidding. Mike had learned the construction business from the bottom up. He reminded Patrick of advice he gave to everyone who worked for him, "Don't be afraid to get your hands dirty."

"You're right, Mike," Patrick admitted. "If I'm ever going to succeed as you have, I've got to take some risks and confront my fear of the unknowns in a big project."

"There you go—confidence is half the battle."

Mike's intercom buzzed. and Gloria announced her father's arrival. "Good thing. He's here now."

"Mornin' boys!" Joe Bohannon smiled broadly. "Already here I see, Patrick. You're very punctuated."

He wore his jacket unbuttoned. It sported giant navy and white hounds-tooth checks, leaving a wide expanse of lavender sport shirt exposed, a black bow tie and ample black wool slacks. He wore a wide-brimmed Indiana Jones hat, which he left on. He stood facing them, legs braced, with his hands spread wide. The impression he made was somewhere between a hyena laughing his head off and a jaguar ready to pounce.

"I can hardly wait."

Mike offered his outstretched hand across the desk to grasp his. "We have some remarkable designs for you."

"Whatcha got?"

"Show Joe your sketches, Patrick."

"Since our last meeting I've walked the site, let the hilly terrain suggest where each building naturally belongs and identified the perfect location, between the lake and the Rock River, where the hotel and luxury restaurant will have views from every window." Patrick stood, rolled up his shirtsleeves and displayed his new color sketches of the proposed complex.

"Here's an aerial view of the entire resort. The casino, really a building which sits on a barge, looks like an old-fashioned river steamboat. It will be permanently anchored in the inlet from the river, accessible from all the restaurants, which front on the lake or the patio. The high-rise hotel rooms look out on either the lake or the river." He pointed out sailboats in the foreground, docks and motor launches speeding past a high-rise hotel on the river and the resort complex beyond. "Lakeside chalets, each with a private dock, are arranged along a cove at the near end of the lake. Between the casino and hotel, a recreation patio forms a central focus for outdoor activity. The hotel bars, indoor and outside, a curving row of cabanas, and several rooms of the restaurant surround the patio. A wading pool, a kids' water adventure area and an Olympic-size swimming pool form the focus of outdoor activity."

"Whoa, fantastic!" Joe walked over to the drawing and started examining the details. A color sketch showed bikini-clad beauties lounging alongside a luxurious swimming pool, white-coated waiters serving drinks and handsome swimmers sitting at an outdoor bar. "Look those gals are swimming—and the guy's over there at the bar ordering drinks. It's a huge pool. You've got the idea."

Patrick propped another board on his easel, depicting the interior of the casino, with elegant men and ladies standing at craps tables and sitting at slot machines. Next, he displayed a color sketch of affluent patrons dining with a view of the lake. "What do you think of that?" Patrick looked hopefully at Joe Bohannon.

"Looks great, but how much money would we'd have to raise

to pull this off?"

"First I need to firm up what we talked about before. For example, how many restaurants did you have in mind and what kinds?"

"I need three restaurants," Bohannon said, "all located off the main casino hall — a snack bar near the pool, an informal dining room with popular bar favorites like chicken wings, Caesar salads, soups, French fried onions and interesting side dishes. The third will be for fine dining ..." Patrick jotted down the program information as Joe reeled it off.

"I envision the fine dining area on a new little island in the lake." Patrick said, "reached from a covered bridge from the casino."

"That's too far for the patrons to walk. I think it will have to be adjacent to the casino, with a just a *view* of the lake," Joe said. "The hotel should have extra-large rooms, saunas, glassed in showers plenty of mirrors, mini bars and deep carpeting in every room," Bohannon continued. "The pool area will be something like what you have drawn there, with food service, jacketed waiters serving poolside drinks at umbrella tables and private cabanas for dressing and, you know, private get-togethers."

"Of course." Patrick mused as he wrote, "VERY PRIVATE" on his pad.

Patrick then went over his long list of potential buildings and site features in the complex.

"This resort has to be really classy to attract the high rollers. If we do this right, they'll come from all over the world," Joe said.

"Exactly my thoughts!" Patrick said. "In fact, we made some diagrams of the number and types of spaces and buildings in the complex. From that I've made a list of all the spaces in each building and suggested some recommended sizes, so we can get a feel for the scope and extent of the project." He handed out his preliminary Building Space Program.

"But what about the *theasibiliity*?" Bohannon spoke slowly, trying to use the proper word.

"What? Oh, the cost and budget. We don't know yet," Mike said.

"The design is exactly the sort of place I had in mind. But when will we know what it will cost to build it?"

"When we get the space program set," Patrick said, "we'll calculate how much building area we'll need to design. Then you can estimate revenue and expenses from each business operation."

"Once you authorize us to get going by signing the Patrick's contract, give him a check to cover initial costs and officially set his team to work, we'll do some estimates. We'll make a preliminary estimate of how much the first phase buildings will actually cost. Then we can calculate financing expense and return on investment.

"The whole idea is to do it in phases," Mike continued, "so you can ease into the project and know what each stage will cost. I imagine you'll want to start with the casino and a couple of restaurants, so you can begin earning money to pay for the rest of the complex right away. Our first phase will give you a rough idea of that. With each step, we'll know the actual cost more accurately."

"Here are copies of the contract," Patrick said, and showed him where to sign.

"It says here you want five thousand dollars to bind the deal. You really know how to hurt a guy." Bohannon grinned, signed the copies and pulled out a fat stack of bills. He counted out fifty, one-hundred-dollar bills. "Sorry about all the C-notes, but I have an all-cash system."

"Can't do better than cash, I suppose." Patrick accepted the stack and took the rubber band Mike handed him. "This is a good faith payment to get us started. The total amount for each phase is spelled out in the contract. We'll bill you monthly, less payments, like this one, already credited to your account."

"For the larger amounts in the next phases," Mike said, "both Patrick's company and mine will need checks. We'll accept a bank cashier's check if you want—but our accountants and the Feds require it."

"Hm-m," Joe said, "I'll have to look into it."

"Now we can start the team going," Patrick said. "Thank you, Mr. Bohannon. We'll make you proud."

"Call me Joe, kid."

"Deal. And don't call me 'kid.' Deal?"

"Deal. Hey Mike, I like this kid's style."

"There, you did it again," Mike said, grinning.

Patrick carefully placed the contract and the bundle of cash in his attaché case. He left the boards with the sketches in the office for Mike to study.

On his way out of the office Patrick patted Gloria on the shoulder, "Nice surprise, all right."

"Patrick, I need to talk to you. Do you have time for lunch?"

He looked at his watch. "Why not? We can celebrate our new project. Let's go."

Twenty-Two

Since the day was cool but pleasant, they walked over to the Berghoff, at Adams near Dearborn, so long established, Patrick had learned, it received Chicago's first liquor license. It was one of Gloria's favorite places, and they sat in the iconic, old-fashioned German interior. Patrick described his plans for the new casino hotel complex.

"Isn't it wonderful?" he said.

"I'm happy for you. You're on your way. But let's talk about *us*."

"Of course, always."

"So…I've been thinking lately."

Patrick choked up. It was never good when they were thinking. "Uh, what's up?"

He inhaled the unique musty scent of the ancient wood interior, mingled with the aroma of roasting meats, rich sauces and secret spices. He placed his napkin in his lap and tried to calm himself. Chicago's oldest remaining restaurant reeked of traditional atmosphere. The room was paneled with dark wood. Ceiling beams had carved and painted coats of arms at the brackets. Leaded glass windows admitted a dim light from what seemed an earlier time.

The chatter of lunchtime conversations contrasted with the sounds of their antiquated accounting system. From the entry to the kitchen emerged the clink-clink-clank of zinc tokens, which superannuated, black-vested waiters plunked down to buy the food they were about to serve, advancing a loan to the house until they collected payment from their customers.

One of their number, Otto, it said on his brass name badge, took their orders for carved sandwiches. When Gloria began to speak, Patrick remained preoccupied, trying to anticipate what she had in mind.

"After being together for over a year, we know we're compatible. When do we take the next step?"

"What you mean? We go nice places, do interesting things, enjoy each other's company. Need I mention how we please each other in bed? There's no reason to complain about any of that, is there?"

"Oh Patrick, don't get the wrong idea. I love you and I want it to last forever. But what about you? Will you always love me and stay with me?"

Whoa, wrong turn. Seems she wasn't really interested in the past. "I haven't given you any reason to doubt that, have I?" Sinking fast, he needed a life preserver.

"Well, Patrick," she began, "you see a lot of women—at your family pub, the office and going around town. I just wonder, that's all."

Oh-oh. The office, certainly, was not an issue. But the encounter at the Art Institute must have stuck in her craw.

"Look, you're a woman." Might as well go for broke.

"No kidding. That's why you noticed me in the first place. You *had* to be my lab partner—in chemistry! Good chemistry, all right. That's why we've become a 'thing.'"

"No, no, I mean…I need to tap into your woman's expertise."

"You haven't already done that?" Her lips and eyes conspired in their sexiest smile.

"Oh that, for sure. But I want to know what else a woman like you *really* wants." Beat her to the punch.

"It's hard to pin down, a kind of yearning—she craves stability, recognition of her status, permanence."

Oh crap, a new concept of their relationship. "What are you getting at?"

"I think we should move in together." Seismic forces were shifting beneath, as if a huge whirlpool had opened in the bottom of the lake to swallow him. The stakes of his involvement with Gloria were climbing fast.

"But, but… there's no room at my place—not for the way I want you to live." Patrick failed to conceal his alarm at the prospect. A few months ago, perhaps, he would have merely shrugged his shoulders, as casually as he would brush the dust off his jacket, ignored it and moved on —a minor annoyance. Now he was in the deep channel without a life jacket, about to go down for the third time.

"We need to get a nice apartment on Lake Shore Drive."

"We do?" It was news to him.

"Oh yes, I've even got ideas about how I want to furnish the place."

"Really? Tell me. You're the client. It's the architect's job to listen."

"Oh, I'll need so many things. In last month's Architectural Digest, I saw the nicest living room. It had a cheery fireplace centered on one wall, with some beautiful eighteenth century French andirons."

"Next to it I imagine we could have a comfortable old chair," Patrick joined in, "with a bookcase along the wall for my favorite books and magazines, and a side table where I could keep my reading light, pens and sketchpad, as well as a place to set a drink."

"Of course," she said.

Patrick was cheered that that she was getting into the spirit of her plan.

"But that belongs in the den."

Patrick gulped his mouthful of beer. "Oh, there's a den, too."

"In front of the fireplace" she continued, "there was an antique coffee table with a crepe-de-Chine upholstered sofa on each side. Behind one of them was a long table with two gorgeous Arabian lamps on either end."

"Don't you think that's a bit too stuffy and formal for relaxing after a hard day's work?"

"Not at all. If I'm going to be doing volunteer work, I need a place for my committees to meet. If we're going to have tea, we'll need tables to set it on."

Couldn't she decide, without consulting a magazine for a model, what she needed in the room and select attractive furniture and lighting? Why clutter the space with heavy tables and hideous lamps, to match some third-rate interior decorator's idea of "good taste?"

Otto brought their plates and unloaded them carefully from both arms. The fuss about food gave him time to conceal his alarm, but the respite didn't last long. He bit into his carved roast beef sandwich—too big a bite—and it stuck in his throat. He had to wash it down with a big swallow of his draft beer. In addition to the bolus in his gullet, he felt a sudden weight on his chest and found it hard to breathe. He scrambled for words, and time. "Wouldn't your father be furious?" Maybe he could play that angle, Joe's resistance. The stakes in this game had risen to new heights.

"My mother is on my side, and I've been working on Dad to look at me, for chrissake. Did he notice I wasn't his little flat-chested fourth-grader anymore? I'm a grown woman now. Dad needs to realize I'm twenty-four years old and perfectly capable of starting my own life."

"After your father's project is finished," he hastened to add, "I think it would be great. By then I should be earning more money." It seemed perfectly logical to him.

"I was hoping you'd be thrilled at the prospect." Her downcast eyes betrayed Gloria's disappointment.

"Of course, I think your wish is perfectly reasonable," he assured her. "I don't see any reason why we couldn't. Just not right now."

"Reasonable? I'm talking love, a life together, and you're this cold, calculating computer brain. You don't love me. You meet all kinds of women at your family's bar. I've heard plenty of stories about you—none of them good. I'll bet you've even fallen for that pathetic, freckled redhead I saw at the Art Institute!"

"That's not fair. I show all the new kids around town—so they feel welcome here."

"You welcomed that woman, all right. I saw her pretty face— and the silly look on yours."

Patrick glanced around the restaurant. Two secretaries at the next table were staring at him. Gloria was creating a scene. Beyond the slight to him, her comments weren't even fair to Kitty.

His perfectly logical objections seemed to have no sway over her groundswell of emotion. A maxim of computer wisdom flashed across his mind—garbage in, garbage out. Then this mental dialog box disappeared, and his internal computer crashed, displaying the Blue Screen of Death.

Gloria's eyes glazed over. She sniffled, and her eyes filled. "I've given you a year in the prime of my life. I'm not getting any younger, you know."

Eager to climb out of the eighteenth century and breathe the fresh air of the modern world, he paid the check immediately, followed by further clinking and clanking from the direction of the kitchen traffic cop. As Otto's supply of zinc tokens was replenished, Patrick imagined he heard the clanking of a cell door. They stood, he retrieved his well-funded attaché case from the floor and they walked back to her office. When they parted at the brass entry to the Old Dominion building, he kissed her very publicly on the lips.

"Thanks for hearing me out," she said, "and for the nice lunch."

"Food for thought." He grinned mischievously.

A smile flickered on her lips. She nodded gamely, waved back and disappeared inside. If they were going to stay together—and he refused to see the alternative—he would have to get with her program. But could he? He felt his heart fleeing in the opposite direction. What to do about his growing regard for Kitty?

Twenty-Three

Monday morning, Patrick's office phone rang. "Patrick, I hate to tell you this, but it looks like your deal with Bohannon has already spun way out of control." O'Malley didn't sound too broken up about it. He was delighted to report more bad news. It was called job security.

"I agree, but I've got to stay on board or take a big fall."

"That's it. We'd like you to continue working as normal, but gather evidence for us about illegal activities. I've called in Radi, a Special Agent we often work with at the FBI."

"Roddy? Rod— who?"

"Piotr Radwinski." O'Malley spelled it for him. "It's a Polish name. Not everybody in town is Irish, you know. We need you to come in Monday to the FBI Office on South Dearborn." The detective soldiered on. "Ask for him."

As if he didn't have enough worries with Gloria, this appointment gave him more reasons to toss sleeplessly in his solitary bed over the weekend.

When he arrived at the FBI Monday morning, he was escorted to a conference room where O'Malley sat with a tall, slender, blond-haired man and introduced the special agent.

"Look, Mr. MacKenna, you've got a problem." Radwinski began. The agent's clear blue eyes bore into him. "We found a handgun registered to you on the casino property."

"That gun was stolen. I told Detective O'Malley about it last week."

"That was last week. The body found in Joe Bohannon's lake was identified as Walter McDougal Howe. That makes you a person of interest."

"I don't get it. Why?"

"MacKenna," O'Malley added, "you were out at the site when they arrived with the body. As far as we're concerned, you're involved."

Patrick couldn't catch his breath. "But I thought you said it was accidental. When he fell, he struck his head."

"It's unclear when he was shot," Radwinski said. "Police at the stadium hustled him out of there, covered, so fast the medical examiner didn't even get a look at him to see whether he was dead or just unconscious. And then the body disappeared."

"But– but, what about the ballistics. I didn't fire that gun, and the bullet in that body could not have matched one from the gun."

"That's still being analyzed in forensics. We won't know results for a couple of weeks."

"Detective O'Malley, you said, while the guards were being questioned the body was carried off in a private hearse. I was on the other side of the arena when the body fell, with Joe Bohannon and his family, and I can prove it."

"With Bohannon? Ha! Not exactly the strongest alibi," Radwinski said.

"Wait, if the body was being guarded by your forces, detective, how could it be released to a private party and not taken directly to the morgue?"

"Good point, Mr. MacKenna. We puzzled about that one for a while, until we looked more into it more closely. We found a witness, a spectator who had gone outside the loading dock to have a smoke. You want to pick it up there, O'Malley?"

"Sure," the detective said. "There was a new officer nobody knew on the loading dock when the police were interviewing the guards. The police figured the unfamiliar cop was a rookie assigned to stadium duty and gave him the job of watching the body."

"But didn't the witness think it was weird that the body was taken off in a hearse and not a police vehicle?" Patrick asked.

"There's the thing," O'Malley continued. "He said he did wonder about it, but he figured, since the cop got into the hearse with four guys in sunglasses, who he assumed were detectives, it was okay."

"He must have been faking it," Patrick suggested.

"You should talk," O'Malley said.

Patrick was on the spot. He was still unconvinced that this dimwit detective knew what he was doing. He squirmed and fired more questions.

"But—but what if somebody wanted him dead?" Patrick was grasping at straws.

"If he owed them money, they'd keep him alive—to pay up." O'Malley said, with a smug smile.

"Owed them money—you kidding? He was an heir to the Clarion fortune!"

"Hey, I just ask the questions. I don't have the answers."

"I've told you everything I know. What else do you expect me to do?"

"Mr. MacKenna," Radwinski said, "let me bring you up to date. You ever heard of La Cosa Nostra?"

"Sure, the nationwide gangster organization that runs rackets in the other big cities. But I understand they're pretty much out of business today."

"Not completely. And 'Chicago Joe' Bohannon, your client, runs the old North Side Irish gang. He's an underboss of the Chicago Outfit."

"Joe, still in the Outfit? He says he's retiring, just in legitimate businesses now."

"We'd like to retire him, for a nice long stay in federal prison. Let me explain what it means to be initiated into 'the life' of the organized crime family, as they call it.

"The family was a closed shop from the 50s until the early 70s, when the ranks were thinned by death, old age and long prison sentences. They only started taking new members after that, and then young Bohannon got his invitation to join. They circulated his name around the five families, to see if anybody disapproved, and he was accepted. But make no mistake. Once you are inducted into the life of La Cosa Nostra—that's Italian for 'our thing'—

nothing comes before loyalty to them. No brother has priority over another, and they claim there is no greater bond among men. And you're in it for life."

"I still don't understand what it took for him to be accepted as a soldier in the family."

"You have to do some useful work for the organization. That includes the possibility of killing someone. Once you've done that you've 'made your bones.'"

"So that's why they call an initiated member a 'made' man."

Radwinski continued. "Then you take the blood oath. You promise to keep the secrets and traditions that you've learned about. You don't violate another member's wife, sister or daughter. You never raise a hand against another member. You must carry out orders, even if that means killing your friend. Nothing is more important than La Cosa Nostra and the life you've taken on."

"Man, that's scary stuff," Patrick said. "But Joe said, since the 70s it's been more civilized, more like a business, with violence used only after all other possibilities have been exhausted, as a last resort. And didn't Senator Estes Kefauver, Elliott Ness, William Roemer and the FBI pretty much wipe out their rackets?"

"Even without those rackets," the special agent continued, "they're into other ones—drug dealing, prostitution, internet pornography and worldwide human trafficking. Those boys from Detroit smell all that money. They're trying to move in on the old mobsters. Before you know it, they'll control your deal, and we'll have a gang war and another powerful gangster organization on our hands."

Crap, no matter what objection Patrick raised, they had an answer for it. "But what do you want from me?"

"You're working closely with Bohannon and his cronies, so we need a little favor from you." O'Malley turned to the special agent. "Radi, please continue."

"Mr. MacKenna, we need you to help us smoke out whoever plotted this murder." Since you have already infiltrated the suspect's organization, we want you to do some covert evidence collection."

"Wear a wire? Oh, God." Patrick could feel his life flashing before him—he was as good as dead. "But that's illegal!"

"For most people, yes." the special agent said, "But not when you're working with the FBI. Now, it's not as bad as it once was. You don't have to strap anything to your body. Do you carry a cell phone?"

"Sure, doesn't everyone? I keep it right here in this little case on my belt."

"Let me see your phone."

Patrick took out his Danger Hip-Hop Sidekick I, the first flip phone, with its full Blackberry-type keyboard, and handed it over. An early adopter, Patrick had insisted to Jason Halliday he needed the expensive accessory to communicate from job sites and back to the office, no matter where he might be traveling.

Radwinski set it on the table and took another device out of his briefcase. "Here, try this one on for size."

He tried to insert it into the bulky case on his belt where he stowed the phone. "It fits," he said joylessly.

"Hidden in plain sight," Radwinski said. "When you go out on location, all I have to do is call that phone and it answers. It won't ring or light up. I can hear any sounds, even a whisper, within twenty feet of the device and record it back in my office."

"B-but, do I have to carry that at all times? That's not fair!"

"No, no," said the agent. "Carry your own phone the rest of the time. Just make sure to turn this one off when you're not with our suspects. I don't really want to know where you are or hear what you say to your girlfriends in bed." He chuckled.

Patrick wondered about that. Did the agent know he was dating Bohannon's daughter?

"When are you next scheduled to see him again?" Radwinski asked.

"I'm picking him up after lunch. He's supposed to walk the site with me this afternoon to approve the locations for the buildings."

"Go in peace, young man. Thanks for helping us out. Let's see what he says when you mention, casually, mind you, that you ran into those fishermen last weekend—the ones who threw that big one back in."

"I-I g-guess I can. I hope he doesn't kill me for asking."

"When these guys find out you know more about them than they realized, you'd be amazed how fast they back off."

Twenty-Four

At one p.m. that afternoon, nervous and jumpy, Patrick pulled up to Joe's Little Place. Bohannon stood in front, smoking a cigar and taking in the street scene. Patrick jumped out and held the door of the Accord for his client. As he drove to the interstate, he described their activities in the past week

"I've got the revised Building Space Program figured out and will give you a copy today. We figured two restaurants to start, with the luxury dining room coming a year later—"

"Nope, I want that restaurant from the start, with a more casual one inside the casino. Then the third can come later, a snack bar on the inside, which also serves the pool."

"Could be done, for sure. I was thinking you could build a finer one after the funds in the casino start flowing."

"I need the revenue at the beginning."

"Fair enough. I'll add it to the program. What I wanted to discuss with you," Patrick continued, "besides identifying all the rooms and spaces, was the site layout. We'll take a walk and see if you think I've found the best places to locate the buildings."

"You know, if this works, maybe I really can retire in a few years and leave something to Gloria — and you."

"Don't worry about me. I already have a job, and Gloria may get tired of me long before then."

Besides, Patrick wanted to be an architect and design a casino and hotel, not run one. He was doubly nervous. For the FBI to hear that he might become part owner of the project along with gangsters was enough to put him away for good. But the prospect of marrying Joe's daughter was even more threatening to his claim of innocence. Now he was cooked.

"We'll see about that, Patrick. Gloria's serious about you, and she won't give up easily."

They arrived at the site and crept up the gravel road. As they got out of the car, he spotted the rowboat, neatly staked down, with the tarp in place. "You know those fishermen you told me about, who use your boat when they're out here?"

"Sure, they come out here all the time."

"Well, last Sunday, I was out here, looking over the site and deciding where we might want to locate the buildings. Two guys took the boat out, threw something very big into it and rode out into the middle of the lake. By then the sun was setting. I couldn't see them anymore in the twilight and we decided to pack it in and go home. Any idea any idea who they might be?"

"Could've been Emil and Axel, local farmers who love to fish. They go out there all the time. I never know when they're there.

"They had dark suits on. It didn't really look like they were fishing."

"Hmm. Emil has a big yellow straw fishing hat. Axel always wears a plaid flannel shirt, a windbreaker and blue denim jeans. Beats me."

Either Joe was either a very good liar or he hadn't heard about all the excitement on his property over the weekend. The FBI would now know that this was news to Chicago Joe.

The rest of the afternoon was devoted to looking at the site and verifying ideas Patrick had considered for placement of the buildings. Joe liked the idea of locating the high-rise along the river with views to both sides—toward the river and to the hills, marina and lake. He agreed that the restaurants should focus on the central outdoor area and pool. Where to put the fine-dining restaurant was the subject of considerable discussion. Patrick wanted to extend a promontory from the lake shore and at its end build up an island out of material dredged from the lake bed, with a picturesque bridge leading to it.

"What if it's raining?" Joe objected.

"We can build a handsome covered walkway from the island right to the casino entrance."

"That's probably five-hundred yards, too far from the gaming space. They'll never come into the casino to gamble."

They agreed to make the restaurant a wing of the casino building, facing the lake shore, overlooking the picturesque row of chalets with their own boat docks.

Patrick was relieved that Joe didn't say anything to raise FBI suspicions that Patrick might be implicated in the murder of this man whose body was dumped in the lake. Still, he wondered what they would think of the prospect of his marrying Gloria, and he feared he would be served up to the law on a platter.

Twenty-Five

In his days at the office and nights alone in his apartment Patrick's thoughts returned to Kitty. Even this brief separation only increased his desire to see her again. On nights he was scheduled to work he would occasionally find she had scheduled her night off. When she was there, she served the busiest corner of the restaurant and took few breaks. When he did see her, she usually held a tray of drinks or plates of food she had to balance and scarcely glanced in his direction. At first he found her neglect and preoccupation with other things amusing. Was she playing a game with him? He didn't know, but it did nothing to cool his ardor.

Only when he had to attend an architect's regional conference in Kenosha, Wisconsin, over a weekend, did it hit him how much he missed her. Through two days of seminars on improving his negotiation skills, understanding zoning codes and learning new environmental regulations, his thoughts drifted away from the dry presentations to a new, soft place, where he felt relieved and comforted. He recalled scenes with Kitty — sketching in the field at Rockville, cheerful moments together during break time at the pub and her excitement and curiosity at the farm and other exhibits at the museum. Her joy in simple things, her lilting brogue and the merriment in her eyes had the power to cheer and sustain him.

Jaded with the attention, physical attraction and fulfillment of his needs with women, this was a new feeling—pining, aching for a glimpse of her smiling face and an intense desire to be with her. Alone in his hotel room, he felt a new sensation — the pain of separation.

Any hope of ridding himself of this obsession was dashed when, on return from his trip, he reappeared Monday night at the pub. Business was slow. Patrick wandered into the kitchen for a late dinner, picked up a burger and cottage fried potatoes and considered his untenable situation. He had not heard from Joe Bohannon, who was not returning phone calls. He still resisted calling Gloria. He didn't see the point in stirring all that up again. It seemed they disagreed on just about everything, including house design.

Kitty's grin when she saw him came as a surprise. Her alluring appearance, even in her modest, crisp waitress pinafore, clarified his problem. He missed her. Like a majestic sunrise after a storm over Lake Michigan, his spirits rose.

He stood beside the help table, where she sat, with his plate and glass.

"Where have you been lately—busy with your girlfriend?"

"Hardly. I was at a conference in Wisconsin, brushing up on my marketing and environmental knowledge."

"Improving your mind, for a change." She cast a blank glance toward him. It landed below his belt line.

"In fact. I haven't seen Gloria for a couple of weeks. We have so many issues these days. Mind if I sit?"

"Why not. Your family owns the table."

He sat down beside her with his dinner. "You seem so distant these days. What is it?"

He couldn't fathom what had become of their easy familiarity, her sense of fun, her friendly manner.

"I didn't think you even noticed me. Since you're here, why don't you tell me something about architecture. You said we couldn't get a tour of that client's house in — where was it? — Kenilworth? What's it like inside?"

"The basic problem with that house, Kitty, is that it's trying to be something it isn't. It's a copy of a manor house in England. Whoever designed the original home arranged the rooms according to the way they lived in those days. It has all the necessary spaces for a different era: a parlor, library, dining room, sun room, drawing room (which is short for withdrawing room) on the main level, and servants' quarters, kitchen, scullery, larders and dry food storage below. Bedrooms and suites were located on the upper floors. These houses were used in certain ways to receive guests, to give parties, balls and dinners, allow the help to do the housework, accommodate visiting family members or honored guests, and to house numerous live-in servants. Different rooms were occupied at different times of day and year, depending on how the sun fell on the building and where the fireplaces were located."

"What's wrong with that?"

"Today a family breaks down activities differently. We don't live that way anymore. Rather than copy an older style intended for different living activities, social customs and psychological impact, modern architects have preferred to start over and decide what kind of a house each individual family needs."

"I see what you mean. Our house in Cross Haven was never designed to be a pub, with living quarters upstairs. There's no place to study, the thatched roof leaks in winter and there's almost no privacy for anyone. If we could have afforded it, it would have been better to start over and build something new."

"For one thing, today's house has no servants," Patrick continued, "so the wife wants to be part of the family while she's preparing dinner. The kitchen, full of labor-saving equipment, like dishwashers, automatic ovens and a microwave, is often open to the space where the family gathers—the family room. Year-round heating and air conditioning makes it possible to ignore climate. And some rooms, like the dining room, often need different kinds of lighting—mellow, for dining, or bright, for doing homework. While most contemporary homes share these newer features, the customs, social habits and design preferences of different families often call for totally different layouts and styles."

"Would you like to design your own house someday?" Kitty asked.

"Of course, although first I'd have to have someone to design it for and occupy it with. I see no sign that will happen soon for me."

"Nor do I," Kitty continued in a detached tone. "But I have a friend who does."

"Who's that?"

"You don't know her. Mary came over on the boat with me. We keep in touch. We had plenty of time together on the long voyage. We've talked about it in great detail."

"What sort of a house does she want?"

"She likes to dream. She'd like to have a flower garden and maybe even space to grow vegetables. It would be wonderful if the house backed up to the woods, with a little stream, where she could go out and catch frogs and turtles, see the birds come and go and listen to the chirp of crickets. If she had a little one, they could go exploring in the woods and gather wildflowers, and even some berries."

"A little one? Unlike you, does she want a family?"

"Mary is on the fence. I think she's in love and doesn't know it, nor what to do about it. She's not ready to marry, either. She's desperate to have her man but she doesn't know how to tell him. Don't you know what a puzzle that can be for a young woman?"

"Maybe the guy isn't interested in her. Otherwise, he might let her know"

Her body stiffened, she took a deep breath and her expression turned sad. "I'd really be sorry about that. She'd be so disappointed."

"I've never thought much about it. So that's what she wants for a yard. What kind of house would she like?"

"All the rooms in the house would have views out toward the gardens and the woods," she said. "In summer, she could open up big glass doors and it would be like living outdoors. In winter they would have a lovely view of the ice and snow on the trees and rocks. But they would all be snug and cozy by the fire."

"All?"

"She and her man and the wee one. She couldn't do that alone, could she?"

"So, what's stopping her?" he asked.

"It's such a dilemma. If she admits how she feels and they decide to marry, she'll be in for the whole public to-do, with families involved. Before you know, it'll spin out of control. All she wants is to settle down with her man and start a small family. This problem might cause her to wither and lose her spirit."

"Maybe they should elope, announce it later."

"I hadn't thought of that."

"If she wants a castle, like the one you asked me about in Kenilworth, I wouldn't be interested in helping her. But, if she ever needs a custom-designed house like the one you describe, I could do that. Perhaps she would select me as her architect?"

"She's just dreaming, Patrick. In that unlikely event, I would make sure you were consulted."

"I would be honored."

"Heavens! It's time for our next set. I've got to go find Sean and the boys."

Patrick sat sipping his iced tea, dreaming a little bit himself. He wondered if Kitty had reconsidered her position on getting involved with men. If so, she'd done a good job of concealing it from him. He wouldn't dare approach her about it unless he was serious and committed. He enjoyed conversations with her, especially a good argument. Until recently, Gloria had seldom challenged him directly. But she let her wishes be known and pouted when he failed to acknowledge her desires. He thought he knew where he stood with Kitty — just friends. But this conversation made him wonder. What would life with Kitty be like?

Who was Mary, anyway? Funny, Kitty never mentioned her before.

TWENTY-SIX

Late Tuesday afternoon, Uncle Mike called and asked Patrick to meet him at the Mid-America Club for a drink after work. He fought his way through a steady rainstorm for the four blocks to the East Randolph location and dripped dry in the express elevator to the 80th floor, touted as "the only club in Chicago with a panoramic view of the city's distinctive skyline." At a quiet table by a window in the bar, he was surprised to find Joe Bohannon sitting with his uncle. Since he hadn't expected to see Joe, he didn't have the FBI's special phone with him. He took the only available seat, facing the windows. There was no skyline visible. The view consisted of gray murk and raindrops racing across the outside of the glass.

"What'll you have, Patrick?" his uncle said. "I'm buying." He and Joe were sipping whiskey on the rocks.

"Any old port in a storm, I suppose," he said with a wistful sigh.

"We have the 1965 Porto Gold," the alert waiter said, without missing a beat. "It's only ninety-five dollars per ounce."

"I'll take a draft beer."

Joe expanded on his plans for the casino. He had always been interested in the entertainment industry, he said. Early in his career, while still on the East Coast, he had provided funds to help start a recording studio, Shiva records, with Mort Feinberg, a New York promoter. Joe put up funds where needed to advance to the talent and became a silent partner in exchange for a fifty percent share in the business.

"I've always enjoyed being part of the music scene," he said, "the stars, the excitement and the chance to earn fairly clean money, flowing like a river from records and shows. I first got interested in the business in the mid-60s, when the Beatles invaded America. After they appeared on the Ed Sullivan show they became an overnight sensation. Elvis had captured the hearts of American teens, and soon rock 'n roll took over. The mobsters were more interested in the old standard entertainers, like Frank Sinatra, Tony Bennett, Dean Martin, the McGuire sisters and Sammy Davis Jr. I had a hunch that rock 'n roll held the key to the future, and I played it."

"What entertainers did you have in those days?" Mike asked.

"Mort had an eye for talent, and he teamed up with another partner, Jerry "Nervy" Winters, who knew how to talk to blacks in jive, dressed flamboyantly, and even walked with a juke in his step—one hip dude. The two of them recorded talent, some of them unknown at the time. It included Janet Jackson, Dionne Warwick, Lionel Richie, the Spinners, the Four Tops, Miles Davis and Patty LaBelle—a glittering array of black superstars. This business was so lucrative that they soon expanded, lost control and immersed themselves in sex and drugs, in addition to rock and roll."

"You told me the mob really frowned on drugs in those days," Mike said.

"Yep, that's when I dropped them. Drugs are always a wildcard, and we didn't want any part of a company we couldn't control. I didn't see Nervy for twenty years, until he and a new partner, Artie Blaine, turned up in Chicago, about fifteen years ago. They approached me again about partnership in the sports agency business. A smooth talker like Winters could use the ready cash to sign a disadvantaged but talented athlete for a five percent share of a professional sports contract. These were running in the millions, sometimes as high as twenty million dollars. It was an easy business to learn, too. The veteran agents in the industry set price ranges for the year. All the rest of us had to do was follow suit, sit back and wait for our athletes to sign and our percentage fees to roll in. Because of the large sums involved in professional sports contracts, it seemed like a sound investment. If you could sign a college player and live with his lower earnings during his college eligibility, there were big bucks to be made when he joined the pros. This business was also a logical extension of our involvement with the gambling and booking business, by giving us direct control over the professional and college athletes."

Joe joined the partnership soon after it was formed, he explained. But this time, he was not permitted to be so silent. In the music business, when a long-term client decided he would prefer to go to a higher-class agency, Artie would step in and asked to be left alone with him. "'I'm disappointed in your decision,' he'd say. 'Why don't you stay with us another six months and see how you feel about it then?' That's all it took — just a hint of a little muscle, and the client would re-sign with the agency. The music business was so saturated with mobsters, this kind of discipline was seldom noticed as out of the ordinary.

"We figured this same logic could be applied to the sports industry," Joe continued. "We started signing athletes, and the business took off. In three years, we were leading sports agents, representing thirty-five players. We even added a little glitter to their careers by mingling them with stars in the music industry, bringing them to award ceremonies and celebrations and introducing them to top recording artists.

"We would advance cash to them, to get around the law. They couldn't be paid, or they'd lose their amateur status. This got their attention to our agency and usually resulted in representing these athletes when they went to college teams. It was low pay for us, since the athletes were paid mostly with scholarships and reimbursed for other educational expenses. We could make it up, however, when the athletes joined professional teams. We ran into trouble, though, with amateur sports. Any payments to the college athletes were a violation of National College Athletic Association rules and were against the law.

"While Nervy Winters would entice the athletes with his hip charm, Artie was the was the bad guy in the negotiations," Joe continued. "The feds eventually heard about Blaine's activities and tapped his phone. They recorded Blaine threatening to have his mob pals, implying my gang, break the valuable arms and legs of an athlete who had accepted his advance payments and then signed with another agency. Blaine also threatened professional NFL candidates, but one player took it further and testified before a grand jury. The rest is history — the nationwide exposé of amateur sports. All kinds of people were indicted, including me. I lost my case, but for the past ten years my lawyers have succeeded in keeping me out on appeal. We'll see what happens, but one of these days I just may have to cop a plea and take a little vacation. I just hope I get sent to that nice new prison facility north of Phoenix, where the time I have to do won't be quite so hard."

Each of Bohannon's revelations further surprised Patrick. He thought he had heard about the extent of their involvement in illegal activities. Wherever there was big money to be found, this crowd had an uncanny ability to get a piece of the action. He was getting a glimpse of the real fate of gangsters. These boys were committing major crimes, and it would eventually catch up with them. If Patrick were convicted of even a single felony count, he would lose his architectural license. Despite the chill off the dripping windows, he began to sweat.

"But I still have lots of friends in the music scene," he said, on a cheerier note, "When we open this casino, I'll parade them through one a week, in a cavalcade of stars!"

"Do you have any plans for funding the casino project yet?" Mike asked.

"Not yet. But I have some appointments in the coming weeks, Maybe even some of these deep pockets from the music business. I can assure you the money will be found."

The waiter brought Patrick his drink, and they toasted to the new project's success.

"I have a plan, Mike, as I've explained to Patrick. If he's smart enough to keep himself in the picture, he stands to gain a big share of Gloria's legacy."

Patrick shifted in his chair. Why was Bohannon bringing all this up now? At the very least, funding for this project would take a lot longer than he, and especially Jason Halliday, had planned.

"By the way, Patrick," Bohannon continued. "Gloria and her mother were talking about you just the other day. Seems they ran into you at the Art Institute café a couple of weeks ago, squiring around a little Irish gal. What's that all about?"

Despite the cool day and the chill off the storm-lashed windows, the room felt unbearably hot. He tried to sound natural and casual in his response.

"Oh, I do that with a lot of the young Irish immigrants. I show them around, introduce them to Chicago, so they don't feel so far from home or get lonesome in a strange new place. I know I would appreciate that in a strange foreign country."

"Your public-spirited concern for your father's employees is touching, Patrick. But don't forget about your future family. Gloria is feeling a bit lonesome these days."

Bohannon smiled at him, but his eyes weren't as friendly as his advice. It wasn't a pleasant feeling, and he wondered how Joe had gotten the idea he was suddenly in charge of Patrick MacKenna. He looked to his uncle for help.

Instead of jumping immediately to his defense, Michael regarded Patrick with an objective stare. "Patrick, I've known Joe for a long time. When he offers you advice, it's always to your benefit to take it."

Crap! Why was Uncle Mike taking Bohannon's side? His discomfort increasing to the breaking point, Patrick looked at his watch and thought about making an excuse to leave. In desperation, he pulled a thought out of thin air.

"Joe, please understand. More than anything I want the best for Gloria. The fastest way I can help her future is to get this project going." Patrick reached for a slip of paper in his wallet. "Recently I met a guy," he said, "of all places, at the Museum of Science and Industry, working in the coal mine. He seemed too smart to be a museum guide and, when we got talking, he asked me if I knew anyone who had a job for him. He called me again today and told me more.

"Sounds like he's got some business sense, and he might know a lot about the kind of folks you know. When I asked him who he used to work for, he said he was an assistant to Jimmy Roma. Does that name mean anything to you?"

Joe's eyes darted around the near-empty lounge. Very few had made the trek over here today in the rainstorm. Still, he lowered his voice before he answered. "Crap, if that's true he could either be my worst enemy or my best friend." He filled in Mike and Patrick on the master criminal and crime boss of Detroit, Jimmy Roma.

"I sure didn't know what to make of the guy at first," Patrick said. "With a big scar on his cheek, he looks like a real rough character. Beats me why was he working at a phony coal mine. For a guy out of a job, he didn't seem that desperate. Then he said he has serious money to invest and needs connections and employment. He seemed to have some business sense." He handed Joe the slip of paper. "His name's Nick McGurk, and he's home evenings."

"Hell, I'll call him. You never know where your next big deal is coming from."

Saved by the distraction but still smarting from his dressing down by Joe and Mike, Patrick was eager to get out of there. He looked at his watch.

"Oh gosh, I just remembered I have a couple of phone calls to return at the office, and I'll have to finish a sketch and get it in the mail before I leave work today. If you'll excuse me —"

"No problem, Patrick," Bohannon said. "We're all pressed for time. Just give my plan some careful thought."

He stood, put on his coat, threaded through the maze of empty chairs and tables and made his escape.

Even in the express elevator, it took what seemed like forever to descend eighty floors to the ground. He felt he had sunk even lower. Outside it was still raining.

He trudged blindly back through the steady downpour. The rain on his face mingled with his tears as he walked the four blocks back to his office.

The streets were jammed with taxis jockeying for position, blocked drivers honking their horns and buses stopping to let drenched passengers clamber onboard and out of the rain. The few remaining walkers reminded him of how he looked—alone, forlorn and abandoned, in a hostile climate on streets with no respite from the danger, isolation and hostility of the uncaring city.

This was Chicago at its most dismal. Comfy if you were sitting by a blazing fire, snug and warm, watching the scene though a window. But if you were outside—exposed, desperate and lonely—the pelting rain, a penetrating chill and the mournful moan of a foghorn on the lake combined to play a dirge of impending doom.

Twenty-Seven

At last he reached the doors to his building and entered.

In the lobby Chet was just leaving the building. "My God, what happened to you?" he said.

"I came back here to to take care of a few loose ends, but to hell with it, we need to talk. Let's get a drink."

At their customary back booth in the Cloistered Oyster bar on Lake Street, Patrick related his tale of woe. For the next hour, he replayed the meeting with Bohannon and his Uncle Mike, for his friend's benefit.

"I've never seen you like this, Paddy," he said. You're usually the cheerful, optimistic one. What am I gonna do with you?"

"You could push me off a bridge. At least you would avoid giving Joe Bohannon the satisfaction of gunning me down. Our project is about to crash and burn, I've got two women mad at me, the FBI is on my case and I don't know what's going to sustain our little team for the next six months. Bottom line, I'm probably going to jail."

"Come on, Patrick, you sound ridiculous."

"What am I supposed to do? Every time I think I'm getting ahead professionally, I get tangled up with another woman and I'm undone."

"Maybe if you'll talk about it, I can help you begin to unravel this."

"Let's just take my last three affairs as an example."

"Whatever helps." Chet took a big swig of his drink, inclined his head and hunkered down to listen.

"First,there was Mona, a pretty brunette who kept turning up like a bad penny. I'd seen her at two or three crime scenes I visited. Then one night I was cooling my heels here at the bar right over there after a particularly busy day. I had ordered a martini, very dry. So dry, in fact, that I had Tony pour in the gin over ice and bless it by holding the open bottle next to the glass and whispering 'vermouth' across its mouth.

"She walked in and sat down with only one empty stool between us. A few sips of the icy brew later, the top of my head felt numb and disconnected—the perfect buzz. When Tony asked for her order, she looked my way.

"'What he's drinking' she said. 'That's not lemonade, you know. It's a very dry martini,' I said. 'It's been a hard day.' She turned to Tony, 'I can handle straight gin. I'll have one of those.' 'Don't I know you from somewhere?' I said. 'Weren't you at the bank robbery this morning?' she asked. 'Not as a suspect, I mean.'

"Then we compared notes about the crime scene, and I told her I had seen the culprits drive off and helped the police identify the getaway car." She had those dark brown soulful eyes, the 'Won't you come home with me?' kind.

"She enjoyed her liquor and didn't care what she wore, as long as it was expensive. She loved to go anywhere that had dancing, as long as they had champagne. I fell hard for her. But before long I found I couldn't trust her."

"Women can be fickle, I guess," Chet said sympathetically.

"It was more serious than that. She was pleased to accept my invitations. She was smart, an overachiever. She spent years of attending tedious City Council meetings, covering lost pets, weddings and funerals. She worked her way up the ladder and was finally promoted to lead reporter.

"I liked her stimulating conversation, not to mention her beautiful body. But whenever I discussed my hopes for the future or new projects, I could never convince her that keeping my job was as important as how she did hers."

"So that was that with Mona?"

"Right. Gloria, on the other hand," he continued, "is a blonde.

She's bright, cheerful, and easy to please. Some might call her needy. I knew her as a skinny, gawky teenager at Oak Park High, before they moved to the north suburbs. She was good at math, poor at spelling, She continually tried to get my attention. I barely even noticed her..

"But when she showed up five years later at Uncle Mike's office, I couldn't believe how she'd changed. She talked more slowly, in a sophisticated alto, and her figure had filled out, to a package of irresistible proportions. I mean, a body of Sharon Stone caliber, that wouldn't quit. And Chet, so comfortable, I've never known anything like it—a perfect fit! Her pale eyes get misty when she talks about her favorite things—bright lights, rock music and wild parties, where she's always a standout. The fact that these aren't my favorite things didn't seem to matter. Her lust for life—and for me—seem insatiable, even now. But she's still needy and clinging. She wants apartments, period furniture, a stylish location—all things that go against my grain, design-wise, and are for now financially way out of reach."

"Whoa—I can see a storm brewing." Chet's brow wrinkled in a grim frown. "This could mean trouble—for you, for our project and for the firm."

"No kidding. A few weeks ago, along came Kitty, this time a redhead, with a fiery Irish temper. She has neither a nose for news nor a Hollywood-style body. But as Ma would say, she's 'pretty enough for all normal purposes.' She defies description—a dream, not even of this world. I can't classify her—as remote and clear as an Irish spring. I've tried to stump her, but she knows more than I do—not in facts or ideas, but in emotions. Her beauty is as indefinable as her hair color—red or orange or auburn, or perhaps burnished gold, depending on the light, or my reaction to her mood. When I'm not with her, I find it hard to recall her face to mind, since she always looks different. Maybe she's like one of those Irish Wee Folk she's always talking about—mischievous, elusive and just out of reach."

"You're pretty good at keeping women happy. Can't you just keep Gloria purring for another year?"

"That would've been fine if Kitty hadn't come along. She's smart, she's strong and she can make me laugh. She's the first woman, besides my mother, who's earned my respect. I can't afford to lose her."

"Oh boy, you've got it bad. I know how that is. When I met Ellen, she was the only girl in the world. All other girls became invisible to me and I had to have her.

"Look," Chet went on, "Joe wants this project so bad he can taste it. It's a monument to his life, a legacy for Gloria and all that. Money has never been a big problem for these boys. If they want it, they'll find it. Maybe even this McGurk character you ran into at the museum can help. Who knows?"

"I'm sure the Detroit boys would love to finance this casino, but Joe and the Chicago mob would have Jimmy Roma on their backs before you could start construction. Might just be simpler to just whack a couple of bankers, empty their vaults and pay for our project. Even if they solve all that, what am I gonna do when Joe finds out his consultant dumped his precious daughter?"

"The solution to this problem is more than a matter of a woman's hair color. The best thing I can recommend is, sleep on it. When you don't know what to do, do nothing. Just please yourself for a couple of days. Watch old Marx Brothers movies on TV. Buy yourself a steak and cook it. Anything. But don't call any women. Would it kill you? Just chill for a weekend. Meanwhile, I'll think about it. Next week, we'll come up with a plan."

"I'll try it, Chet, but I don't see how it can help."

"Be careful driving home. You've got a great life ahead of you!"

"Don't worry, I'm okay," he assured Chet, waved back over his shoulder and walked into the garage entrance.

But even to himself, his voice sounded weak and his resolve unconvincing. He started the engine and sat shivering until the car warmed up. At last he gathered the courage to put it into gear and venture out into the street.

Twenty-Eight

The rain had settled into a cold drizzle. Patrick's shouted farewell had been shaky reassurance at best.

By the time Chet walked the wet, chilly three blocks to the Dearborn subway, it was 6:30 p.m. He reached the underground platform and crowded into the rear car just as the doors were about to close. Smothered by the radiant heaters on the subway car and the body heat of a hundred humans oozing out of downtown, he barely found room to stand, much less sit. He hung on a sturdy pole as the car lurched and veered around curves. He rode the glowing snake out of the ground, alighted on the elevated platform and descended. He'd safely escaped from the concrete hive to the comparative openness of his residential neighborhood in Rogers Park.

As he walked home, streetlights clicking on early in the gloom illuminated apartment buildings with identical floor plans. Lamps glowed from apartments, once designated by the builder L-D-K and MBR, BR2, BR3 and Study, arrayed around a common stair hall. The rain had stopped, and children ran outdoors and played in the twilight. Their chatter, screams and laughter reminded him of his own friendly neighborhood back in Newark. Neat front yards, welcoming porches and cheerful homes on the regular grid of streets sang out the soothing refrain of Order, Calm, Peace.

Sarah and David greeted him joyfully on the front steps. Ellen took his coat, handed him the day's Star-News and brought a glass of golden beer. He sat down to read, but not even the murders dominating the front pages could hold his attention. He stared at the page as the bold headlines and narrow columns swam before his eyes. He needed less, not more, trouble.

"What is it, Chet?" Ellen sensed his unease.

"It's Patrick again. The usual, and then some."

"It's not your day to watch him, you know. You're allowed to lead your own life."

"It's always my day, honey. Not only do our lives and livelihood depend on it, I like the guy." He flashed a broad smile. "When do we eat? I can't wait to hear about your day."

"Thirty minutes, tops." She returned to the kitchen. The smell of baking bread and broiling meat wafted in when she pushed through the swinging door.

He had his own life, true. But so much depended on Patrick MacKenna. His job, their professional reputation and his career. He couldn't bear to share the burden of his latest troubles with Ellen, and there was no one else he could talk to.

He tried to be objective about his main worry, Patrick, and reviewed the principal facts about his life. A young architect recently licensed, he craved material success, the admiration and envy of his peers and sexual conquests of beautiful women. His practical pub-owner father had insisted he get a better job, and his East Coast education helped him land a junior architect position at Halliday & Robb. His mentor, his uncle Mike MacKenna, successful construction contractor, helped him see beyond his father's more practical outlook and indulged his fantastic dreams.

While he had youth, optimism and the advantages his hard-working parents and well-connected uncle had given him, Patrick also was weak. He was vain, self-absorbed and lacked judgment where women were concerned. In keeping with this weakness, he was easily detoured from his coveted goals — by those in positions of political power, wealth or influence—with scant regard for the conscience his parents had tried to instill. And yet he possessed the devotion of a puppy dog.

He worried about Patrick. He could get too deeply committed

to clients, was passionately loyal to them, whether justified or not, and found it hard to say no to their excessive or even legally questionable requests. Chet had to be his regulator. When Patrick went quiet on him and withheld key information, Chet often found out when it was too late. Then he worried more, unable to do anything about it.

He'd seen it coming. He had never much liked Gloria. Her language was crass, her tastes low and her education poor—not that acquiring it had been cheap. She attended Stevens College for Women in Columbia, Missouri, an exclusive finishing school in those days. They even had riding stables where a girl could bring her own horse. The town and its University of Missouri were nationally renowned for their liberal arts and journalism degrees. Very little of that culture had rubbed off on Gloria, except perhaps when she sneaked out of her dorm at night and stroked the egos and the other parts of the football players. Besides, her parentage was totally disreputable, not the young woman from a good family Lily and Seamus still hoped Patrick would marry.

Patrick was too good for her, dammit. Why couldn't he use the organ between his ears instead of the one between his legs to select his women? Maybe he was improving. Kitty was smart, assertive and self-assured. But was it too late? How could he dump Gloria now, when both their fates were tied up in the success of her father's project? And what about Joe Bohannon as a client. A retired mob boss — really? That's not exactly the kind of career you can retire from, unless it's feet first. He was sorry he had made light of it. He felt responsible for Patrick's wrong turn.

Now with the signed contract they were committed. Not only were their own reputations on the line, but also those of Jason Halliday, his family name and that of their distinguished firm.

"Dinner's ready. Come and get it."

Ellen's cheerful call ended his musing. He joined his upbeat family around the dinner table.

"Dad, I made the middle school soccer team!"

"Way to go, David!"

"I got an A on my history paper," Sarah said.

"See, I knew, if you just sat down and got started, you could do it!"

"How was your day, Chet?"

"Good news, I suppose. We got our contract signed to do a multi-million-dollar casino and resort."

"That's wonderful," she replied. "Isn't it?"

"Depends on where it goes from here," he said cryptically.

The bad news was, they had to find a way to get it done. He was confident the money would be found. But could Patrick untangle the people problems standing in the way? He was his own worst enemy. After dinner, he retreated to the study with his own disturbing thoughts, feeling sorry for himself. *Why me?*

PART II: STORMY WEATHER

TWENTY-NINE

Patrick stopped on his way home from his pity party with Chet to park beneath the high-rise grocery store. He rode the elevator to the retail floor and picked out the thickest strip steaks they had, well marbled throughout, some mixed salad and a bottle of dressing. He grabbed a bottle of a favorite wine—a Washington state, Lake Chelan Pinot Noir. Chet was right. It was high time he holed up for a night, took stock of himself and reflected on who he had become.

At home, he lit a charcoal fire on his balcony grill, prepared one of the two steaks he'd bought with olive oil, a spice rub and fresh ground pepper. When the fire reached 450 degrees, he placed the steak on the hot grill, covered the kettle and set the stove timer.

What a shame he had promised not to call any women. This meat was too fine—he should share it with someone special. But a promise to Chet was sacred. Chicago Joe had taken a blood oath. His own bond with Chet was equally strong, based on their mutual trust, forged in the hard work they'd done together.

He respected the way Chet's family had struggled. When he called him his best friend, Chet always brushed it off. "I doubt it," he'd say, "judging by some of the scrapes I've gotten you into." He was too modest. Rather than being part of the problem, he was often the solution. They'd met shortly after getting their first jobs at Halliday & Robb and had stuck together. Chet's folks had worked hard for their kids, the way Patrick's parents had. As much as he wanted to break his promise and spend the night with a woman, he had too much admiration and respect for Chet to let him down.

Patrick feared many unanticipated outcomes, any one of which could cause his fall from grace. Other added terrors lurked hidden in the deep shadows of Chicago's man-made canyons. Any false move could topple this house of cards, shakily built on incorrect assumptions, false confidence in his mentors and foolhardy reliance on his own instincts, which were daily proving to be wrong. He might be forced out of his beloved job, lose his hard-earned architectural license and betray his well-meaning family. Behind him would trail the ruins of his failed ventures and soured human relations — familial, business and personal.

He opened the wine, poured himself a glass and sipped thoughtfully. He chuckled at what the placard on the wine shelf had said— "dry and earthy, with overtones of pear and ripe plums, and just a hint of cinnamon." To him, it tasted a bit harsh and needed air. He set it aside for a few minutes to mellow.

He struggled to find an ounce of courage within his frightened, rambling thoughts. He didn't trust fate, and he certainly had never believed in the supernatural. Why then had his luck been so good for so long and then run out so fast? He had never found his mother's faith satisfying nor adequate to explain one's good or ill fortunes. Even in this case he dismissed destiny and divine benevolence as influences on his life. It was hard to blame fate, the divine or bad luck for his arrival at this turning point.

Maybe his predicament came from within — a product of the innate, unknown elements which made up his very being. His life had always been singular, unlike that of his peers. He was haunted by a sense of impending disaster, arising from his restless, critical father, who never seemed to accept his son's earnest efforts to please him. Patrick had been impatient in school, absorbing the point and the substance of the topic immediately, bored with the remainder of the semester. And he too was restless, never satisfied with his own work. His best efforts always felt inadequate to any task, and he seldom took to heart the praise of others for his achievement. Disappointment, his constant companion, was the expected outcome of most of his endeavors.

His loins ached for Gloria. He dared not call her. The way he they had parted at lunch would prompt her to bring up the same subjects, which he wasn't ready to discuss all over again. It had been building up for a long time. They were certainly built for each other, no doubt about that. But their mismatch in outlook was fundamental. Their tastes, personalities and hopes for the future were as different as night and day. He was of solid merchant parents, rising to professional class. She was elite in some respects, lowbrow in others. She held herself above poorer people, less brazen individuals and those who would stoop to common labor. She was afraid of scandal and the low opinions of others and had a mortal fear of the law. He wondered whether she wouldn't be happier with someone matching her station in life, whatever that was.

He might never have discovered these differences if Kitty hadn't come along. Her outspoken courage of her convictions, her aspirations in life and the way they could make each other laugh opened a new world of possibilities. Perhaps there was more to this relationship with the opposite sex thing than he had ever dreamed possible. He'd never given it a chance, always shortcutting the process by hopping into bed with a girl before he'd even gotten to know her. Once that happened, it became a power struggle—what he had to have, versus what she was willing to give. This was no way to live.

He wanted desperately to talk to Kitty, listen to her musical brogue, enjoy her purr of contentment with simple things—the sun shining on a garden, breakers on the beach and a fragrant breeze across the flowers. Why, she even thrilled at thunderstorms, more excited by their majesty than frightened by their force.

The timer reminded him to flip the steak. The seared side bore grill marks and an even brown. He set the timer again, dished out some of the pre-mixed salad on his plate, heated a half loaf of day-old French bread he found in the refrigerator and put on a Mozart Symphony. He couldn't bear to turn on the news. He preferred to savor the remains of his days with Kitty, that day at the Art Institute and the picnic at building site, when his life had changed forever.

He refilled his glass. This unfortunate turn of events put him in a double bind which not only gripped his chest, it confused his judgment. Two women, whom he loved for different reasons. Which one should he choose? Would either one of them still have him? Or was it too late to have either one?

The timer sounded again. He tested the steak. One cut through the thickest part told the story—medium rare, deep pink at the center. He turned the meat again to inspect the second side, an even brown just short of black char. He plated the steak, set it aside to rest and put Greek dressing on his salad. He removed the half loaf from the oven, sliced diagonal nicks in it, mixed some butter with garlic and spread it liberally in the slots. Placing the napkin over a basket, he set the bread on it and folded it over to keep it warm. He replaced the kettle cover, closed the air vents and returned to his well-set table. Thank goodness he'd been trained in his mother's kitchen. Not a bad meal for an hour's work, even if he did say so himself.

He flipped his Mozart vinyl disc to Side Two, *Eine Kleine Nacht-Musik*, a Little Night Music, one of his favorites, and began to eat.

Joe Bohannon left little doubt as to why he wanted to build on the casino project. It was to cap a lifetime of struggle with a little personal glory and to pass something real and lasting on for Gloria. If Patrick wasn't for her as well, his architectural services would no longer be required. If the firm lost the casino and restaurant project, fees already incurred just for the preliminary work to date would be hard to recover. Not to mention the loss of future work for their team to prepare working drawings for construction and design of future buildings in the complex. Would the fees earned so far even be collectible? Would Bohannon try to pay his bill with hundred-dollar notes and trigger a federal Suspicious Activity Report? Without a happy reunion with Joe's daughter, all these adverse results were likely.

Kitty, in her first performance at the pub on that makeshift stage — green dress with a lace collar, her perfect form and the voice of an angel — dominated his attention. Kitty brought out his best qualities. He wondered if she would ever change her mind about marriage. In the meantime, she would be no help with his manly needs. She wasn't interested in a relationship. He had accepted that, and they'd even joked about it.

If she would accept him, as he secretly suspected, she would offer, not just the hot, lush indulgence of other women he'd known. She also promised to be a friend, a partner in his life's striving and a homemaker, continuing the stable homestead he had enjoyed with his birth family. Her presence overcame all the terrors he faced — the unpredictable mob, his critical father, his risk-prone uncle and his boss. Other cheer-leading, fair weather friends encouraged him to take chances but would not be there when his luck ran out. His mother had warned he was spoiled by too much attention, his easy acceptance by those he pursued, and the sexual favors granted by so many women. Frankly, he was scared to change. He didn't know who he would be if he settled down with one of them. Could he give them all up?

Others also came to mind. There was the friendly brunette teller at his downtown bank. Her top half looked good enough. Perhaps her bottom half, which he'd never seen, was equally nice. He recalled watching a pair of shapely calves retreat from him in a downtown office building toward the outside doors, hips undulating smoothly. Where had he seen her?

Aha, in the elevator, at the murder scene.

The ugly vision returned—the lawyer Angionomo, sprawled on his swivel chair, with his head blown wide open. The Verdict Reporter. What was her name, Angela something? He reached for his wallet and found her business card. There was her business phone number. Damn, in the frenzy of recent days, he'd forgotten to call her. She had important clues to the case and knew how to get in touch with the lawyer's secretary. With all the flurry over the new casino resort, he had totally neglected the issue of finding out who could have killed the lawyer and a wealthy dog-walker client, murdered a few days later. Even if it meant he could not remain as architect of this questionable project, perhaps he ought to go in the other direction. He would do as the FBI wished him to do and help solve all these mysterious crimes. Not that he had a choice. But now he would take it seriously and give it his full attention,

He owed Angela a phone call anyway. Maybe she would even join him for lunch.

Thirty

The next morning Joe Bohannon got a visit at his bar from Nick "Scarface" McGurk.

When he was ushered in by the waitress into his private office, Bohannon looked up.

"So you're the wise guy Patrick MacKenna sent me?"

"Yes sir. He said I could contact you about a job."

Who was this McGurk, anyway—a skinny, crooked-nosed kid, with his eyes set too close together? He projected a kind of hunger that food alone could never satisfy. He looked like a case of arrested development, or at least, arrested.

"Patrick said you already have a job. Why are you here?"

"I want a better one."

"So, what's your story, kid?"

"I never wanted trouble. I just wanted to make it in life. See, I wanted to be like my Pa, an autoworker for forty years. Then he got laid off. Everyone was buying Japanese cars. He never worked again — left home. Mama held two jobs. Hotel maid during the day, office cleaner by night. One night she was waiting for the bus. Two wise guys grabbed her, raped her and left her for dead. She survived and supported my sister May and me."

"Tough luck, kid. How'd you get that scar?" he asked McGurk.

"I got in a knife fight, back in Detroit."

"Who did that to you?"

"The boss's enforcer. I tried to work my way up in the Detroit Outfit. But I was going nowhere. Couldn't wait to get out of there."

"So, you've got scores to settle?"

"Oh, yeah, I'd been studying auto repair, sheet metal work, all kinds of metallurgy in my high school's auto shop program. Mom's health got worse and she couldn't work. I had to quit school and find work wherever I could. I fell in with the gang helping with drug deals, driving for them, doing odd jobs. My sister, who worked in a downtown office, was robbed and stabbed to death coming home from work. I swore I'd kill whoever did it. I got even, all right. I knew some of the boys in that gang. One night I caught them bragging about their exploits and found out who killed my sister. Got in a knife fight with the sonofabitch who did it, killed him and got the scar. Proud of it, too. I vowed I'd never lose a fight again. See"

With lightning speed he pulled out a knife and flipped it in the air. Bohannon flinched as it landed point first on his desk and stuck. "Feel how sharp that is. It can really hurt."

Joe sprang up and leaned forward, both hands on a .38 caliber automatic pointed squarely at where McGurk had sat, but he was gone. He had dropped beneath the surface of the desk. Bohannon stared, his steel grey eyes hard and beady, at McGurk as he climbed from the floor. "Not bad, kid. You know how to handle yourself." He lowered the pistol. "Now, don't you ever pull a weapon on me again, or you're dead meat. You got that?"

"Yes, sir."

Bohannon removed the knife, smoothed the nick on his polished mahogany desk and laid it down, point toward McGurk, on the surface. "Put that shiv where it belongs," he ordered.

McGurk retrieved the weapon and placed it back in its ankle sheath. The pistol already back wherever it came from, Bohannon sat again, loosened his tie and leaned back in his chair.

"Thanks for the personal history. Again, why are you here?

"I'd been running errands for Jimmy Roma. That included delivering packages to this hideout in the basement of an abandoned bank, where they stored their cash. I helped myself—I figured they owed me after they killed my sister."

"Your lucky you lived to tell about it. What the hell are you doing working in the coal mine at the museum?"

"It's a long story, but—"

"Okay, okay. Out with it."

"You remember when they moved to the Boeing 727 into the museum?"

"Yeah, a big deal — all over the papers and TV. Flew it into Meigs Field. Towed it somewhere to work on it."

"Right—Indiana, near the lake. Most of my work for the Partnership was at night. In the daytime I read all the papers. I learned they planned to take off the wings and prepare it for an exhibit at the Museum of Science and Industry. While I was still working for Roma, I signed on to the repair crew and commuted there to work on weekends. Told him I was visiting a sick aunt. Since I knew all about sheet-metal. I used all my auto body skills to build a hidden compartment in the cargo hold. Little by little, I transferred cash I'd lifted from the hideout in Detroit to the cargo bay of the aircraft. When they floated that airplane back here, I quit working for Roma and stayed on to help install it. Then I took a job at the Museum so I could get the money out. That's how I got the money to Chicago. Now I'm ready to invest it."

"You figured out all those moves yourself?

"Right, pretty clever, huh?" McGurk smiled.

"Maybe too clever. By comin' to me, you forgot one thing. There's no way I want to get crosswise with another family. You sure you're not in hot water and want me to bail you out?"

"No, but I couldn't stay there. I got even for my sister's murder. Sooner or later, Roma would get even with a dude who whacked one of his boys. I just have to chill for a while and put the money to work."

"It ain't a good idea to wake a sleeping giant. What have you got to invest, anyway?"

"Cash. Millions, transported in that plane. Now it's well-hidden in a safe place. "

Bohannon's eyes opened wide. "And why do you think I would care?"

"MacKenna says you've got a big project, a casino and resort you want to build that will print money from here to eternity."

"And what if I do?"

"He says you might consider taking in an investor to get it

rolling—pull off a big deal."

"He talks too much." Joe got up and walked to the window. He studied the three parked cars and two trash dumpsters in his view. He returned to his desk and stood, gazing at the family photos behind it, and sat again. "I don't know. It's pretty risky, if you ask me."

"Of course, if you're not interested, I could go somewhere else..."

"Hold on, kid. We may need to talk after all." If this strange dude was for real, this could be a no-strings deal. "How long you think you got until Roma figures out who made off with his dough?"

"Maybe a year, maybe two. He's got so much cash lying around, and his accounting is so sloppy, he may not miss it. If I hook up with somebody like you—a strong man who can fight them off, maybe forever. I've got all kinds of skills. My job lately has been to guard the precious cargo that came in that airplane."

Bohannon listened carefully and then made a sour face. "Oh, crap," he said. "My intestines are calling. Please excuse me."

He left McGurk staring at photos of his family while he went into his sound-isolated bathroom. He punched in a number on his private phone.

"Hey, this is Bohannon. I gotta talk to Sal."

He waited a minute or so. "Yeah?" The line crackled and popped. Sal's voice was distorted.

"Hey, Sally, how goes it?" Between rushes of static and noisy snow, the boss's distant voice came through in bursts.

"Joe, Baby, what's rockin' on the North Side?" His voice was gravelly, barely audible over background noise that sounded like a concrete mixer.

"Look, I was checking on this deal we talked about. Have you boys decided about investing in this resort project?"

"We looked into it..." His words were broken by a crunch like gravel tumbling in the churning tub... "Frank says... the heat's on in Springfield. Soon as the gaming commission discovers we're involved... the project is dead in the water, and probably us in the bargain. You know the drill, 'organized crime influence' and all that crap. Why?" The speaker might have pulled the lever to pour in the cement.

"Because I got an offer on the table, some guy from Detroit named McGurk, says he knows Roma. Says he's got millions in cash he can put in."

"No way...." The scrunching sound got louder. "I'm not starting another war."

"That's what I thought—at first. This is money he says Roma doesn't know about. Looks to me like it's arm's length—no strings."

"You might have to run with it… but don't give away the store. When Roma finds out …his boys are serious. They might want an arm and a leg—plus your head—in return for the caper…" The roaring increased, as if the driver started his engine, to add to the clamor.

"Good advice, Sally. I'll explore it further, but I'll watch it."

"Joe…you didn't tell me this…and I don't know a goddamn thing about it. Anybody says I do … I'll deny it. Got it?"

"You bet…"

A loud, final roar of static like a ready-mix truck driving away, and then a dial tone, told him the conversation was over.

He hung up. That was a yellow light, and in a way, his blessing. With a warning—proceed at your own risk. Time to put on his Big Boy pants and make his move.

Moments later, Bohannon came out, relieved and smiling.

"Forgive me for the delay. I hate asking folks to bear with my intestinal distress. I don't want to create dysentery in the ranks."

"No problem, Mr. Bohannon. So, how much you lookin' for anyway?"

"Call me Joe, kid. The first phase is the casino, pool, boat dock, restaurants and all the trimmings. Including architect's fees of three hundred grand, the architect and contractor tell me it's going to total a cool five million. We could swing it with a bank loan, but that would slow us down quite a bit and give me a whole bunch of partners I don't want, if you know what I mean."

"I get it."

"What can you do for me?" Bohannon asked.

"One million down," McGurk said, and thought for a minute. Three million more after the construction contract is signed, paid out by percentage of completion, and the last million, when construction is complete."

"And what do you want in return?"

"One million sugar—you know, interest—and a half owner-ship in the land and the casino. What do you say?"

"Ouch, that hurts. I'll have to think on it, crunch some numbers. You know, see if it's theasible."

"If you like this deal, I'll pay you a hundred-grand right now, to get the project started, and we'll work out the details." He opened his briefcase. Stacked neatly in rows filling the entire interior were hundred-dollar bills. Bohannon flipped through two stacks, count-ed and totaled the cash: 20 stacks of 50 one-hundred-dollar bills each—all there.

Bohannon's eyes lit up while he did a quick total in his head. This would keep the MacKennnas off his back while they designed and bid the project.

"I guess I could accept this as harness money." Bring me the rest of the down payment in a week. We'll work out the details and sign an agreement."

The kid seemed awfully eager for the deal, but Joe couldn't pass it up. McGurk handed over his briefcase containing the cash down payment, and they closed it with a handshake.

"Call me in a week."

"Thanks, Joe. You won't regret this."

After McGurk left, Bohannon congratulated himself.

His elation didn't last long. What if Roma found out and wanted full ownership? Not a problem, he figured. Gloria's history teacher told her about that French ruler, Napoleon Bonyparts. He had a good old saying: "Always have a plan, leave nothing to chance. Better yet, have two plans. Leave something to chance."

Thirty-One

In a last-ditch effort to patch up his relationship with Gloria, Patrick invited her to the groundbreaking ceremony for the Chicago Casino and Resort at Rockville. On a Saturday morning at the end of June the sun shone brightly, although a cool front and a dense cloud deck were quickly overtaking the land.

At the turnoff for the gravel road in Rockville, he eased into a line of cars. Expecting a large crowd, it seemed Joe had brought on additional help. A man in dark pants and a matching windbreaker and a peaked cap directed him ahead to a similarly dressed attendant, who motioned with both arms to turn left into a row just forming of parked cars. A third standing at the next empty space guided him to turn right next to the car that had just parked. Patrick waved thanks to him and alighted from the car as the man returned his gesture with an informal salute, the arm raised to his sunglasses, as he moved up the row to park the next car.

His uncle Mike's carpenters had built a platform and set out folding chairs on an emerald green tarp to protect the ladies' high heels from sinking into the rain-softened turf. The Mayor of Rockville, Population 1,292, took a seat with his wife on the raised stage. Standing in front of the platform, Joe and Candy Bohannon, Mike and Rose MacKenna and State Representative Ferguson were chatting. Patrick's display boards were set up all along the dais, taped to the front rail against a fresh breeze. A black limousine roared up alongside traffic on the gravel road and special guest, Mayor Robert J. Dooley, Jr. got out and walked up, accompanied by the Chairman of the Illinois Gaming Commission. Standing by the front row of folding seats, Archie Scott cast a significant glance at his photographer and nodded toward Mayor Dooley and the other dignitaries to make sure to capture these shots. The Star-News reporter Margaret Larson chatted with Joe Bohannon and jotted notes between questions. Mona Strong approached the mayor and interrupted his conversation with Mike MacKenna. A dozen chrome plated spades leaned against the folding table where a brick anchored a stack of descriptive brochures Patrick had prepared for the occasion, including images of his color sketches depicting the project, with the headline:

Chicago Casino and Resort

Your vacation getaway

One hour from downtown

Patrick and Gloria approached the group gathered in front of the stage. Dressed in his best charcoal gray suit, Chet walked up to them.

"Where's Ellen?" Patrick asked.

"She has to take Mary to get her shots, and David has Soccer League at eleven."

"Of course. I forgot how busy those two keep her."

"Joe and Candy," Patrick said, "this is Chet Neuzing, your Project Manager. He'll be running the show to produce your working drawings."

"Chahmed, I'm shu-ah." Candy said.

"You the one who keeps Patrick in line?" Joe grinned as he shook Chet's hand.

"Most of the time," he assured him. "We're a great team."

Chet turned toward Candy. "I'm from New-uck, by the way. You?"

"Well, whaddaya know—a homeboy!" She asked about his favorite places and nightspots. They chatted cheerfully—it was old home week.

"Who's that?" Gloria had spotted a tall, hungry looking young man lurking at the edge of their little group. He wore the uniform and cap of the parking attendants.

"Hey, MacKenna," he said.

He looked familiar, but Patrick had trouble placing him. Then he noticed the scar. "McGurk, I didn't know you without the miner's overalls." Patrick said. "What gives?"

"Joe and I hit it off. We've got a deal, and I've got a job. Today I'm supervising the parking crew. Thanks for the intro."

"Sure, no problem."

The platform had two sets of low steps, arranged on either side of its front edge. Off to the right, a path improvised with precast concrete pavers foot-stepped across the adjacent field toward the old farmhouse. Uncle Mike's carpenters had thoughtfully provided a handrail along one side of this walkway so the women in heels could balance on the pavers without muddying their pretty shoes.

Patrick regarded the darkening sky with a nervous glance. Mike MacKenna climbed to the platform and took the microphone as master of ceremonies.

The speeches were predictable. Mike introduced Joe Bohannon, congratulated him on his "visionary project" and introduced the guest of honor, Mayor Robert J. Dooley Jr. The mayor praised Joe and his bold venture as a first in ensuring Chicago's future, not only as a tourist destination, but as a year-round vacation getaway. The Illinois Gaming Commissioner brought greetings from Governor Reamer and conveyed his message that he had a previous, commitment and regretted not being able to attend in person. He was addressing the state legislature on his tax cut program. "He also wants everyone to know," the commissioner continued, "that gaming projects such as this one form a keystone of his economic program," to make up from the private sector the funding which, "the taxpayers should not have to provide." In his revenue-starved, limping state economy, Patrick figured, it was a miracle this commissioner had gas money to make today's trip. Mike introduced Patrick, who stepped up to the podium.

"Thanks, Mike," Patrick said, "As land planners and architects for the Chicago Casino and Resort at Rockville, we at the long-established firm of Halliday & Robb are proud to be selected to realize Joe Bohannon's bold vision for a new kind of year-round vacation getaway, about an hour from downtown Chicago.

"The drawings displayed here before you, illustrate Joe Bohannon's plan to create daytime recreation, with fun for all ages, as well as nighttime amusement and entertainment for the adults. We are honored to have Mayor Dooley, Representative Ferguson and the head of the Illinois Gaming Commission, a representative of Governor Reamer, here today to show their solid public-sector support for this worthwhile project. It is expected to contribute considerable funding for public projects and many new, local jobs. This beautiful country retreat will be set among the rolling hills and waters of this lovely site, amidst the glories of nature—"

His speech was rudely interrupted by Mother Nature herself—a terrifying, simultaneous lightning and thunderbolt set off another roar, this one from the assembled crowd. Beneath the blackening sky the foam-core board containing the overall view of the casino complex broke free from its taped restraints and flew into the air. Patrick lunged for it and missed, toppling off the platform and landing on his face. Huge raindrops pelted his back and the rest of his suit. Chet offered him a hand to help him get up. When he caught his breath, he instructed, "Grab the boards!" He snatched the view of the high-rise hotel and the river. Chet grabbed the drawing of the villas, the marina and the dock and put it on his stack, while Patrick made an end run around the platform in pursuit of the sailing overall view. He would have caught it, except for a collision with Mayor Dooley, who had just descended the steps in one of his classic escape moves and was dashing toward his limo.

While he offered embarrassed apologies, he watched a display board take flight toward the platform and plaster itself in the face of Mayor Brown's wife, and, like a sail, blow her backward off the platform, chair and all. Mayor Brown made a valiant leap for her, but the legs of her chair had lost their footing, as did she, and she toppled from the stage, landing on her rump on the ground below, legs flailing wildly in the air atop her crumpled metal folding seat.

"Run, Gloria! Here, follow me to the farmhouse." Patrick led the way down the path. He balanced the clumsy illustration boards, which blocked their view. They quickly abandoned all hope of preserving their shoes. She followed him blindly, only occasionally glancing down, the only direction where her sight was unobstructed, to inspect her ruined pumps. When they reached the farmhouse front door and burst through it, a white-jacketed waiter greeted them cheerfully, accepted their rescued illustration boards and greeted them: "Good afternoon, sir. Please help yourself to the hors d'oeuvres. What would be your preferred drinks?"

"Scotch and soda, but that's not important right now," Patrick exclaimed. "Rescue somebody!" He pointed out the open door. Candy Bohannon, whose perfect, not-a-hair-out-of-place coiffure had become a birds' nest atop her dripping face, led the throng dashing toward the farmhouse, attempting to shelter their heads with purses, jackets and blown-out umbrellas. Like a swamp creature, Candy limped along on one stockinged bare foot and one mud-encrusted spike-heeled shoe.

The farmhouse living room and the dining room, where an elaborate buffet had been set out, were now crammed with soaked, dripping visitors. Patrick spotted a Staff Only sign on the closed, double stained-glass doors to the formal parlor.

"We can't go in there," he warned Gloria. "That's probably the caterer's serving space."

"The hell we can't! I need space to dry off." Gloria pushed through the doors and entered, closely followed by Patrick and then Chet, who closed the doors behind them.

There among wing chairs, a dusty needlepoint upholstered sofa and Tiffany-shaded lamps, Piotr Radwinski sat at an aluminum folding table, with a radio receiver, recording equipment and lots of wires and cables. Adjacent, at a card table, Detective Sergeant O'Malley interviewed a young woman whose back was turned to them. She turned to see what all the commotion was about.

Patrick faced Kitty O'Connor.

"Top of the mornin', Patrick," she said. "Wet enough for you?" She took in his muddy, rain-soaked suit and Gloria's elegant white sheath dress, with its deep décolletage. Along with Gloria's skimpy underwear, it had now become quite transparent, leaving no bodily feature to the imagination.

Gloria, who must have been accustomed to interrogations in her family, recovered and spoke first. "Why, if it isn't the little barmaid! In trouble with the police already?"

"Hello, Kitty," Patrick said. "Sergeant, what in hell is going on here?"

O'Malley looked up from his notes. "Radi here asked me to help out today. He wanted to be positioned to interview anybody who attended this distinguished gathering. Just to back up your story, I wanted to interview Kitty.

"Let's see," he read to her from his notes, "you said, 'We spent the afternoon, out here, Patrick sketching his ideas for the project. I took the opportunity to catch up on my letters back home to Ireland. We had a little picnic lunch. It was an unusually warm, sunny day. It was just nice to spend some time outdoors together—'"

"You…what?" Gloria glared at Kitty. She didn't wait for a response but wheeled around to face Patrick. "No wonder you're not available on the weekends anymore. You're getting a little on the side! You, you… bastard." She stalked away.

"For your information, you spoiled bitch, he's not getting a damned thing from my side, or my front, or any other part of me," Kitty retorted to her bare-looking backside now disappearing through the stained-glass double doors.

As Gloria bolted from the parlor, O'Malley followed, explaining. "I have to secure this building, so nobody else we need to talk to leaves unexpectedly."

"Your comments should be sufficient, Ms. O'Connor, to confirm Mr. MacKenna's alibi," Radwinski said. "Mr. MacKenna, it appears you have some urgent matters to attend to, so I'll let you get to it. Thanks for your cooperation today. I collected what I need." He nodded toward the surveillance phone on Patrick's belt. He dismantled his radio receiver, packed it into the aluminum case on the table and turned his attention to his written notes.

As Patrick accompanied Kitty out into the crowd, he said, "You didn't learn such words back in the convent school."

"I'm a Chicagoan now." She smiled mischievously. "A quick study, don't you know?"

He looked for Gloria in the living room but couldn't find her in the milling crowd.

The rain abated, and visitors saw their chance to escape. Despite O'Malley's demand to remain, they burst through the front door and hastened to their cars. Patrick saw no sign of the helpful parking attendants. The many cars they had so compactly stored now formed a massive tangle of vehicles, which sputtered, whined and spun their wheels in their drivers' attempts to unearth them from the mire.

As the crowd thinned, he searched again for Gloria, so he too could escape. After checking every room of the house, the grounds and the occupied cars waiting to leave, in case she had accepted a ride with someone else, he returned to the farmhouse.

Joe Bohannon emerged from the parlor-interrogation room, shaking his head. "Look what happens when you try to do something right in this crooked town." He turned to face Patrick. "Have you seen Gloria?"

When Patrick reported he couldn't find her anywhere, Joe lost it.

"I told her to meet us here afterwards. She would never ignore such a request." He stuck his head back into the parlor. "Radwinski. What's going on here? While you fiddle-farted around with your fishing expedition, my daughter disappeared. Earn your keep, dammit!"

THIRTY-TWO

When the rain stopped and the crowd sheltered in the farmhouse began to leave, Nick McGurk looked for Joe Bohannon in the old farmhouse. He entered though the kitchen and approached the door to the dining room. He felt an iron grip from behind on his right upper arm. Someone else grabbed his left upper arm and the two of them bent him over the kitchen table and pinned his wrists with cable ties behind his back.

"What the hell?" he exclaimed. "Let me go!"

It hurt. They tied a blindfold over his eyes, marched him out the kitchen door, and, in this uncomfortable position, threw him into the back seat of a sedan parked alongside the rear porch.

He discovered he was not alone. He heard whimpering on his left, and felt a soft thigh compressed against his leg. The door slammed, and they were momentarily left alone together.

"Who's that?" A young woman's voice asked.

"Nick McGurk. You Gloria?" he guessed.

"Look what they've done to me!" She uttered between sobs.

"I can't see a damn thing. I'm blindfolded and tied up."

"So am I. Where are they taking us?" she asked.

"Nowhere I want to go."

"I'm so scared, I want out of here!"

"Sh-h.. Here's what we have to do. No complaints, or threats. Curses are okay, I guess. But let's shut up and learn as much as we can — find out who they are. I've got a hunch, but we'll have to figure it out."

"Who could they be? How did they get into this crowd?"

"Easy." McGurk said. "I think they were personally invited by your father."

"No, impossible."

"You think? Remember, he was shorthanded. Maybe he asked Sal Falcone for help. He got it, all right. I think there's something fishy about that parking crew I was assigned to supervise. I've seen that big bruiser with a limp somewhere before. The skinny guy with the hooked nose said he was local. I'm not sure I believe that either."

"But where did they come from?"

"How about Detroit?"

"Oh crap. Daddy was fighting them off. I can't believe he fell for that."

"Maybe one of his boys did it, Anyway, it's just a theory. Sh-h-h. I hear them coming back. Now shut up and try to remember everything you hear. We're facing north now. Count the turns if you can and try to figure out what direction we're headed."

The front car doors opened, and the two thugs climbed in.

"Okay, you two," the driver said. "We're going for a little ride."

"Can we get some heat in here?" Gloria said. "I'm wet and cold, you sons of bitches."

McGurk kicked her shin to remind her to be quiet.

"Pipe down," the driver said. "The heat will come on in a minute."

"You know what's good for you, you'll listen to Bulldog," said the other, whose voice was thinner and higher. "Let's go."

"Hold your horses, Buttafumo. I gotta get out of this mud and steer clear of all the stuck cars in our way."

Nick knew the driver.

Slowly at first, Bulldog started the powerful car moving. After spinning his wheels several times in muddy patches, they reached one side of the gravel road. McGurk could tell from hearing the crunch of gravel and honks from other cars that they had to ease their way slowly into the stream of vehicles leaving the site.

Amidst the noise and distractions of their exit from the property, McGurk leaned his head to the left and whispered in Gloria's ear.

Rain pelted on the roof of the car. Gloria squirmed on her left side so her tied hands faced McGurk. With some struggle he maneuvered his leg near her hands. Following Nick's whispered instructions, she tugged on the handle of the knife sheathed on his shin and worked it free. She set it on the seat between them.

By sliding his head against the door handle, McGurk worked his blindfold upward and managed to see. It was late afternoon by now, and thick clouds further dimmed the sky. The darkness inside the car would help conceal their movements. He grabbed the leather handle of the knife in his teeth and inserted the blade, slowly and carefully in between the ratcheted ties that restrained Gloria's wrists.

"Careful now, no sudden moves," he whispered. "I'm trying not to cut your wrists"

Gloria froze, holding her breath.

McGurk worked his head toward and away from the gap between Gloria's wrists. He was grateful he kept his weapon honed like a razor. With the weak leverage he could muster with his teeth in his contorted position, it took a lot of effort to keep sawing until the ties gave way. At last her wrists fell apart.

"Now, very slowly, roll over and face me with your hands in front of you. He moved his head into the rear corner of his seat and flipped onto his knees

"Hey, stay still, back there! No funny business," Dugan warned in a gruff bark.

"Hard to do that with you lurching this car like a maniac," Gloria said.

That shut Dugan up for the moment. In the murky light, she edged up her blindfold, took the blade in her hands and sawed at the ties binding McGurk's wrists.

"You got it," he whispered, as the car lurched again, he rolled into a seated position, flexing his tingling hands to restore feeling. "Good job," he breathed into her ear.

He waited until the car lined up to merge into traffic on the gravel road, fully occupying Dugan's attention, he leaned in her direction and whispered, "When they get us out of the car, grip your hands together behind you, so they won't notice they are untied."

"Thanks, Nick," she whispered. "It feels so much better."

With partial vision restored, McGurk could maneuver and think better.

Like a flash of lightning, the puzzle pieces fell into place. Jimmy Roma wanted to move into Sal Falcone's turf in Chicago. Then Nick recalled where he had seen that limping, big bruiser before. Bulldog Dugan, Jimmy Roma's toughest enforcer. He hated to distress Gloria further, but he had to warn her.

"Gloria," he whispered in her ear. "These are Jimmy Roma's Detroit boys. Be careful."

"Oh crap," she muttered in a frightened whisper. "We're in deep shit."

McGurk knew the longer he allowed these goons to establish control, the more difficult it would be to escape. He was outnumbered and outgunned. He tackled his problems in reverse order.

Dugan maneuvered the sedan out of the field, around numerous mired and disabled cars, back to the gravel road. They proceeded haltingly, hemmed in on the left and right by idling cars, each pressing for its chance to turn down the gravel track. Any route around the single exit lane was blocked by other idling cars, all jockeying for their shot to turn into the exit lane.

In his Dugan's rough handling when he was dumped into the car, McGurk had felt a holster with a gun under his captor's windbreaker, strapped to his left shoulder. He didn't know about sidekick Buttafumo, but he'd bet he was unarmed. Just as Dugan stopped, waiting to turn onto the gravel path, McGurk lunged forward toward the driver's seat, grabbed the pistol and delivered a powerful blow with its butt to Dugan's temple. Bulldog slumped in his seat, unconscious. McGurk leveled the pistol at Buttafumo. "Don't make a move." With his left hand he grabbed the man's necktie, yanked it around behind his head and secured it to the steel supports of the seat's head rest.

"Ow! Your choking me," the skinny guy said gasping, and reaching for the noose.

"That's the idea," McGurk snarled. For good measure, he whacked him on the head with the gun barrel, knocking him out. He reached around his inert body and unlocked the car doors with the switch on the passenger door and grabbed the driver's car keys, which he threw hard across the rubble- and car-strewn field.

"Hey—" Dugan protested weakly, before he passed out again.

"Okay, Gloria, climb out."

He followed her out the left rear door. "Quick follow me."

A bolt of lightning struck, instantly followed by a loud thunderclap. The skies opened again. A steady rain poured down. From the point where they had driven on the gravel road, he led her back toward the rear of the farmhouse, a mere 500 feet away from their starting point. Nonetheless it was a slow slog, even for McGurk. Gloria hobbled behind him, then removed her filthy pumps and held them in one hand until they reached the shelter of the roofed back porch. The white van sat another 100 feet beyond. They made a dash for it in the downpour.

He let her in and ran to the driver's seat. He started the engine and drove in a wide circle, across the hilltop field where a few parked cars remained, toward the main road. He located a break in the rail fence and a flat spot spanning the ditch alongside the main road. He turned right, in the opposite direction from exiting traffic and took his first left, heading south at the next county road. He doubled back eastward on the next crossroad toward the expressway.

THIRTY-THREE

In the gloom, dusk fell early. The storm subsided to a steady, gentle drizzle. McGurk reached behind him, retrieved a blanket he used when he slept in the van and handed it to her. The dashboard clock showed it was already 6:15.

"Hey, cover yourself! People can see right through that dress. Besides, it will keep you warm until this bus heats up."

"Such a gentleman! But you're the only 'people' who can see me."

"I can't take you anywhere looking like that."

"Where did you want to take me?"

"Seems a shame to end a day like this without celebrating our escape. Are you hungry?"

"Starved."

"I know a club in Skokie, hidden among the lagoons. My buddies take their girlfriends there. We could stop to eat on the way to your place, have a drink, look out at the lagoons. Their food is good, and they have a nice little dance band."

"Oh, Nick, that sounds so sweet!" She checked her hair in the rear-view mirror. "I'm a total mess, but I have an idea. Just drive to the restaurant."

The rain had stopped, and a half-moon peeked through a

break in the clouds. When they arrived at the parking lot of the Bit & Bridle, Gloria took a plastic rain poncho from her large purse purse, which she'd had no time to open earlier, and draped it over her soaked dress

Nick escorted her out of the car and into the restaurant, where they were seated on a banquette at a small round table. They ordered a pitcher of martinis, which arrived right away.

She excused herself to the ladies' room. Twenty minutes later, she emerged, both her appearance and her disposition visibly improved.

"You look great," Nick said. "What did you do?"

"I monopolized the hand dryer and dried my hair. Then I dried as much of my dress as I could."

"It's almost opaque white again."

"You were very brave today," she said. "You probably saved my life."

"You came through like a champ, too."

"But I hardly know anything about you."

"Not much to tell. Some days I felt like a capo, a diamond in the rough. At other times, nothing I could do in the Outfit succeeded in getting me ahead—I felt dumb and worthless."

"The Outfit? Certainly not here, or I would have heard of you."

"No, Detroit."

"Oh, my God. Have you ever considered a different career?"

"What choice did I have?" He filled her in on his family's misfortunes, his rocky career in the Outfit, his sister's murder and his rough life in Detroit. "How about you?"

"Nick, you're not from Chicago, so you don't know a lot about my family. But everyone else does—we're notorious, known for all the wrong things. I've seen more bad shit go down in my short life than most girls my age."

"You poor kid."

"Not exactly poor, but unfortunate. It is what it is. How did you get here?"

"You remember when they moved to the Boeing 727 into the museum?"

"Sure, it was all over the news."

"I helped do that." He described his role in fitting and moving the plane to its new home.

"See, you weren't dumb, or worthless."

"Wait, there's more. With some cash I could have a good car, a decent place to live and maybe even attract a girlfriend. With a lot of cash, maybe I could swing a really big deal. Nobody loved me, not ever, since I was a kid. My mother maybe, she took care of me when I was young. But when I got older, she had bad luck…

"And those wise guys owed me. Every time I think about it I get angry. I want to be somebody: respected, admired and self-suf-ficient. I'm no dummy, so I got even."

"I shudder to hear you say that. If they find out they'll kill you in the blink of an eye — they're ruthless. But tell me how you learned your trade."

"I was good with my hands. I could make anything I could vi-sualize, out of metal— welding, brazing, casting, even sculpture. It was all due to Mr. Robinson, my metal shop teacher, one of the few who ever cared, who took an interest. He made sure I stuck with my projects, did perfect welds and finished every one. One Friday night, in a fit of anger, I stayed late after school, past lockup time, working on an idea. I made an armature of steel — an animal. I attached sheet after sheet of custom cut metal — strips, long trian-gles overlapping, nested, gently rounded — to form a sleek body, legs, haunches, abdomen, swelling chest and finally a proud head with feline ears."

"How did you eat during all that time?"

"I improvised with food from the vending machines in the hall, using a tool I made from sheet metal for tricking the coin acceptor. All weekend I gobbled peanuts, crackers, candy bars and soda pop. By the time it was dark on Saturday night I had formed the rough shape of a big cat, poised to spring. As a finishing touch I took some thin steel tubing and formed it on a brake into a gentle curve, welded on a rounded tip and attached it to the back of the piece, a defiant tail. By sunrise on Sunday I had a 5-foot-tall animal poised to spring. The alternating pattern of rusted and shiny seg-ments turned the finished piece into a striped tiger."

A waiter arrived and set silver-dome-covered dishes on a tem-porary tray next to their table. He uncovered the lobster tail for Gloria, beautifully presented, with delicately browned scalloped potatoes, green beans and a cup of drawn butter on the plate. He placed Nick's prime rib with roasted potatoes and horseradish sauce in front of him. He held the bottle of champagne for Nick to approve, popped the cork and filled their flutes. After this talk of subsisting on vending machine food and their vigorous day they attacked their meals with a vengeance.

"I'll bet you're proud of your sculpture," Gloria said.

"When it was done, I said out loud in that workshop, 'That's who I am. It expresses me!' That morning as the sun rose, I swore I would never be a flunky or a go-fer again. I knew what I had to do and had an idea how I could do it. Since no one, except Mr. Robinson of course, would help me, I had to help myself."

Exhausted but satisfied, he told her, he lay down early Sunday evening on a tarp by his workbench for a long nap. At dawn, he awoke and put his masterpiece in the trunk of the Bluebird, a 1985 Chevy he had reconditioned in auto repair class, which he had stowed in the service bay of the school's auto shop. When the alarm system was turned off at 6:30 a.m. Monday morning for the maintenance staff, he cautiously raised the garage door and drove his creation home.

He finished his roast beef, poured them more champagne and resumed his story.

"Indeed, in the following months I did help myself, generously, to a weekly portion of Jimmy Roma's treasure. Each week, I told the boss, I spent Friday and Saturday visiting my 'elderly aunt,' who was ill in Indiana. I filled my battered fake leather suitcase with cash, stashed some clothes and essentials in my backpack and drove the Bluebird to my rental apartment in a Gary tenement."

"I can't believe you're telling me this. If Roma ever finds out, he'll kill you."

"I have to tell someone. I-I trust you. Do you think you could ever trust me?"

"I already do. Don't worry, I'll never tell a living soul."

They danced to the combo's swing and jazz favorites. When they played Duke Ellington's "Deep Purple," Nick led her in a slow foxtrot and Gloria melted into his arms. "Do you still have your big cat sculpture?"

"Sure do, I brought it all the way from Detroit."

"Let's go see it."

"Now? Tonight? No!"

"Why not?"

"I can't do that to Patrick. He has helped me so much. You two are a couple. And I can't let down your parents. Joe's my future…"

"I'm not Daddy's little girl anymore. Tonight, they're all tied up at Rockville. I can't face them at this hour. You can take me home in the morning and be properly introduced."

"But your clothes. You have all the wrong ones, again."

"Not a problem. I brought this big purse, just in case Patrick wanted…" Her thought trailed off. "Please take me home with you. I'm so-o-o tired."

Nick was overwhelmed. He had plenty of experience with women, but not her kind. He felt she was high class, above him. He hoped to win her respect someday, but never like this. "Okay, you can have my bedroom and I'll sleep on the couch, but I'm taking you home first thing in the morning."

With trembling fingers, he picked up the check, examined it and put some Franklins on the silver tray to cover it. With racing heart, he gently escorted her back outside.

When they got to the entry porch of the club, the rain had resumed.

"You sit here, Gloria, and I'll get the van. No sense you getting soaked twice in one day."

She sat on a cozy wooden bench beneath the shelter of rustic stone piers and deep, overhanging eaves. The reassuring sound of the rain on surrounding bushes and trees lulled her into a serene peace.

A pair of headlights appeared out of the murk and a car squealed to a halt at the porch. She stood to meet McGurk. When her eyes adjusted to the gloom after the glare of headlights, she realized too late the car was black. Two men emerged. One took each of her arms tied her wrists together in front of her and thrust her into the back seat."

"Oww, you're hurting me!"

"That'll teach you, bitch," the scrawny one said. "You don't fuck with Bulldog Dugan!"

"Oh crap, you two again. How did you find me?" Gloria demanded.

"We followed you, stupid!" Dugan whirled around and yanked the purse from her shoulder. He dug in and retrieved her cell phone. I'll take that now. It served its purpose. He threw the purse back at her. "Here, take your money, you won't be using it where you're goin.'"

Thirty-Four

Patrick returned Kitty to the Hunters' house in Winnetka a little after 6:30 p.m. Ross Hunter greeted them at the front door. "Kitty, I don't understand. You left with an FBI agent and you've returned with Patrick."

"Hello, Mr. Hunter."

"What happened?"

"It's a long story. Our outdoor groundbreaking ceremony got out of hand," Patrick explained. "With almost no warning, the cloudburst made a mess of everything, and people dashed for the old farmhouse on the property. It was total confusion, I assumed Glo—the others I came with—had all left together. The detective was still busy, and it was easier for me to give Kitty a ride."

"We're all safe and dry now. We had cocktails at Ravinia and were planning to have dinner and attend the concert. We would've had to walk quite a distance in the rain to the concert pavilion. We decided to pass."

Ann Hunter joined them and invited everyone to sit in their informal family room to chat while they dried out. "I've got a leg of lamb in the oven," she said. "You're welcome to join us, Patrick."

"As a single man, I can't afford to refuse such a fine dinner invitation," Patrick said.

"What exactly is your involvement with the FBI?" Hunter asked. "It seems my reservations about Kitty's association with you weren't unfounded."

"Ross, for heaven's sake, lighten up!" Ann was apparently used to his excesses.

"No, no," Patrick said, "I can appreciate your concern. My client for the new casino and resort out in Rockville has some old associations which the FBI monitors. In this case, there was also suspicious activity on the site, which Kitty and I happened to witness. I've been helping the FBI and the police solve a murder case."

"You are not reassuring me here." Hunter shook his head in dismay. "When it starts involving Kitty as I warned you, you're way out of bounds."

"Wait, Mr. Hunter," Kitty interrupted. "They merely wanted to know why Patrick and I had visited the property where the resort is being built. A few weeks ago, while I was still living with the other girls, Patrick showed me the project site and we sat all afternoon. Patrick sketched his design concept for the project, while I wrote letters home. Then at dusk, when we were ready to leave, these two men drove into the site. We saw some fishermen, or so we thought. They went out in a boat."

"Exactly," Patrick said. "Kitty and I were safe. We stayed out of sight, since I didn't want to discuss the project with outsiders. I just thought I should observe why intruders were trespassing on my client's property."

"Protecting your client's confidentiality and interests," Hunter said. "I understand completely."

"I only learned later that the two were disposing of a body, of Walter McDougal Howe, an heir to the Marvell-McDougal estate."

"I've been following that case in the papers," Hunter said. "There's entirely too much organized crime in this city. I'm pleased to know you're trying to help get rid of it."

"Thank you, sir. I try to do what I can."

"Kitty, I can't tell you what to do, but under the circumstances are you still totally comfortable with seeing Patrick?"

"I'll admit, today's experience gave me quite a turn. But it was the sudden storm that caused all the confusion. It's quite different from my boring life back in Ireland, and Patrick is funny and very talented. You should see his drawings."

"I'd show them to you," Patrick offered, "but we lost most of them today in the sudden wind and rain. Good thing we still have the originals back at the office."

Patrick considered saying more to justify taking on this risky assignment with a known mobster. But he would probably dig a deeper hole for himself.

When dinner was ready, Ross Hunter turned to a wine cooler under the bar and selected a hearty cabernet to go with the lamb. They moved to the dining room.

"I used to think I wanted to be a criminal lawyer," Hunter said, "but both the pace and the type of people I had to deal with were not to my liking. Frankly, the corporate work also paid better, but it wasn't nearly as exciting as criminal trials."

"Likewise, I chose architecture for my profession, but I have a fascination with solving crimes. I guess I just can't stand to see people wronged and criminals getting away with it."

"Just recently, I had to turn away a case. A man from Detroit called my office and wanted to know if I would undertake some work to recover misappropriated funds. The phone connection was poor, with a lot of static, so I wasn't quite sure I heard the man's name correctly, Rosa, or something? Anyway, he said a man named Candicci would be in town soon and asked if I would meet with him. I told him that's not my line of work and thanked him for the call. That was the end of it."

"Could that name have been Jimmy Roma?" Patrick asked.

"Yes, that was it."

"How long ago was that?"

"Oh, about two months ago, I guess," Hunter said.

"Bingo! That may help us find the man who killed Walter Mc-Dougal Howe and his attorney, Fabrizio Angionomo."

"Oho, let's retire to the study. I'd love to hear more about the case. Maybe there's something I could help you with."

Kitty helped Ann clear the table, clean the roasting pan and put the plates and silver in the dishwasher. Hunter poured Patrick some of his good cognac, helped himself and soon they were deep into a discussion of all the events that had led Patrick up to this point. After about a half-hour, Ann and Kitty had finished cleaning up and joined them in the study.

"Kitty has been telling me about some of your explorations

around the city," she said. "She says you've really helped her get to know Chicago."

"We've had an enjoyable time exploring together," Patrick said. "But I think it has a lot to do with Kitty's interest in trying new things, like Chinese and Vietnamese food, and her adventurous spirit."

"There are lots of other things to explore in Chicago, Kitty," Ann said. "Patrick, you might both go down to the University of Chicago campus in Hyde Park. You could explore the Oriental Institute, visit Rockefeller Chapel and even see Stagg Field. In a lab under the bleachers of that stadium, Edward Teller and the other scientists on the Manhattan project produced the first sustained nuclear chain reaction that led to creation of the atomic bomb. In fact, a couple of blocks from there, you could stop by and see the Robie House—"

"Ann, he's an architect! You don't have to tell him about the Robie House."

"No problem," Patrick said, "I hadn't thought of taking her over there, but it's a great idea." Ann continued to ramble on about her favorite Chicago attractions, art museums, special exhibits, the aquarium. The wine and the cognac were having their effect. He caught himself letting his eyes close. His head drooped, once, twice...

"Patrick, we've worn you out," Ann said. "And now it's probably too late for you to drive home."

"Don't worry about me. I'll be fine." He got up to leave, but his knees were unsteady.

"Ann is right," Hunter insisted, "it's not a good idea for you to drive home right now. We have plenty of room upstairs. You can have our son's room. I'm sure there are pajamas in his dresser and extra toothbrushes and razors in his bathroom."

"Patrick, please don't drive home." Kitty said. "You'll be more alert in the morning."

"It's unanimous, then. I'll follow you, Ann."

She led him upstairs to their son's room, set out a pair of his pajamas and turned down the covers on a handsome, queen-sized fourposter bed. Ann puttered, closing blinds, turning on the bedside light and plumping pillows. "You know, Patrick, Kitty is very fond of you. She's been so shy about saying anything, because she doesn't know where she stands with you."

"She is? We have a great time together, true. The first thing she ever told me, though, was that she doesn't ever plan to get married. And Mr. Hunter defends her like his own daughter."

"Don't believe everything she tells you. And don't pay any attention to my husband. He loves Kitty, as I do. Deep down, he doesn't want to hurt her chances for a happy relationship. But he can be infuriating at times—all bluff and bluster."

"You all had me fooled."

"Just sleep on it. I'll let you get some rest. Goodnight, Patrick."

"G'nite Mrs. Hunter. Thanks." He donned the pajamas and got ready for bed. He wondered if Hunter's facts were vital clues to solving the mystery. He needed help, and he was running out of time before O'Malley and FBI Agent Radwinski cut off his access to the case.

THIRTY-FIVE

Kitty slept soundly for six hours. When she awoke at 3:58 a.m. by the digital clock, the events of the previous day raced through her mind and chased away any hope of returning to sleep. She couldn't get her mind off Patrick, who lay in bed, not twenty feet away from her across the hall,

She crept silently, bare feet gripping the carpet, out of her room into the hall. The door creaked as she swung it slowly inward. Patrick sat bolt upright as a ghostly presence, his large form silhouetted against the glow of the moonlit narrow-slat blinds.

"Patrick, are you awake?"

"Kitty! What are you doing in here? If Ross Hunter catches us, he'll kill me!"

"They're in their bedroom downstairs, at the other end of the house. Even when they play their television loud, no noise comes up here. They both sleep quite soundly."

"I woke up too. I'm trying to figure out who the other parking attendant was."

"Good, you can worry about that in the morning. I've been tossing and turning. Something is bothering me, and I had to talk to you.

"I don't really know you, Patrick. Tell me about your family."

Moonlight filtering through the partially open blinds revealed his impassive face. He turned his large, hazel eyes on her, awaiting what she had to say. Her breathing quickened.

"I can't get you out of my mind, I want to get close to you, but I'm afraid I can't trust or rely on you. Maybe it's because I don't really know you, Patrick."

"We're just innkeepers. like your family. You know what we're like to work with," he said, "and we're really pretty much as we appear."

He told of their immigrant history, their various moves through neighborhoods on the South Side, and finally to Oak Park. "My mother fears for me, rightfully so, considering some of the reckless things I do. My father is realistic, strict and demanding—too much so at times."

"But you've achieved so much," she insisted.

"I suppose so. I'm twenty-eight." Patrick said. "Uncle Mike convinced me I could have a professional career. He showed me I was meant to be an architect."

"And you're still alone?"

"What you mean? Do I live alone? Yes, most of the time. And I've got to get married eventually."

Kitty laughed. "You make it sound like going to the dentist. Do you think it will be that bad?"

"It doesn't do to take a date to a professional party, dinner with a client and his wife or a public reception. Most unmarried girls become the topic of the conversation, and they just don't fit in with all those wives. Besides…I can't bear the thought of a humdrum domestic life, at least not with any of the American girls I've met.

"Foreign, then? European, Asian?"

"Maybe that's why I hang out with the new arrivals from Ireland. Someone more exotic than your normal American woman."

She wondered about this man. It was clear he knew where he was going—he had drive, earnings and artistic achievement. In the glow of dawn, she admired his handsome features. Despite a callow attitude about women, in some respects he had an understanding much older than his years.

"Do you know anything about your Irish ancestors?"

"In fact, my mother's people lived in Balleyvourney, an isolated valley north of Cork. They were mostly bards and priests—an ancient people, older, it's believed, than the Anglo descendants who raided Ireland in a later era from the adjacent British isle. My father was from good peasant stock, in the locale of Cork." His fathomless hazel eyes under high-arched eyebrows and a thin, determined expression on his lips evoked their Old World, fatalistic outlook

"No wonder you're different, you know," she said at last. "And a loner."

"And you're not? I've never met a woman like you. So distant—so alone, and aloof."

"But I rather like you, and I can't explain it," she said.

When his eyes met hers in the growing light of dawn, he looked puzzled. "Well, that's something, anyway."

"You know that girl Mary I told you about, my friend from the boat?"

"The one who can't talk to her boyfriend?"

"That one. I made up that story — that's really me, Patrick. I've become attached to you. I've been trying to find a way to tell you for the longest time. But you always shut me out, change the subject or turn a serious conversation into a trivial joke. Besides, you love that Gloria—"

"No, no. Gloria has been the object of my affections for some time. But I can tell you—lately I've been using every excuse I can think of not to call her, so I can spend time with you. That performance at the farmhouse was the last straw."

"Really? Then, why do you act this way toward me?"

"I thought that's what you wanted — no men in your life—nothing to do with me personally. I thought you just wanted to be friends."

"We are, very good ones, But the fact is — and I don't know how this happened — of all the men in the world, I want you."

"But…you said you didn't want anything more."

"A woman has the right to change her mind, doesn't she?"

He stood and put a finger to her lips. "I can't take my mind off you, either."

"Patrick, hold me."

"Kitty, I can't. When you come to me like this, I can't treat you the way I've treated other women. I don't want to hurt you."

"I'm not some Barbie doll who would break if you dropped me. I'm tougher than you think. Try me."

"I—I … the words stuck in his throat. "Chicago is so—brutal. I feel I need to protect you."

"I'm so lonely. Reckless as you are, I trust you."

"But, but—why me?"

"I've been looking for someone just like you for a very long time. You're creative, with imagination, vision and ability. You're more gentle and kind than you act. I think you just hide it from others, so they won't think you're weak. Can I depend on you?"

"Oh, Kitty!" He put his hands on her shoulders and pulled her to him. Her smooth cheek rested on his, and her soft breast melted into his. He pulled away, moved over and patted the bed in front of him. "Sit here and talk to me."

"Can't you show me how you feel?"

"Kitty, I'm overwhelmed that you want me. But we're in someone else's house, not in a proper place for this, sneaking around."

He had certainly been in bedrooms with many women, but he acted unsure of himself. His insistent desire seemed to relax. His notorious lust seemed to have left him. Contrary to the predictions of her new friends at the pub, he was acting brotherly, protective, entrusted with a great treasure he didn't want to break.

"Then just listen to me for a change. I want to spend more time with you, I look up to you. And I think you're too good for that stripper's daughter." She spat out the words.

"Don't, please, don't be angry with me. She's a person, with hopes and dreams, just like you and me. But I've learned—over a year or more, she's not the person I want to spend my life with, not the one for me"

"Really?"

"I'd stake my life on it. In fact, I did."

"I'm so lonesome in Chicago. I feel so close to you. Will you hold me once in a while? I need someone I can depend on. For some crazy reason I feel I can depend on you."

"You can. You have my word." He sealed it with a kiss.

Thirty-Six

Kitty left the room to shower and dress. Exhausted with the emotions of the past twenty-four hours, Patrick fell back on the bed and dozed. The characters he'd met in the previous weeks rose up and haunted his dream—the detective, the dead lawyer, the underboss, the henchmen. He saw four men greeting them at the Bulls game. One of them had no face, just dark sunglasses. I'm a specialist, he said in a hollow voice, *I have no name. Death's my game.*

Like file cards, possible suspects flipped through his vision: Bohannon, fully occupied with his hosting duties, the dignitaries and his exhaustive interrogation by the FBI and police. The new strangers on the scene were parking attendants. Which of these seemed likely suspects?

There was one more card under M, for mob connections. He flipped it to face his eyes. It was blank, but then blurred text appeared which slowly came into focus. The name Candicci glowed on the card — the man Jimmy Roma had mentioned in his call to Ross Hunter! The file cards flew into the air and then resettled into an orderly pile.

When Patrick entered the kitchen, Kitty was seated at the breakfast table. Ann was making pancakes, and the savory smell of bacon filled the kitchen.

"Hello, Ann. Thank you for taking me in last night. As you

said, it was a life-saving idea." He winked slyly at Kitty.

"Did you sleep well, dear?" she asked Kitty.

"Like a dream," she said demurely.

"How did you sleep, Patrick?" Kitty asked.

"Never better," he said staring into her deep, green eyes.

Ross Hunter arrived at the breakfast table. He was trying make sense of his new clue. "Ever since you mentioned it, I've been thinking about Candicci's possible involvement the case."

Hunter 's remark diverted Patrick's eyes from Kitty. "But where does he fit in?"

"A double cross. Your client Bohannon ordered a couple of extra parking attendants. He got them from Detroit, with a heap of trouble in the bargain. Could be somebody out there didn't like the way he forgot to clear it with them."

"One of them seemed familiar, maybe local. The big man was probably Roma's enforcer. But the other stranger might be behind it. Patrick scratched his forehead. "What was the first name of the guy Roma mentioned on the phone—that Candicci?"

"Marco, I think. I'll check my notes, run a search of police records and let you know of any results."

Later, when Patrick pulled out of the Hunters' drive, the early morning sun outlined the crisp architectural shapes of the houses and trees. After the rain, everything looked fresh and new. He had never felt such kinship with all of nature, all buildings, even the birds and the squirrels. A new life force coursed through his awakened body and animated all the world's creations.

Lucky thing—he faced many challenges, with his client of dubious virtue, with his employer and with the law. He would need all the energy he could muster.

THIRTY-SEVEN

At 10:30 a.m. Sunday, Patrick was back in his apartment. He had bought the weekend papers on his way back home, including the Clarion. The front-page headline read:

SPRING STORM SOAKS SPA SPLASH
Five missing at casino site

By Mona Strong

A ceremony meant to launch the illusive Chicago Casino and Resort at Rockville ran aground Saturday, when a sudden thunderstorm sent terrified guests scrambling for cover. After drenched dignitaries escaped the muddy mess, five persons were missing, regretfully not including this reporter.

Mayor Robert J, Dooley Jr. had just finished praising the vision of Joseph Bohannon, North Side businessman and suspected mob underboss, when a thunderbolt and cloudburst dispersed the crowd and chased guests into a ramshackle farmhouse on the property for shelter. Mayor Dooley and the Illinois Gaming Commissioner escaped the fiasco, but the wife of the Mayor of Rockville was blown off the platform, broke her right arm and suffered numerous contusions. She remained overnight in Boone County Hospital, under observation. Missing after the storm were Gloria Bohannon, daughter of the property owner, and four parking attendants.

Display illustrations prepared by architect Patrick MacKenna were scattered in the sudden windstorm and drenched with rain, perhaps as an omen foretelling the fate and future of yet another MacKenna project. The present fortunes of his ill-fated architecture firm, Halliday & Robb, were also uncertain. Their team and that of MacKenna Construction, contractors for the building expansion project for the Star-News, a struggling newspaper, were halted last week when a construction crane fell into the Chicago River…

"Blah, blah, blah…" Patrick threw the newspaper on the floor in disgust. He was sure the Star-News version of events would be fairer and more informative. But it had him thinking— as regarded his new client, whose side was he on? Whose side should he be on?

At 11:15 Joe Bohannon called.

"Patrick, have you heard from Gloria?"

"No."

"She's disappeared. Radwinski, O'Malley and I searched everywhere."

"Oh my God! Didn't she call?"

"No, Candy is beside herself. She's been crying for the last three hours. I've got all the boys out trying to find out what happened. She doesn't answer her cell phone. I don't know what the problem is."

"She might have been kidnapped," Patrick suggested and then bit his tongue

"But, dammit, the police and the FBI were there when she disappeared."

"I had no idea. It was a confused, messy situation, with people and cars all over the place. What do you suppose happened?"

"I'd never seen two of those parking guys before. I assumed they were on loan from Sal Falcone. The boys said they were all right. I even put Nick McGurk in charge of them, just to in case they tried to pull anything. Now, both McGurk and Gloria have disappeared. None of the parking attendants showed up to get paid. And Nick hasn't called me to talk about the project yet. He's not answering his cell phone. With you two on the outs, I'm just wondering," Joe said, "if Gloria and Nick ran off together."

Patrick hadn't thought of that.

"As soon as you hear anything, let me know."

"Of course, Joe, and you call me when you know more.

"Sure, sure."

The poor man was frantic.

Patrick stared again at the morning paper, but he couldn't concentrate. What had become of Gloria? Where was McGurk? Why didn't the the parking attendants claim their pay for the afternoon's work? And what about the bruiser with the limp? And that sidekick wearing sunglasses on a cloudy day seemed awfully familiar. Who were the two others with Arnie at the basketball game? Since the dog walker had really been shot, not accidentally killed by the fall from above, who was his killer working for?

Why were these new players unfamiliar to Joe Bohannon? Special Agent Radwinski had worked all afternoon, reviewed Patrick's cell phone transmissions and talked to everyone. He reported that Joe came off clean. Was someone else operating in this area, another faction they didn't know about?

He called Nick McGurk's cell phone and got no answer.

THIRTY-EIGHT

Patrick had still not heard from McGurk when he arrived at the office Monday morning. Desperate to do anything to solve this baffling case, Patrick called Angela Atkins at her office, down the hall from the scene of Fabrizio Angionomo's murder.

"Ms. Atkins, this is Patrick MacKenna. You may recall meeting me in the elevator that day of the unfortunate demise of your client, the man on your floor."

"How could I forget?"

"You said you could tell me how to contact his secretary, Gertrude Simms."

"Oh yes, of course. Let me look up the number… Here it is." She read it to him.

"You also mentioned you did some business with the victim. Could you spare a few minutes later today to tell me a little about him? Perhaps at lunch."

"I have to attend a court case this afternoon. With any luck, I'll only be tied up until about three. I could meet you for coffee at four—there's a little café in our building. I usually sit in the booth to the left of the door."

"I really appreciate it, Ms. Atkins. I'll see you at four."

He tried the number Angela gave him. No answer. He then called Angionomo's office. He got the recorded greeting, in a woman's voice: "You have reached the law offices of …yada, yada,

yada…at the tone." With nobody left to call him back, he hung up.

The intercom emitted its ominous beep. "Patrick, can you come in here, please?" Jason's tone conveyed panic.

Gathered around Halliday's desk were Detective O'Malley and Special Agent Radwinski.

"Patrick, what is the meaning of this?" Halliday demanded.

"Detective, Agent Radwinski, we meet again. I thought I had answered all your questions on Saturday." Patrick looked quizzically at Jason Halliday.

"These officers have been asking me questions I can't answer." Halliday turned to the detective. "Sergeant, please proceed."

O'Malley picked up his cue. "Okay, we were at the groundbreaking Saturday. We have two unsolved murders. Your gun was found at the casino property in Rockville. We can't pin anything directly on Bohannon. We would appreciate anything more you could tell us about this puzzling case."

"I trust I don't need to remind you, Patrick, of the distinguished reputation of Halliday & Robb. We could be dragged under with the bad press alone on this project, not to mention the sum of ninety-five thousand dollars owed to us so far in fees for the preliminary design."

"I'm well aware of the situation," Patrick began. "I've been struggling with the same questions. The mess that the thunderstorm made of our groundbreaking ceremony was merely the icing on a badly botched cake."

"So," O'Malley said in his driest tone, "what gives?" His pencil poised above his notepad, he cocked his head expectantly.

"You are aware of the disappearance of Joe Bohannon's daughter Gloria after the cloudburst?" Patrick asked Radwinski.

"Yes, as well as the missing parking attendants and Nicholas Mc-something."

"McGurk," Patrick said. "In all the chaos after the storm, Gloria, McGurk and the other parking attendants hired for the occasion went missing. We couldn't find them either. Joe called me Sunday morning, panicked. I told Bohannon I couldn't find her either and hadn't taken her home with me. He said his wife Candy was inconsolable. That's when I called and left a message for you, Sergeant O'Malley."

"And here I am, just now returning your call." O'Malley simpered. "You sure you didn't just spirit her away for the weekend?"

"No, when I left she was nowhere to be found." He looked toward Special Agent Radwinski. "But you had brought Kitty O'Connor out to the Bohannon farmhouse for questioning. Then, afterward you were busy with the situation at the scene. As you will recall, I offered to take Kitty home to Winnetka. We left about 6:00 p.m. and went directly there. You can verify that by calling Ann and Ross Hunter at their home."

"So far, so good, "Radwinski said, "but both Gloria and this McGurk fellow are still missing. Anything else?"

Jason Halliday's eyes darted among Patrick and the two law officers like a spectator at a tennis match, hanging on every word.

"Saturday afternoon, Bohannon hired three additional men to park cars. Since he had already met McGurk — in fact, I introduced him to Joe — he put him in charge of their crew."

"You did what?" O'Malley said.

"I introduced them. He was a guide in the coal mine at the Museum of Science and Industry. I was showing Miss O'Connor around town, and he approached me about finding a better job. I told him to call Joe."

"Okay, okay. So, then what?" O'Malley said, impatient.

"Now let me get this straight," Halliday said. "You made these discoveries and found all of this out. What, may I ask, does this have to do with architecture. Your job, remember?"

"Now Jason, I can explain." Patrick looked at Halliday. "You recall how you encouraged me to get to know clients, to cultivate relationships with them, so they'll trust us."

"Right, right. Go on."

"That's why I helped him plan the groundbreaking ceremony, made sure the dignitaries were invited. That's why I was at the stadium that Saturday when Walter Howe died. My uncle Mike MacKenna, contractor for this project, helped with all that. We used his Bulls tickets."

"Go back and tell me more about Saturday morning," O'Malley said.

"I realized I didn't recognize two of those four guys. One was a big bruiser with a limp. Dugan. Next was a tall, well-dressed fellow

I didn't know. The third was tall and gangling, vaguely familiar. The fourth was Arnie, a regular associate of Joe Bohannon. Nick McGurk, the guy Joe put in charge of his temporary parking crew, made five. Every one of them wore sunglasses, even though it was a cloudy day. Bohannon told me none of them showed up to get their pay for their afternoon's work."

"I didn't recognize the tall gangling one at first. Then it dawned on me — it was Tom Buttafumo. And the burly one—"

"Our former employee?" Jason Halliday stared at Patrick, incredulous. "What am I running here, an architectural firm or an employment agency?"

"Or a detective agency," Radwinski chimed in. "Patrick has provided us with some valuable information today, Mr. Halliday. His observation skills may lead to the arrest and conviction of the murder suspects. If so, there is a substantial reward, which might help you cover your unpaid bills."

"That would certainly be welcome." Halliday shook his head in dismay.

"This Bulldog Dugan, the burly one with a limp, is a known gang member," Radi continued. "He's an enforcer for the Detroit Partnership, also called the Outfit, part of La Cosa Nostra."

"As if Joe doesn't have enough trouble launching this project." Patrick shook his head He had revealed enough today. He hoped he would never have to disclose where McGurk really came from. He still wasn't sure how he had come by his hoard of cash. And hoped he would never have to find out.

"In fact, we've noticed another pattern," Radwinski continued. "Further evidence has come out that the Detroit mob has been using the old Victorian house they bought a couple of years ago on the Northwest side. It's been mostly unoccupied since then. That could be Dugan's local headquarters."

"What about Bohannon?" O'Malley said. "Can't you nail him while you're at it? His North Side gang has been our headache for years."

"With Patrick's help we gave him a pretty good going over. As far as these murders are concerned, he appears to be clean. Patrick, you can return that surveillance phone you've been wearing for us. We're done with that phase of the investigation."

"You're welcome to it. What a relief." Patrick removed the phone from his belt pouch and handed it over to Radwinski. Then he reached in his pants pocket and replaced it with his own cell phone.

"You've been doing surveillance?" Halliday exclaimed. "My God, I am running a detective agency!"

Thirty-Nine

Later that Monday morning, Detective O'Malley and special agent Radwinski paid a visit to Joe Bohannon at his bar and grill.

"I'm relieved to see you at last. Can you help me find my daughter Gloria?"

"We came as quickly as possible after you called," O'Malley said. "How long has she been missing?"

"She disappeared after our groundbreaking ceremony Saturday, in all the confusion when the thunderstorm hit. A new man I hired, McGurk, is also missing. As I told you both, I couldn't find them after the groundbreaking."

"Yeah, and there's been no word from her?"

"No. She arrived at the ceremony with Patrick MacKenna. He doesn't know where she is, and she hasn't been at her apartment or our house since that day."

"How terrifying it must be for you and your wife," O'Malley said with a hint of sarcasm. "We'll get more details from you and get right on it. But first, could we discuss another matter?"

"Go ahead."

"Mr. Bohannon," Radi said, "we appreciate your cooperation so far. However, we can find no logical explanation for the untimely deaths of two men involved with the heirs of the Marvell-Mc-

Dougal fortune: first an attorney, Fabrizio Angionomo, and then his client, Walter McDougal Howe. What can you tell us about their unfortunate and coincidental demise?"

"I read about it in the papers. I have absolutely no idea how they happened."

"What about the second one, Walter Howe?" O'Malley asked. "We understand you were there at the basketball game where he died."

"Those were not my regular seats at the Stadium. In fact, I'm a hockey fan and seldom attend the Bulls games. My wife and I were guests that afternoon of my architect, Patrick MacKenna, using his uncle Mike MacKenna's tickets."

"So we understand," O'Malley said, "but we also learned that four men visited you at those seats before the game."

"The funny thing about that visit was that I only knew two of them. The other two were unfamiliar to me."

"So, who were they?"

"One of them was my busniness associate, Arnie. The other was a character they called Bulldog, who doesn't work for me. But he always turns up when there's trouble. The game was about to begin. There was no time for introductions. They all wore sunglasses. I'll have to admit, those lights on the basketball court are bright."

"What did they have to say?" Radwinski asked.

"My associate Arnie kidded about proper behavior at a sporting event. He assured me they would be polite."

"I see," Radi said. "Were you aware of the fact that a man fell from the upper deck to the floor below?"

"There was no way to avoid knowing. They delayed the second half for twenty minutes while they removed the body. So sad for his family."

"He didn't have immediate family in town that we know of," O'Malley said, "He and his family were from D. C. He lived alone with two dogs," "He was an eccentric, aging bachelor, a dog walker by trade."

"It was not an accident," Radwinski said. "When we found the body on the lake at your property, we learned the man was also shot. Police assigned to the stadium hustled him out of the arena before they were aware of that fact."

"I hadn't heard that," Bohannon said.

"You have any idea who might have killed his lawyer, Angionomo? It was an assassination, with a single shot to his forehead."

"Absolutely not. This was not us."

"Well, Joe," O'Malley said in a sarcastic tone, "if it's not your boys, who could have done these guys in?"

"I don't have a clue. I'm positively baffled." He grabbed for his gut with both hands. "Oh, my insides are calling. Can you excuse an old man to use the facilities?"

"Yeah, go ahead," the sergeant said.

◊

While they waited O'Malley studied the family photos on the credenza behind Bohannon's desk. Joe was powerfully built, about five-feet-eight in height, with hair once jet black, now sprinkled with gray. His early family photos showed a short, bull-necked man, with close cropped black hair, a stubbly five o'clock shadow on his chin and squinting eyes. Even when smiling with his wife and kids, his eyes seemed to penetrate and burn like a demon's. His hefty two-hundred pounds were all muscle, and his pit-bull-ugly appearance still revealed his street thug origins.

In more formal poses with the mayor and business associates, he appeared clean-shaven, with longer hair, carefully styled, and sideburns flecked with distinguished gray. He beamed with a contented smile, more refined as he grew older and more successful in legitimate businesses. He wore expensive, tailored suits, snug fitting overcoats and a crisp fedora with the brim cocked upward and pointed black shoes. The obligatory Mafia diamond pinky ring sparkled on his right little finger. It seemed the higher he'd risen in the Chicago crime family, the more handsome his appearance became.

For O'Malley, the photo collection was a good review of all the years he had spent sparring, playing cat-and-mouse and jockeying for advantage with Chicago Joe Bohannon. He felt he knew him pretty well. The man said he didn't know who was behind the killings. Based on what they'd learned so far, he was prepared to accept Bohannon at his word. His body movements and manner had evolved over the years—from the clunky, brute force of a street soldier, when he could freeze even a fearless hit man with an icy stare, to today. Now he could suppress the beast within and appear charming, graceful and harmless. He'd learned to adapt himself to his situation, whether among the top gang hierarchy, the affluent or the nothing-to-lose killers, he could fit in with his milieu and quickly establish control. Studying the man before him, O'Malley observed that this quality could be extremely useful on the shifting sands of Chicago's lake shore.

◊

Inside his soundproof inner sanctum, Bohannon reached for the phone on the wall next to the stool and made a call.

"Hey, it's Bohannon. Get me Sal." A couple of minutes later he heard a scratchy voice and static on the line, with chopping, pounding and roars in the background, this time like machinery at a rock quarry.

"Joey, what a pleasure, as always! His words sounded furry, changing from thick to thin.

"Yeah, hi Sal. Look, I got O'Malley and Radwinski… yeah, the FBI guy … in my office right now. You know anything about this lawyer Angionomo, who got whacked, and his client Walter Mc-Dougal Howe, who had that so-called accident at the Sunday Bulls game?"

"I heard about it."

"And my daughter, Gloria, she's been missing for three days!"

"Frankly, I smell a rat. That's not us either…" The chopping and pounding resumed.

"Yeah, something stinks. We had trouble when the storm hit at our casino groundbreaking. Gloria disappeared. There's no way I would've staged that."

The thuds and roars got louder…"So I hear — so sorry. We didn't know a thing about it." The cacophony increased in volume and drowned out his voice

"Hey Sal, you're breaking up."

"Yeah…" More roars. "We're broken up about it too… But I told you, with that casino crap, you're on your own …" Chop, chop, bang, thud… "Look, we don't have a clue who is behind that, but I can tell you this… Somebody's trying to horn in on our turf …

Big bruiser named Dugan… You can't miss him—must weigh over 200 — all muscle…. He's Jimmy Roma's enforcer… Let me know if you need …any …" One final crash overwhelmed the rest of Sal's conversation.

"We sure as hell need help, Sal… Sal? SAL! … Dammit!"

The line went dead. Joe heard nothing else and hung up. He flushed the toilet and went back into the office.

◊

Bohannon re-entered the room.

"Sorry for the interruption, boys, but I feel much better now."

"Okay, Mr. Bohannon," Radi said. "Anything else you suspect, like who's behind this?"

"Something is rottin' in Denmark—or maybe in Detroit. Someone else is trying to move into Chicago. I think it would benefit us all if we could keep them out."

"I hear you," O'Malley said. "We got enough problems right here without asking for more." They stood and headed for the door.

"Wait, there's one more thing…"

"What's that?' O'Malley turned back to face him. Radwinski stopped in his tracks.

"To deal with the crowds on Saturday I had Arnie, one of my main men, hire some extra help—to park all those cars, you know? So along came this bruiser named Dugan, a well-put-together tough guy, plus a pretty boy I didn't recognize and some other local kid they called Tom. I put my new manager, McGurk, in charge of them, especially the new guys on my staff, just in case—"

"Bulldog Dugan?" Radwinki asked.

"Yeah, that was what they called him. Funny, he didn't show up after work to collect his pay. None of them did. And that's when I discovered my daughter Gloria and McGurk were gone."

"Bulldog Dugan — he is from Detroit," Radwinski said. "Funny, what's he doing here?"

"'Tain't funny, McGee," O'Malley said. "See what I mean? You gotta stick with local folks — somebody you can trust!"

FORTY

At four p.m. Patrick joined Angela Atkins at her table in the café. At close range, she looked older than he recalled — he now guessed about forty-five. She had crow's feet at the corners of her eyes. Her blue serge suit had shiny patches at the elbows. Her expression was weary and strained.

"I can only stay until 4:30. I have to catch my bus to Maywood and get home in time to let out the dog and make dinner."

"You live at your family home?"

"Yes, with my mother. She's slipping away—dementia and early Alzheimer's."

"Sorry."

"She was such a lively, active woman. It's painful to watch her go. I don't know what I'll do when she can't take care of herself anymore."

"You can call the Alzheimer's Association." He hated depressing talk, so he changed the subject. "How well did you know the murder victim?"

"Before Mother started failing, I used to see him regularly. His wife died, and he was lonely. I haven't seen him as much since Mother fell ill. Before that we would have lunch together."

"Oh? How often?"

"Once a week, on Fridays. We used to sit right here."

This was turning into a real hard luck story. "What did you

learn about the Howe case?"

"Very little. There was some question about bearer bonds and preferred stock in the Clarion Company. The bank where he had a safe deposit box holding the certificates was taken over by a bigger fish. I believe it was Anchor Capital."

"You don't say? That company is reputed to be controlled by Salvatore Falcone, the Chicago Mafia boss."

"That might explain a thing or two. When Fabrizio started looking into the case, they claimed that Scott had no forwarding address. The bank said they turned over contents of his safe deposit box to the State of Illinois Department of Unclaimed Property."

"Was he getting anywhere with his search?"

"The state had no such property. That turned out to be a dead lead."

"And it resulted in a dead attorney." Patrick was immediately sorry he'd said that.

"The last time I saw him, the week before his — as you put it, demise — he said he was on to something. He might have found Howe's bearer bonds. They had a face value of two million dollars, today worth even more. The police went through the office after the murder, but I wonder—"

"—if they knew what to look for, right?"

"Exactly. He said he'd been threatened on the phone by some thugs. He died five days later." Her eyes filled, and she shook her head, as if to rid herself of the horrible memory.

Patrick put his hands on her arm. "I'm so sorry," he said, at a loss for words.

"Fabrizio looked after me, sort of a guardian angel."

"An angel's angel. Thank you so much for sharing your story, Angela. By the way, I tried calling Gertrude Simms. There was no answer, either at her home or her office here in Chicago."

"I haven't been able to catch up with her either. She was visiting her sister in California. She talked about going to live with her someday."

"This can't be easy for you, but if it makes you feel any better, your information may helped track down these criminals. Here's my card. If there's anything else you think of, please call."

He felt like Sergeant Joe Friday, droning on about the facts of the case, when he should have been much more sympathetic. He was beginning to understand how Detective O'Malley had become so hard. A million stories lurked behind the shuttered windows of this city that never sleeps. This was only one of them.

Back in the office at closing time, Patrick was just settling in to complete a drawing of the casino building he had intended to work on early that morning when his phone rang again .

"MacKenna?" The voice was only too familiar.

"Yeah, McGurk, what the hell happened to you?"

"Long story—short version, Gloria and I got kidnapped, we got free, but then Gloria wasn't so lucky. They tailed us and nabbed her again."

"How could you let that happen?" Patrick demanded.

"It was raining. I was trying to keep her dry, so I went—"

"You left her alone?" Patrick shouted into the phone.

"For thirty seconds. They were on our tail, and they grabbed her again."

"So, what do we do?" Patrick said.

"Find a way to spring her loose, I guess. But first we've got to find out where they took her."

"Yeah, the cops are working on it."

"Not fast enough. Can you give me any hint of who's behind this?"

If they really were holding her captive, she must really be suffering. That girl's idea of roughing it was staying at a five-year-old luxury hotel. Whether or not they would even resume their relationship was beside the point. As Gloria had said, she'd given him one of the best years of her life. If there was to be anything left of this life, he had to find her and set her free.

"Well, there's one possibility. You ever heard of a guy named Dugan, from Detroit?"

"No, who is he?"

"He's an enforcer for Jimmy Romas's operations. He's in town, and he was parking cars with us. They may be trying to muscle in on Chicago operations."

"Wait—my Pa has run into them. I'll check it out and get back to you.'"

"Do that, and we may find Gloria."

"Okay, I'll call you. soon."

"Wait, I need more advice."

"Look, Nick, we're desperate to find this girl, I don't have time to run an employment agency here." That was Halliday's line, but maybe it would get him to the point.

"I need a lawyer."

"I figured you would, sooner rather than later."

"No, no. Nothing like that. I'm starting a business, in fact two of them. I need to set up a couple of companies."

"I'm not a management consultant either. I don't know any corporate lawyers."

"Who can I ask?"

Patrick thought for a moment. If he didn't try to help McGurk, he'd never get him off the phone. "Well, I did meet someone today who knows a lot of lawyers."

"See, I knew you had the answer. Who is it?"

"Her name is Angela Atkins. She's a court reporter. Probably knows them all. Here, let me find her business card." He fumbled in his wallet, found it, and gave him the number."

"Thanks, MacKenna."

"Don't mention it. Just watch my back if I get in trouble with the Outfit."

"Not to worry."

"By the way, McGurk, that gal's been through a lot, and her mother's ill. She could use some paying work."

"No kidding? I could use a Girl Friday to keep track of a whole bunch of businesses."

"Give her a call. She might be the person you need."

"By the way, you know any reporters? I need some free publicity for all my good works."

"Now I'm a public relations consultant? I've got to get back to work. Since you're Joe Bohannon's new best friend, couldn't we talk about this the next time I meet with him?"

"Sure. Why not?"

"And by the way, will you please tell Joe Bohannon what you know about his daughter? It will save you some—uh, embarrassment—and he'll be able to fill in the police and the FBI."

"Thanks, will do. Talk to you later."

At last he hung up. Maybe that's how he could get Bohannon to call him about the project. Nothing else seemed to be working.

At 5:30 p.m., Chet wandered in, carrying a bowl of ice. How about a shot?"

"You're still here." Patrick tossed his felt tip pen back on the uncompleted drawing. "Might as well. What's the occasion?"

"We're back in business—and celebrating."

"We are?" He filled two glasses with ice anyway, took his fine Irish whiskey from the credenza behind his desk and splashed both glasses half-full. He added sparkling water and handed one to Chet,

"Here's to getting paid!" Chet raised his glass.

"Who paid us?"

"When Jason opened the afternoon mail, he found a check from Chicago Casino and Resort for ninety-five thousand dollars, covering the preliminary design phase."

"Hooray!"

"Along with it was a letter from Joe Bohannon authorizing us to begin preparing construction working drawings for the casino."

"He must've mailed it before the groundbreaking," Patrick said, "while we were still on speaking terms. How could he have made such large bank deposits without attracting FBI attention?"

"Oh, it can be done." Chet said. "Back East the mob has found many ways to turn a surplus of cash into legitimate bank deposits. You make them look like business proceeds. It's simple money laundering. They've been doing that in New Jersey for decades."

"How does it work?"

"Easy. You just open a legitimate business, mingle your real revenue with profits from the rackets with your regular business deposits. The Outfit has a holding company called Anchor Capital, and they also own a bank. In Jersey, even a laundry like that little storefront featured in The Sopranos will do. That really exists, you know. I've seen it. Anyway, we're authorized to begin the casino building."

"How do you plan to begin?"

"I've got to nail down the main floor plan — all those specialized rooms: restaurants, kitchens and casino functions. We'll need a meeting with the client to get his approval on placement of all that equipment before we can start the structural, plumbing, mechanical and electrical engineers going on their system designs and layout drawings."

"By the way, how is Joe going to do that? Does he know anything about casinos?"

"We'll find out soon. We'll have to wait until Joe calls us about it. Right now he can't think about anything but finding Gloria."

Part III: Follow the Money

Forty-One

Nick McGurk had too many problems.

Monday morning, he sat in his tiny apartment above the store on Jeffery Avenue, eating a bowl of cereal topped with a sliced banana, reading his copy of the morning Clarion and worrying about Gloria.

By trying to treat her right, he had let Gloria slip through his fingers. After the weekend's groundbreaking fiasco at Rockville, he should have taken her straight home and left her there. She most likely would not have been kidnapped and would be at home and safe with her family.

He didn't know where they were holding her, or he would attempt her rescue. But he couldn't set her free without help, and he couldn't just call the police. Joe Bohannon, the key to his future, must be frantic by now. Patrick wanted him to call Joe. But he couldn't call him until he had a plan to rescue her. He'd have to think about that one.

His other main concern was never far from his mind. He had to find a way to process his cash and get it into circulation, like a real businessman, without making any suspicious bank deposits. That's what Jimmy Roma had done in Detroit. He created dozens of legitimate businesses, restaurants, nightclubs, delivery services, union pension funds, jukeboxes and taxi companies, which hired people, paid salaries — even taxes — and wrote big checks, to suppliers, wholesalers, lawyers and accountants. McGurk figured if he could do that he would be able to put this hoard of cash to work, impress Bohannon and get a position of responsibility. If given a chance, he could make the man some real money. But how could he make his mark and get his serious attention?

The front page featured the headline: Grade Schoolers Killed on Front Porch. Its continuation page also carried a feature story by Mona Strong, listing this and other drive-by shootings over the past year and the failure by police to curb gang warfare. She quoted a University of Chicago sociologist who said, both legal and illegal guns in the possession of teenagers and adults throughout the South Side were not the problem. Citizens had to arm themselves and scare off gun-wielding assailants. Nick didn't know the answer, but he didn't think more guns would solve the problem—it was hard enough to sleep at night with all the random gunfire interrupting his rest.

He finished his breakfast and packed his shirts, pants and one coal miner's uniform in his laundry bag. It was another gloomy day in Chicagoland, the sky again threatening rain. Nick checked his reflection in the shop windows as he strutted along—he looked like Santa Claus. He was beginning to feel like somebody, his free time his own, his money working for him. He had done something to better himself, both now and in the future. It was the first time in his life he felt he even had a future.

He pushed through the door of a store with the name painted in gold letters on the glass, Abe's Laundromat, and greeted the attendant.

"Hey, Henrietta, how's it going?"

"Hey, Mistah Nick. I see you got a bundle for me today."

"Big load this week. Guess I stayed away too long."

"The bigger the better, I say. I gotta keep thirty machines busy."

"You've got a hell of a business here. How many shops does Abe Goldstein have?"

"He got twenty-five across the city, and not enough he'p. At my shop alone, three washers and one dryer are broke down. The old man complains when bid'ness fall off, but he cain't keep up and repair 'em all. I tell him, 'You want mo' money, Mistah G.? You keep all yo' machines running, you improve yo' take big time.'"

"What does he say to that?"

"He say, he old and tired. He'd like to sell the whole ball of wax. But he don't do nothin' 'bout it. Top of that, we got robbed last week. Third time this year. Startin' to scare away the customers. I'm gettin' too old for this."

"Did you know, I'm a whiz at repairing machines—all kinds? I got an idea, might help you folks out. You got Abe's phone number?"

She took a pencil off her ear and jotted the number on the back of a laundry slip. While she was at it, she weighed Nick's bag and wrote another slip. "I'll have these for you tomorrow night, Mistah Nick. Bring me some good news, hear?"

This got him to thinking. He stared at the gold lettered sign on the storefront window: Abe's Laundromat. What a crummy name for a store.

When he returned to his flat, Nick called the number. Abe Goldstein was all ears. They closed the deal later in the day for one-and-a half million cash and a plane ticket to Miami. Nick drove with the cash in numerous cardboard boxes to Abe's home office. In exchange, McGurk loaded his van with three green metal file cabinets of bank account records, property leases, deeds and machine warranties for his twenty-five stores.

Later in the week, McGurk drove Abe and his wife to Midway airport. Abe shook his hand, thanked him and pronounced him a *mensch*. He grabbed his fine new briefcase—giving a new one away with the cash when he closed a deal was McGurk's new thing—now full of bonds, cashier's checks and stacks of hundred-dollar bills. Abe Goldstein was on his way.

So was Nick. The next day he set up two bank accounts at the South Shore branch of that same downtown bank, one for The Machinery Works, d/b/a The Mommy Laundry, and a second for a company called Lawn Order, depositing five-thousand dollars in C-notes. in each. He was in business. All he had to do was stick to his detailed business plan. As an established owner of a cash business, Nick would now be able to deposit large amounts of cash without question— in his various business accounts in local banks throughout Chicago.

Forty-Two

Patrick was about to explode. Joe Bohannon pressed him for news of Gloria. Kitty wanted to spend more time with him. Chet pushed him for help with design issues—questions their distracted client was too preoccupied with his missing daughter's fate to answer. Jason Halliday wanted to know when the firm would be paid for another month's work by a half-dozen architectural and engineering personnel, as well as charges from consultants for site surveys.

Meanwhile, however, he had to fulfill a steady stream of requests by Radwinski of the FBI and O'Malley at police headquarters. They made so many demands, for meetings, information and clues on the unsolved murders of the lawyer Fabrizio Angionomo and celebrity dog walker Walter McDougal Howe he could hardly think straight. Only then would they attend to the "minor detail" of of Gloria Bohannon's kidnapping. Early on Tuesday of the following week, the two lawmen appeared in the office lobby at 8:30 a.m. Without prompting, Yolanda brought coffee into the conference room. O'Malley took a lot of sugar and Radwinski preferred a lot of cream, which she had begun stocking in the break room refrigerator for just such visits.

Radwinski had traced Howe's movements to Chicago and back home to D.C. He had a local FBI agent checking on his activities there. He had also learned from his Chicago bank that whenever he had needed to transfer money from the Barnes estate to personal accounts, he had been in the habit of arranging it from home and drawing cash on a debit card. However, in the latest bank acquisition, something had gone wrong with the re-issuance of the debit card, and the new bank required him to appear personally in Chicago to arrange for a new drawing account. Judging from the results of that trip, Patrick figured, his life was too high a price to pay for a simple visit to Chicago, so he could continue using his own money

O'Malley had followed up on his search for Gloria Bohannon. He had several theories of her whereabouts but lacked a motive. Joe had not received a demand for ransom. The detective presumed she had met with foul play and was wary of outspending police resources. He limited his efforts to searching among recent murder and accidental death reports for clues on her disappearance.

He and Radwinski arrived at the office again.

"MacKenna," O'Malley began, "I need to know more about the last time you saw Gloria Bohannon. Her father won't let us alone until we find his daughter."

"Look, Sergeant, I've told you everything I know. In the confusion caused by the storm—you were there—I looked for Gloria throughout the rooms of the house, upstairs, downstairs, everywhere. When I finally caught up with Joe, I learned she had not left with her family."

"Was there anything else?"

"Yes. Since we last met, McGurk told me something that may help us. He said he recognized one of the parking attendants. He remembered this heavyset muscle man called Dugan."

"So we heard," Radwinski said. "He's one of the most ruthless of the Detroit Outfit. He's an advance man and enforcer for their family of the mob. Bohannon told us that on Monday. At various times when Jimmy Roma was after something over the past ten years, they've made efforts to move into Chicago."

"When they tried a few years back, we had a couple of gang killings," O'Malley said. "They bought a house somewhere on the Northwest side."

"Right," Radwinski said. "I heard about it. Since Chicago police were watching it, I never learned where that house is located."

"Sergeant, can you find out where it is?" Patrick said.

"Yeah, I'll check it out and get back to you."

"Please do. If they have Gloria there, the sooner the better."

Patrick hoped the detective would pay more than his usual casual attention to his promises.

Patrick walked over to the MacKenna's pub for a late lunch. His father sat at the family table poring over food orders for the coming week. His mother was sorting the bills. He made himself a roast beef sandwich in the kitchen and sat down with his parents.

"Pa, do you know anything about the Detroit mob?"

"Don't I, now? When they were trying to move into town a few years ago, didn't they try to shake us down for protection money?"

"They did? You had to pay?"

"For a year or so. But then the police got after them. I'll never forget Detective Mahoney, a fine gentleman, if I ever met one, and a very good officer of the law. They chased those rascals clean out of town. Serves them right, too, for harassing law-abiding citizens."

"Did you learn where they hung out?"

"Didn't I, now? We had to deliver cash once a month, to keep them from demanding it at the pub."

"Where was it?"

"I'll never forget. It was in old Irving Park on the Northwest side. Why do you ask?"

"We're still looking for Gloria. They could be holding her there. What's the address?"

"Oh, my goodness!" He went into his office in the kitchen, looked up the address in a old ledger and returned with a slip of paper for Patrick. "Be careful. Those men will stop at nothing."

"Don't worry, Pa. I have my trusty Glock with me." He patted his side pocket.

"Just don't put any bullets in it," his mother said. "You might kill somebody."

"Well, Ma, better them than me."

FORTY-THREE

Another Monday arrived with no sign of Gloria. Joe Bohannon called Patrick daily to see whether he had any news.

"Patrick, what am I gonna do?"

"Keep the faith, Joe. I'm working on a plan to find and rescue her. I hope we'll have her back to you. Then we can get together at the farmhouse. Chet has a million questions for you about design decisions—arrangement of slot machines, placement of the cashier's cage and counting room, access to the restaurants, and location of the common kitchen. This is all critical stuff, which will ensure smooth operations. And we can't proceed on structural, plumbing, heating-air-conditioning and electrical design until we make these decisions."

If he could keep Joe busy with these key matters for another twenty-four hours, maybe he could relieve Joe's worry about Gloria. He had a hunch. He called McGurk and discussed his plan.

"That's risky, Patrick," McGurk told him. "If you're correct, we might tip off the kidnappers and get her killed. Jimmy Roma could find me and call down the wrath of hell on our heads."

"Nick, are you going soft on me? None of your plans to get employed by Joe will proceed unless you can get this solved. You need to scare the hell out of these kidnappers. Fear is the only emotion they understand. Then we'll take matters into our own hands."

"Okay, genius. What do we do next?"

"Pick me up at six p.m. tonight. Bring your tools. We'll plan our attack on the way over there. I'll wait for you at the steps of the Art Institute, between the lions."

After closing time, Patrick walked from the office to the Art Institute steps. He stood by the North lion, the friendly one, according to Kitty. When McGurk arrived with the white van, Patrick picked his way among the pedestrians heading for the Grant Park garage and the Illinois Central station and slipped into the passenger seat. He directed Nick toward the Outer Drive where they turned on Belmont and headed for the Northwest side.

They passed through blocks of rusting industrial buildings in various states of decay along the North branch of the Chicago River. Soon they found the formerly fashionable neighborhood where captains of industry had once lived. On a street of aging Victorian homes, he looked for the address his father had provided. His online search of city records had turned up a property plat at this address registered in the names of Serafina and James Romano. Close enough. They cruised up the street of tall, gingerbread encrusted frame houses, with wide porches, corner turrets, steep, dormered roofs and tall dark windows. They came to the address.

"There it is," Patrick said. "Pass it up." They parked in the next block and walked back along the front sidewalk. The darkening sky barely afforded a view of the bric-a-brac bracing for porch columns, half-round wood shingles on the roofs, with their many peaks and valleys, and deep shadows in the recesses of the front porch. Lights shone from the back windows of the first floor and in two rooms upstairs. They crept up a half-dozen steps to the veranda.

From the front window, Patrick peered past a heavy Victorian davenport, upholstered wing chairs and wooden-armed side chairs along the walls. A thin man passed through the kitchen door into the dining room carrying a tray and disappeared through a wide opening, beyond the dining table. Patrick joined McGurk at the sidelight of the front door and watched this man climb the main stair. He patted his pants pocket to make sure his gun was there.

"He's taking food to a prisoner!" Patrick said. "It could be Gloria."

"Maybe so, maybe not. Could be his invalid wife."

"I don't think so. No gangster would bring somebody like that along on a mission. Their prisoner has to be Gloria!"

"In that case, we have no time to waste," McGurk said. "That's probably Dugan in the kitchen. I'll keep him busy. You go upstairs, surprise his buddy and grab Gloria." He inspected the front door hardware and quickly picked the old-fashioned deadbolt with a skeleton key. Then he reached in the vest pocket of his suit jacket, produced the right burglary tool and picked the modern cylinder lock above. Within minutes they were inside. Beside the hall tree stood a chest covered with junk mail, a man's fedora and a ring of keys.

McGurk raced silently through the dining room toward the kitchen. Patrick faced an ornate Victorian stair, its design marred by a round iron post, added no doubt, as a remedial measure, a midpoint support for the sagging stair hall above. A banister curved around it at its lower end to join the newel post. Patrick climbed the stairs in silence.

At the end of the upstairs hall the door to a rear bedroom was ajar. He peeked in—Gloria!

The gangly thug held the tray of food in front of her.

"You expect me to eat this mush?"

"That's all we got, bitch. I didn't take this job to be a babysitter. You don't want it? I'll take it away."

He turned toward the door with her dinner. Patrick barged in and pushed the tray into his face.

"Patrick!" Gloria screamed.

Holding his gun by the barrel, he clobbered the thug on the temple. The man crumpled to the floor, unconscious, his face buried in the tray of food.

"Come on, kiddo. Let's move."

As they clambered down the Victorian stair, wails emerged from the kitchen.

"I'll get you, McGurk. You'll pay!"

"I don't think so. Here's a little remembrance of me."

"No, No-O-OO— O-w-w!" the victim bellowed.

Then came the sounds of a scuffle. At last the wounded Dugan's whimpers subsided. After a long minute, McGurk emerged from the kitchen, pushing a manacled Dugan in front of him. "Got him." He handed a paper napkin to Patrick. "Here's a little DNA sample for the cops."

Patrick examined the bloody piece of flesh on the napkin, the lobe of an ear. He folded the paper carefully and stuck it in his jacket pocket.

"That's my little earmark. Ha-ha, B-WAAH-HA-HA," McGurk burst into a full-throated belly laugh at his own joke.

"The other guy is up there," Patrick said. "I knocked him out, but I don't know for how long."

"Bring him down here," McGurk said.

Patrick took the stairs two at a time and disappeared into the back bedroom. He returned a minute later with the other thug, groggy. He secured the man's hands behind his back with his own necktie. They descended the stairs.

Meanwhile, McGurk had tied a dishtowel tightly around Dugan's mouth and ears.

"That should stop the bleeding until the cops pick them up and deal with him." Here, take charge of your man while I hook this guy up."

"You bast—m-m-ph—" Dugan uttered, his last intelligible words for a while. McGurk stuffed the end of the bloody dishtowel in his mouth. unlocked the cuffs and refastened Dugan's wrists behind him and around the steel post.

Patrick wiped the blood and the mush he'd served to Gloria off of the taller man's face. His features were revealed—a hawk nose, close-set eyes and a sour expression, now turned bitter.

"Buttafumo!" Not surprisingly, it was his former employee. "Serves you right, you son of a bitch. But why Gloria?"

"Ask Bulldog. That's what you get from me for your abuse and foul treatment."

"You haven't seen anything yet," Patrick snarled. He grabbed his captive's wrists and wrapped them behind the opposite side of the post while McGurk fastened him to it with a second pair of cuffs and used another dishtowel to shut him up.

The remedial post that ruined the Victorian look of the stairwell now animated the architecture with two squirming gargoyles, resembling the grotesque figures found on the exteriors of Gothic cathedrals.

"Just the touch this ugly house needed," Patrick said. "Now I'll check for anything else left upstairs."

He climbed the steps again and scanned the furniture in Gloria's bedroom prison. On top of a dresser he found a white cell phone and grabbed it. At the other end of the hall, he pushed through a closed door and found a made-up double bed, a dresser and the door to a closet. Inside were two dark suits, a belt, dress shirts, and on a top shelf, two fedoras. One looked familiar. with a red feather in the band. He tried it on—it was too loose. He left it on the shelf and looked around the room. On the bedside table he found a note, in a bold scrawl:

> *Marco,*
>
> *Tony wants you to squeeze Bohannon about the*
> *broad. Call him. —Bulldog*

He put the note in the pocket of his jacket and bounded back downstairs.

"Here, recognize this?" Patrick held the phone out Gloria.

"My phone!" She caressed the white phone in its pink outer shell like a long-lost friend.

"All done. Let's beat it." McGurk turned to Gloria. "Forgive me, ma'am, if I don't pick you up at the door. It would be safer for all of us if we simply look like normal people and walk up the block to my van."

Gloria smiled at Patrick. He agreed. Normal people, ha—that was a stretch.

McGurk offered his arm to Gloria, and they left through the front door. Patrick closed it behind them, double-locked it with the ring of keys and placed them under the doormat. The group straggled up the street to the white van.

FORTY-FOUR

When the three of them reached the Dodge Caravan parked up the street, McGurk took the driver's spot, Gloria rode shotgun in the bucket seat and Patrick sat on the rear bench cushion. He caught up with O'Malley on his cell phone.

"Detective, I have a little cleanup job for you and a couple of Chicago's finest. Your kidnappers and suspects in other crimes can be found in an old Victorian house in Irving Park on the Northwest side. McGurk and I tied them up. One of them might need first-aid. I've covered the wound, but he was bleeding like a stuck pig." He gave O'Malley the address.

"MacKenna, I told you to leave this cops and robbers stuff to us."

"Certainly, Sergeant. But while we were waiting, Gloria became extremely unhappy with her captors. It seems she didn't like the food."

"Gloria! You found her? "

"Right. If you act fast, before they break out, you can nab the kidnappers, including one Bulldog Dugan."

"Bulldog Dugan—the murderer?"

"Yes and no."

"We'll send the wagon out as fast as we can."

"If you want to catch them, you'd better do it now. I won't wait to tell the newspapers."

"Sure, MacKenna, You just want credit for catching the murderer."

"No, it's your case. And I don't like that idea anyway."

"What? He surely killed Angionomo and Walter Howe."

"I don't think so. Getting a close look like I just did, he's not the guy I saw on the scaffold. My sources say Bulldog is just a muscle man, anyway—the Detroit boys normally send somebody else out to do the dirty work.

"You can ask Dugan what he knows know about the deaths of Walter McDougal Howe and Fabrizio Angionomo" Patrick continued. "Then you might want to charge them with the kidnapping. You can also pick up his accomplice, Thomas Buttafumo. Sadly, he's a former employee of mine, who helped out as her jailer."

"Well, if not Dugan or your ex-employee, who's the hit man?"

"You're asking me?"

"Yeah."

"Fifty will get you a hundred his name is Marco Candicci, from Detroit. You'll have to put a twenty-four-hour watch on the house for when he comes back. He's got a few suits in the closet of the front bedroom. On the shelf is a hat with a red feather. Make sure and collect it. I recognize it from the crime scene."

"Okay, MacKenna. Thanks."

"By the way, make sure Radi hears about this. He'll be a big help in cleaning out Detroit influence in this town."

"I'm on it."

He hoped so. They had one chance to catch Candicci. He placed another call to make sure. He filled Radwinski in on the events of the night. He hadn't troubled O'Malley about the note that clinched his identification of the perpetrator. Such deep thinking was above his pay grade. Nor would he mention it to Bohannon. All Joe needed in his fragile state was to know how close his daughter had come to a hostage crisis. But he made sure to tell Radi. He'd been lucky to intercept the message before Candicci got it, and he'd made sure the FBI knew about it.

McGurk asked directions to Patrick's apartment. When he told him, Patrick added, "Just drop us off, Nick, and I'll take her home. You would be unfamiliar with the route to Gloria's."

"No, Patrick," Gloria objected, "that won't be necessary."

"What? I need to explain to your parents exactly what happened."

"How do you propose to do that?" Gloria objected. "You weren't there. Nick and I went through this together. They need to hear it from both of us." She looked at Nick with a smile of pure adulation.

"Gloria will show me the way. "Besides, I feel responsible for getting her into this mess after we managed to escape once."

Although disappointed at Gloria's choice, Patrick was relieved. He was bone tired from his ordeals of recent days. Despite his role in the rescue, he didn't really want to face Joe and Candy at this hour.

They rode in embarrassed silence until they reached the Outer Drive. Gloria broke the ice.

"I appreciate what you both have done for me, especially you, Nick." She explained what she meant by her comment — his dramatic struggle with the thugs to free them, the elegant dinner at the Bit & Bridle and tonight's rescue after her second capture by the crooks.

"Gloria, we have to talk. I'll call you tomorrow."

"No need, Patrick. I think I understand. You didn't want to move in together with me, you have a new woman in your life — that sharp tongued Irish barmaid we met at the art museum, and then at the farmhouse— and you've...stopped calling me..." Her voice broke and trailed off.

"Gloria, it's not like that —"

"It isn't? For some reason, I don't think she's a member of your Girl-of-the-Month Club. She said you haven't touched her, yet. That would be a first. But I believe her, and it's very unsettling to me."

"Gloria, can we please have this conversation in private — later?" Patrick could feel his face heating up and turning red, even in the darkness of the car.

"I don't need to hear all this." McGurk said.

"It's all right, Nick," she continued. "You might as well know it."

"We can't break up like this. I *do* care for you..." What she said was all true, but he couldn't leave the situation like this. "After all I've done for you, all we've done together —"

"We're finished, so far as I'm concerned — both with the conversation — and our relationship…" Her words were interrupted by sobs. She paused until she recovered her voice.

"And Patrick, you need to hear what a gentleman Nick is. He cares how I look, how I think. He admires me, treats me with the utmost care and respect. Even when he rescued me, when we were tied up in the car, he was so gentle, and even tonight, he was so careful not to hurt me more. You just don't respect me!"

"Enough, Gloria! I get it."

The van approached Patrick's street, and he guided McGurk to his front door. "This is it, McGurk. Good work! And, both of you, don't forget to fill in Detective O'Malley."

"Will do. And Patrick, I couldn't tell you while you were talking to the detective, but I think you're right about Candicci. He's the meanest sonofabitch in the Detroit operation, and Tony Roma's top hit man."

"I think so too. But as O'Malley says, 'Leave the cops and robbers stuff to us.' This time, he can have it."

"Where to, ma'am?" McGurk was playing chauffeur to the hilt today. He started his engine.

"Kenilworth, please, driver," Gloria replied. "Get us to Edens Expressway, and I'll guide you from there."

Patrick took one last look at Gloria and got out of the car. The little pad he called home never looked so good to him. He sighed with relief and climbed the stair.

It was the outcome Patrick wanted, anyway. She had met someone from her own station in life — a neglected kid, a gangster, a murderer, but smart enough to make his own way — and for once, she was content. He could also appreciate that, humbling as it was to be dressed down by a woman, he should let her have the last word. Despite the risk to himself, his life and his well-being, it was the outcome of his dreams. It could be a turning point, to salvage his happiness and save his life.

Forty-Five

Gloria directed him to her parents' street in Kenilworth. They pulled into the secluded drive of the Bohannon estate. Nick parked the van in the circle drive by the entrance

Before Gloria could even climb the steps, Candy Bohannon flung open the front door with open arms and stared with disbelief at the reappearance of her missing daughter.

"Oh my God, Gloria. Why didn't you call? Where have you been? Who's this?"

"One thing at a time, Mom," she said, joining her mother's embrace. "The main point is I'm free, and Nick here can tell you all about it."

"Hello, Mrs. Bohannon, it's nice to meet you. I'm Nicholas McGurk."

Joe Bohannon clattered down the stairs, breathing heavily with the sudden exertion.

"Gloria, you're back! How wonderful." Looking at McGurk he asked, "You rescued our daughter?"

"Yes — well, actually I had help, from Patrick MacKenna."

Candy stepped aside and let them in. Nick stared in awe at the crystal chandelier in the two-story hall and the curved staircase leading to the second floor. She showed him into the living room, the walls hung with expensive looking oil paintings of Dutch and Italian cities, furnished with oversized sofas and an abundance of brass and silver wall sconces and lamps "My mother is fascinated with culture," Gloria explained.

"Wow! What a high-class setup. As fancy as those hotels I saw in Miami Beach."

"Trust me, Nick," Joe said. "It took many years to get here."

"You poor dear," Candy told her daughter. "You must be exhausted. Let's get you upstairs, in the shower and into some fresh clothes, and you can tell me all about it."

"I'll be back soon, Nick. Don't go anywhere." Gloria followed her mother upstairs.

Bohannon led Nick into the den, where a whole wall was devoted to electronic equipment, including a large screen television set, a four-speaker hi-fi system and classy furniture, just like those Biscayne Boulevard hotels. If it hadn't been for Joe Bohannon's barrage of questions, he would just have wandered around, marveling at Joe's display of wealth. This was a status in life Nick had scarcely dared to imagine.

"Nick, please make yourself comfortable. Can I get you a drink?." Joe stepped over to a bar built into the bookshelves of the wall beneath a large wine rack. He poured himself a stiff scotch and drizzled a little seltzer in it.

"Maybe a little bourbon with plenty of ginger ale?"

"No problem, kid. We're celebrating." Bohannon fixed the drink, handed it to McGurk and took a seat in an easy chair next to the sofa.

"Nick, how the hell did Gloria get herself into this situation?"

"She didn't 'get herself' into anything, Mr. Bohannon. We did our best had to stay out of trouble, but they kept coming back at us." He explained how they been captured twice in the aftermath of the storm, by Bulldog Dugan and his accomplice, the inept and bumbling Tom Buttafumo. How first Gloria, and then McGurk, had been manhandled, tied up and shoved into the back seat of Dugan's sedan. How they had cooperated to cut their bonds and escape the pair once. After celebrating their liberation at the restaurant, how the thugs tracked her own cell phone and recaptured her.

"I was trying to treat her right, Mr. Bohannon, believe me—and I almost succeeded."

"Don't beat yourself up, Nick. You did everything you could.

That bastard Dugan is slippery, and he's backed by one of the slickest bosses in the Outfit. But how did you find her and spring her loose?"

"Patrick deserves a lot of the credit for that. It seems his father, who owns MacKenna's Irish pub downtown, had to pay protection to those Detroit guys when they were trying to move into town. They had to deliver the payments to a house on the Northwest side. Seamus MacKenna had records of the address. That's where we found her, tied up these two birds and sprang her out of there. Then Patrick notified police."

"Ha, they'll have their hands full for a while. Great work, Nick! I'll tell Patrick the same when I see him."

"What happens next, Mr. Bohannon? Do I still have a job?"

"Call me Joe, for cripe's sake, kid. I've been thinking. You've got a head on your shoulders, and I need someone to help me run this casino resort project. I'm sure Gloria will help me eventually with the numbers and the day-to-day management, but you know your way around. I'm starting to get a dozen phone calls a day about materials, deliveries, decisions. I'm getting too old for this crap. I need a project manager. Want to give it a shot?"

"Holy shit, Mr. Bohannon — I mean Joe. You'd really give me a break like that?"

"You want it, you got it. Fifty grand a year to start. In addition to your percentage of the deal."

"I can hardly believe it. You're on." They shook hands.

Gloria and her mother reappeared. She walked into the room, her blonde hair clean and shining, in a white tennis dress she kept here so she could play on Joe's clay courts.

"Wow, you look gorgeous," Nick said. "No wonder Patrick fell so hard for you."

"How is Patrick, by the way?" Joe asked "After helping rescue you and all."

"Since you ask, as usual, Patrick's health is excellent," she said in an icy tone. "I have no further thoughts about him. He is history as far as I'm concerned."

"What about your engagement and future plans?" Joe asked.

"We never were engaged, and we have no future plans. Meanwhile, Nicholas has been a perfect gentleman, and we plan to be seeing each other quite a bit."

"You mean it's over between you and Patrick?" Candy Bohannon said.

"During my ordeal I've done a lot of thinking. It was never meant to be. I'm so tired and fed up, I just want to get out of here for a while. Then, when I return I'd like to make a fresh start. It would be such a delight to be treated with the respect and honor for a change, the way Nick treats me."

She winked at Nick, inclined her head, gently held his neck and kissed him on the lips.

FORTY-SIX

On Friday, Patrick again sat at his drawing board, attempting to finish a floor plan for the main casino building. He was relieved he and McGurk had been able to return Gloria to her family. Estranged as he was from her, he hadn't wished her kidnapped or harmed. He'd wanted to let her down gently. Before he even had a chance to begin, she had disappeared, leaving no trace. Now that she was back, however, despite her brave words in the car in front of Nick, he feared she would want their relationship to resume.

After his awkward break with Gloria, he was unsure of his relationship with Joe Bohannon, He half expected never to hear from him again.

His phone buzzed, and he reached for it mechanically, expecting another of the multiple office calamities which divided his typical workday into dozens of unproductive segments.

"Hey, Patrick, we need to meet and discuss the next step in the project."

"Joe? Is it really you?"

"Hey, thanks for rescuing Gloria. Nick said it wouldn't have happened without you."

"I just did what I had to, Joe. She meant too much to me, and to you. Were you surprised to see her?"

"When she walked in through that door, you could have knocked me over with a fender. But once she was back, with her and her mother around, I could barely think straight. I've sent them both to Miami They're sailing Saturday on a cruise to Europe."

"No kidding?" Patrick said, "Gone. She didn't even call me to say goodbye." She'd meant what she said he van. "How come?"

"After her ordeal, Gloria deserves a break from Chicago. Candy has been wanting to go to Europe for years, except I could never take time off. This way, I can focus on our casino resort project in peace."

"You're not upset she broke up with me?"

"Hey, she's as stubborn as her mother. When a woman like that makes up her mind, nobody can change it."

"What do you know?" A surge of relief swept over Patrick, making him positively giddy. "Hey, I'm happy for everybody. And thanks for the payment. What happened to turn the project around?" He had a pretty good idea, but he wanted to hear it from Joe.

"It's a long story, but you need to hear it directly from good ol' Nick McGurk."

"Good, old? He's young and he's a murderer. What do you mean?"

"Hey, nobody's perfect. Nick's my new project manager now. He even understands the Detroit method of processing cash."

"I thought you were done with Detroit."

"Oh, we are, if we can help it. It's just that you've gotta have a few legitimate cash businesses. The bank expects you to—look, I can't talk about it on the phone. What say we meet out here this afternoon?"

"Sounds fine. Out where?"

"We've set up project headquarters at the site in Rockville."

"In all that muddy mess?" He recalled the condition it had been left in after the cloudburst on Saturday.

"Not a problem. Mike sent a crew out here at dawn on Monday morning with a bucket loader, a dozer and a couple of dump trucks. By nightfall they had the site looking better than before. Come on out and meet my team. Say, at one o'clock."

"Your team? What the hell?"

"You'll see."

"One o'clock, then, Joe."

It was already 11:30 a.m. Patrick left his cubicle to search for Chet and found him in Marty's office, discussing the project.

"So that's why we can't schedule production for the casino building yet." Chet spread his hands and shrugged.

"Darn, I sure hope you find out soon," Marty said. "I've got a man finishing up another job. We were hoping he could start designing the final grades—"

"Hold everything." Patrick cut him short. "I just got off the phone with Joe Bohannon. Looks like were ready to roll again. We'll need it yesterday."

"No way!" Marty said.

"Way!" Patrick replied. "Chet, what are you doing about lunch?"

"Brought it from home."

"So did I. Bring it with you. We've got to be in Rockville by one."

Marty shook his head, picked up his phone and called Yolanda at the front desk "Babe, you're not gonna believe this!"

"What happened?" Chet asked on the ride to the site.

Between bites of his steak sandwich and shaking it at impatient idiots passing him at 85 miles an hour, Patrick filled Chet in on what he had just learned—Joe's change of heart toward Gloria, Mike's restoration of the building site to its pre-fiasco appearance and some sort of new project team.

"What team?" Chet asked.

"Whatever he means by that, we'll soon find out."

When they pulled into the gravel road, all traces of the platform stage, splintered handrails and muddy tracks were gone. The field where the buildings would be located had been restored to its smooth, gently rolling contours.

"Whoa, Mike's crew did one heck of a job. What's all that hay doing everywhere?"

"Looks like they've seeded it," Chet said. "They usually use a ground cover of alfalfa, overlaid with a layer of hay mulch, to hold moisture and promote germination of the seed."

Inside, the old farmhouse showed no signs of Saturday's shambles. All traces of the buffet, posters and trampled rugs had been removed. The Victorian furniture had been restored to its original arrangement, rugs restored, hardwood floors cleaned and polished and even the knickknacks repositioned on their former shelves. When they entered the dining room, now full of people, Joe addressed them from the head of the table.

"Welcome to our new project office," Joe said. "Here's my new General Project Manager, Nick McGurk. This is his executive assistant, Angela Atkins." She sat next to McGurk. In this new context, Angela glowed with confidence. Her tailored jeans, in the current mode, conformed to her well-shaped legs and buttocks, leaving little to the imagination. An oversized Mundelein College sweatshirt hung loosely on her shapely frame.

"Yes, we've met. Hi Nick. Congratulations on the new job., and to you, Angela, as well. You both seem to be coming up in the world." He turned to Joe. "What happened?"

"We've found a new investor," Joe said.

Patrick guessed he'd found a way to use Nick's hoard of cash, consisting of reams of hundred-dollar bills. Nick explained. "We're just doing what we always do about cash. By using all of Joe's small businesses, he could make legal cash deposits, the actual cash proceeds of the business, along with other cash he may need to clean up and make legal."

"Nick also saw another business opportunity," Joe continued, "and he wasted no time putting it into action. Why don't you tell the rest, Nick?"

"So, I was taking my laundry to Abe's Laundromat on Monday. It occurred to me, he'd built a huge business with lots of stores, but he was doing a crappy job of running it, with a crummy name. He's got machines all over town that need repairs, he can't control the crime problem and he's missing out on all kinds of profits.

"The guy had no promotional sense at all. Abe's Laudromat, mat, for cryin' out loud," McGurk continued. "What kind of a crappy name is that? He was anxious to bail out and retire, so I just decided to oblige him. I call it The Mommy Laundry. Our slogan is, 'Bring your dirty duds, Mommy's got the suds!'"

"The money-laundry?" Patrick asked.

"Don't get the wrong idea. That's just my business name. My repair company is called, The Machinery Works. With a little tender loving care from me, pretty soon all the machinery will be humming. Thanks to the lawyer Angie found, we applied for all the official documents, opened two bank accounts, and we are in business!"

"Two accounts?" Chet said.

"Right. One for the laundry and another for my handyman crew. There will be a Mommy in every store, to accept bundles of laundry, run the machines, collect the money and do the ironing." The handyman crew will repair washers and dryers, do neighborhood landscape work and also provide security at my stores. I call this the landscaping and security operation, Lawn Order.

"You've thought of everything," Patrick said. "How will these people be paid?"

"Depending on the number of eight-hour blocks recorded on their timesheets and approved by the store manager," Angela said, "Lawn Order workers will receive a corresponding number of hundred-dollar-bills bills deposited in a bank account in their names, accessible only with personal debit cards, which can be used to buy anything they really need. This lack of cash should discourage street buys of drugs. Store managers, called Mommies, will receive double those amounts for the same time blocks. Henrietta, General Manager of the Mommy Laundry, will receive triple that amount for each completed time block."

"Are you okay with all this, Angela? I mean, legally speaking," Patrick asked.

"Look at it this way," she said. "Nobody knows how Nick got these funds. He's using them for the benefit of society and to ensure that the people are employed, protected and returned to the workforce as law-abiding citizens. The government will insist, based on their bank deposits, and that they pay income taxes. Now, I'm no lawyer, but it seems to me this is the whole point of having laws in the first place."

"Patrick, you promised me when we would get together," McGurk said. "you would connect me up with a reporter to help me tell this great story."

"Yes, that would be Margaret Larson, at the Star-News. Don't go near the Clarion with the story. I'll let Margaret know you'll call. Tell it in your own words, Nick. Just clean it up a bit when it comes to where you got the money. Other than that, I don't think you need any help from me with promotion."

"Now that the briefing is finished," Joe said, from his seat at the head of the table, "it's time for our progress meeting on the Chicago Casino and Resort at Rockville. Nick will run the meeting, and Angela, his executive assistant, will keep the official meeting notes. Since I will be sort of a general partner, I'll just provide input here and there. My main goal is to get this project moving, fast. I would like to see construction documents and firm construction bids within ninety days."

On the way back to town in the car, Chet asked. "How did Mc-Gurk get so smart, so fast?"

"Kitty thinks he's in touch with supernatural spirits, Personally, I think he was always smart. He just never had a chance to use his brain. Besides, he was understudy to one of the most effective La Cosa Nostra bosses in the country. Roma's right up there with Murray "Curly" Humphries, who worked his way up in the Capone days from a job as the boss's driver to the financial genius behind the mob. In the Fifties, he was their best legal mind and the money man. At the McCarthy hearings, and then in the Kefauver investigation, which brought the old Outfit down, he came up with the concept of taking the Fifth, and the famous phrase, "I refuse to testify, on the grounds that it may tend to incriminate me.""

Forty-Seven

On this bright spring Wednesday morning, Patrick arrived early at his office on the corner of Wabash and Lake and opened his office window. When the clamor of trains squealing around the corner of the elevated tracks died down and the persistent odor of burning oil and asbestos abated, a fresh lake breeze wafted through the opening

At ten o'clock Central Time, the earliest he considered it polite to call the West Coast—it would be two hours earlier in Oakland—Patrick placed a call.

"Hello?" The thin voice of an elderly woman answered.

"May I please speak with Gertrude Simms?"

"Just a moment, please. Gertie, it's for you."

"Ms. Simms, my name is Patrick MacKenna. I want to offer my condolences on the unfortunate passing of your employer, Fabrizio Angionomo."

"Passing? He's dead?

"I'm afraid so, Ms. Simms. A couple of weeks ago. I'm sorry to be the bearer of such bad news, and so late at that"

"Oh no! I haven't been able to get him on the phone. I supposed he was just twice as busy while I was away, but this—"oh, poor Fabrizio… It was that awful man —"

"What man are you referring to, Ms. Simms?"

"And who did you say you were, Mr. MacKenna?"

"I'm an architect in Chicago. I happened to learn of his murder and was helping the police try to solve it."

"His murder? Oh, dear. A man came to our office and threatened Mr. Angionomo. We had just called the previous day to inform our client, Mr. Howe, that is, that we had obtained the bonds he hired us to search for and retrieve. Then I left on my scheduled visit to visit my sister here in California."

"You say the man threatened him. What did he say?"

"That man wouldn't let us alone. He kept calling. He said he was coming. I warned Fabrizio he'd better watch out, but he wasn't worried. You should have heard the terrible things that man called me."

"What things?"

"Oh, I can't repeat them — obscene things. Names you would never call a lady. Just because I wouldn't tell him where the bonds were located."

"The bonds?"

"Yes, bearer bonds of the Clarion Company. They — oh, I can't face the thought that he's dead. Murdered, you say?"

"I'm sorry, Ms. Simms. Can you describe this man?"

"Oh, he was terrible looking, and so mean."

"Can you be more specific? His build, hair color? Distinguishing features, you know."

"He had no hair color. He was bald, medium height and very stocky."

"Stocky? You mean, fat?"

"Oh no, muscular. He wore a black T-shirt with the Detroit Pistons logo on it. I'll never forget. His trousers were black he had something on his right arm. A very fancy tattoo, with a red heart on it that said 'MOTHER.' Fabrizio once called him Bulldog."

"Bulldog Dugan?"

"That sounds right. He wouldn't tell us his name, but Fabrizio knew. The other man wore a suit. He used polite words but threatened, like, 'Play ball with us or you'll develop a bad headache.' I left the room and went back to my office. They got into an argument: I could hear it through the door. He had a nasty, gravelly voice. They said they'd be back, and they wanted to get the bonds. They were very valuable."

"Like, millions?"

"Yes. We found them in a safe deposit box Walter Howe forgot he had. Fortunately, we had a key in our file. They're filed safely in my filing cabinet. I had removed our portion — fifteen percent — or three of the twenty bonds. Mr. Angionomo's share alone was worth at least three hundred thousand dollars. I put them in a file folder and laid it on his desk before I left."

"Did Mr. Angionomo have a will?"

"Oh, yes I believe he had a colleague prepare it for him. Angela, our office neighbor, was one of the witnesses of his signature."

"Angela Atkins?"

"Yes, the court reporter down the hall."

"I've met her. I'll ask her about it. I understand they had lunch together every week."

"They were very close. She must be so upset. I tried to call her, but we've been missing each other on the phone."

"When I see her, I'll tell her to call you."

"Please do."

"Do you know where Mr. Angionomo's will is kept."

"Of course, in the first file cabinet drawer, top drawer, labeled "A to F" the same one where the bonds are stored. Under 'A,' not under 'B' for bonds, you understand."

"Naturally. You have a unique filing system."

"Ah yes, all kept under lock and key."

"When do you plan to return to Chicago, Ms. Simms?"

"Next week, to break up my apartment and arrange for shipping. My sister needs me out here. She has a heart condition. I'm moving in with her."

"Did Mr. Angionomo have any next of kin?"

"No, no immediate family."

"What about the heirs of Walter McDougal Howe, his client?"

"He was the last of his branch of the McDougal family. But his parents are still living, in Washington, D.C. They are probably mentioned in Howe's will. He said he would leave sufficient money for a lifetime supply of Milk Bones for his dogs."

"Of course. Will you call me when you get in? I would like to meet you, and the police will need a statement. And perhaps we can look at your well-kept files."

"Why certainly, Mr. MacKenna."

"I'll talk to you next week." He gave her his number and ended the call.

He spent the next few hours finishing a master main floor plan. It showed the casino deck, a bridge from the gaming floor to the main lobby area, which featured indoor "sidewalk cafes" along an interior main street, passing bars leading from the casino entry past each restaurant and to a grand entrance to the hotel and its lobby. All wrapped around the outdoor pool and recreation patio. The ideas flowed freely and resulted in a grand vison of the interior he had never quite grasped before.

He worked through lunch, proud that at last he had steered the project to its final resolution. At about three in the afternoon he cleared his desk of original sketches and carried them over to Chet's desk. It was time for his team to take over. They would a develop a detailed design and coordinate it with the engineers' structural, air conditioning, plumbing and electrical systems. Once approved by Bohannon, the project would then shift to the Construction Documents phase. They would transform it into drawings and specifications for the contractors to use in constructing the first building.

He spent the next hour with Chet, making sure he understood his intent in the final master main floor plan. He looked at his watch. It was time to leave. This was Ladies' Night again, and he was needed at the pub.

He helped himself to a plate of his mother's corned beef, cabbage and cottage fries and sat at the help table. As he savored the excellent dinner, he idly picked up a copy of yesterday's Star-News. Glancing at the headline he could hardly believe what he read.

ARCHITECT AND GUIDE RESCUE KIDNAPPED GIRL
Perpetrators and Murder Suspect Captured

Exclusive to the Star-News

By Margaret Larson, Senior Reporter

An architect and a museum guide combined forces to rescue Gloria Bohannon, kidnapped daughter of businessman Joseph Bohannon Monday night. Architect Patrick MacKenna and his acquaintance, Nicholas McGurk, an employee of the

Museum of Science and Industry, working on a hunch, raided a North side house believed to be owned by the Detroit Partnership, a notorious Mafia crime family, reported Detective Sergeant Matthew O'Malley, of the Downtown Division of Chicago police.

Ms. Bohannon was unharmed and reunited with her family later that evening. She was abducted last Saturday evening at the Bit & Bridle restaurant in Skokie, while waiting to be picked up by McGurk during a rainstorm at the restaurant's entrance. Mr. Bohannon expressed his gratitude to the rescuers. "Thanks to bravery of Patrick MacKenna and Nicholas McGurk, our daughter has been turned to the family, safe and sound. The Chicago police are also to be commended for their prompt response."

Her captors, one Finn "Bulldog" Dugan, of Detroit, and Thomas Buttafumo, of Highwood, were taken into custody at the house where Ms. Bohannon had been held prisoner.

Unlike Mona Strong, Margaret always seemed to get the story straight.

Kitty breezed into the kitchen to pick up a tray of orders. She brushed past Patrick, ignoring him, and disappeared again through the double doors with her tray. She came back for drinks, Patrick stopped her.

"What's bothering you?"

"Oh, nothing. I see you've been risking your life for your girlfriend again."

"Hey, *her* life was at risk. What would you do? And she's not my girlfriend —"

But Kitty swept back through the doors with her tray of food. She barely heard his protest. He intercepted her the next time she came through the kitchen and said, "That's not fair! After all she had done for me, the least I could do was save her life."

"Patrick, it really hurt me that I had to read that in the paper. Even the Hunters asked me questions about it."

"Kitty, I'm so sorry. There's no excuse for not telling you. But I've been so busy this week, I haven't had a chance to think. I 've been glowing all week, meaning to say how wonderful it was to talk last Saturday night. I still meant what I said. And now, everything's good, and my worst problems are solved. We should be celebrating."

"Well, that's a little better. What do you suggest?"

"Where would you like me to take you for dinner? Anyplace you want."

"Not a restaurant — I get enough of restaurants in my job."

"Well, what if I fix you a fine steak dinner at my place?"

"Now that is a lovely idea!"

Forty-Eight

Sunday night, Kitty arrived by cab and rang his doorbell promptly at seven. He opened the door and stared. Compared to her elegance, he felt under-dressed, in shirtsleeves and his grilling apron.

"Thank you so much for coming, Kitty. "Is that a new dress?"

She blushed, hesitating in her response as he stood, his mouth agape, and looked her up and down. She wore her new strapless sheath in changeable green taffeta, which revealed hints of her lovely décolletage. The fabric glinted with hues matching her copper-colored hair, which fell in waves upon her cream-tinted shoulders, now reddening as well.

"It's such a temptation to work near all those fine department stores, and I had nothing to wear."

"I like it—it's really you. Please sit down. I've picked a special wine for us tonight."

Beyond his window, the sun hung low in the western sky over the residential skyline of the Near North side. Mozart played on the hi-fi. His dinner table was set, with a centerpiece of fresh pink carnations floating in a bowl. Flames of two pink candles guttered in a breeze from the balcony. Hickory smoke wafted from a kettle grill into the main living-dining-kitchen from a sliding door open to the balcony. Bright-colored Chagall, Picasso and Dufy prints, simply framed in brushed chrome, adorned white walls. Scatter rugs on natural oak floors, throw pillows on a gray studio couch and his reading chair complemented the décor. A bookcase and an extra captain's chair, matching two at the dining table, comprised the living area furniture. Through an open door she saw a wide, comfortable-looking bed.

"What a cheerful apartment," she said. "In Cork, a modern, simply furnished place like this would be rare and come dear."

She took a seat on the couch.

He opened a Chateauneuf-du-Pape 1989 Cuvée Reservée. He walked to his grill on the balcony, put on the steaks and set the stove timer. He returned and poured two glasses of the ruby red wine.

"So extravagant," she said, "and such a pretty container." She stroked the embossed glass patterns on the traditional bottle.

"Here's to us," he said.

"To our health and happiness," she said

He sat next to her, raised his glass and they sipped.

"Mmm, marvelous," she said, and paused. "Did you—um, are you still working on the project with Joe Bohannon?" She hated to bring it up, but she had to know. "Because of your issue with Gloria, I mean."

"It turns out Joe needs an architect more than a daughter, at least right now. He sent Gloria and her mother off on an extended tour of Europe."

"Certainly, you joke." She raised her eyebrows, incredulous at the news.

"It's true," he said. "It seems Joe finds it hard to focus on such a complicated project with too many women around."

"What about her job with your uncle?"

"Mike has hired a new secretary."

"Can this one type?" She'd heard about Gloria's spotty secretarial skills.

"Can she! Gladys Plunkett, middle-aged and devoid of any sense of style in makeup or dress, types sixty words a minute. She turns out letters, job memos and critical path charts for construction so efficiently, she looks around for more to do. The staff can hardly keep her busy. Now Mike's officers have more time to find new clients and bid new jobs."

"Gloria, gone." She shook her head in disbelief. "It's the last thing I'd have expected."

"Big changes are happening everywhere." He told her about the signed contract, McGurk's new role in Joe's company and the new project team. "In fact, now that the resort is planned and the major buildings are designed, I've turned over almost everything to Chet for preparation of construction documents."

"So, what are *you* going to do now?"

"You know how Uncle Mike is always looking toward the future, trying to scope out future markets? He announced casually to me this week, he has opened an office on the on the downtown riverfront in St. Louis, within walking distance of the Gateway Arch National Park, He and Rose have bought a house in west suburban St. Louis County. He started up a branch of his company and has begun building office and industrial facilities, while he's placing his Chicago operations in the capable hands of his engineers. They'll run his Chicago jobs for highways, bridges and private developments, like Joe Bohannon's Chicago Casino and Resort."

"My heavens!" Kitty could hardly wrap her head around such alarming news. "How will that affect your business?"

The bell on the stove timer rang and Patrick got up to flip the steaks, leaving her in suspense. He brought over the bottle of wine, refilled their glasses and sat again.

"Mike recognizes the strategic location of St. Louis in the center of the American heartland and believes the region's potential will soon be rediscovered. Mike was less concerned with crashing computers at the turn of the millennium, but he's paying close attention to the money to be made in the new century. St. Louis has natural advantages — a transportation crossroads, outdoor recreation amidst natural beauty and untapped natural and workforce resources. He moved to take advantage of a market ripe for expansion. If you count the city and Missouri and Illinois suburban counties, it's the ninth largest city in the United States."

He took a bowl of salad from the refrigerator, put garlic bread from the oven in a basket and set them on the table.

"Don't you depend on him for some of your best projects?" Kitty said, afraid to hear the answer. "Why would he want to do that?"

"Good observation," Patrick said.

It would be a huge disappointment for her, now that she had Patrick's full attention, if he were to leave town.

"If business prospects in Missouri are as strong as he thinks they are, I may have to follow him down there." The bell rang again and Patrick plated the strip steaks.

"They look and smell marvelous, if I do say so myself."

"But, but—" she stammered.

"But that would only happen in the future," he added.

"What do your parents think about losing you?"

"They're not thrilled, but the thought that both Mike and Rose would be there softened the blow."

"Which reminds me," he went on, "if that ever happened I would have to ask them about you, too."

"But...what *about* me?" she exclaimed, with her heart in her mouth. He was speaking in riddles. She couldn't make sense of it.

"You have to admit we've been almost inseparable lately."

"Not exactly—you have to be together more often than we are to be inseparable."

"But that's how I feel—I can't do without you. Last week at the Hunters' you said you'd like to have me around too... ."

"So you're leaving me. I don't get it." Her meat sat ignored on the plate, getting cold.

"No—I have something much more important to do." He reached in his pants pocket, drew out a velvet box and set it before her.

"So I was wondering... if you'd... if you could see your way to..." "Damn, I'm no good at this," he cursed under his breath. Finally, he blurted, "Will you marry me?"

He opened the box.

She gazed in disbelief at a solitaire diamond in an elegant silver mount, probably a couple of carats, glittering in a ray of sunlight. In her weeks of ups and downs, she'd had hopes of winning Patrick for her very own, only to have them dashed when she had met Gloria. When she'd learned about her claims on him, aesthetic, physical and financial, she had despaired of ever seeing him again, much less turning it into forever after.

"Oh, yes, Patrick, yes!"

He slipped the ring on her finger, meeting no resistance. She reached for his shoulders, pulled him nearer and shyly kissed him.

He grinned. "It's all very exciting, but we have to eat! *Bon appetit.*"

"Ah well, the meat needed time to rest, anyway," she said. He led her to the table and held her chair while she sat. Still in shock, Kitty dished some salad on her plate and waited for Patrick, almost too excited to eat.

Kitty took a bite, savored the juicy, perfectly seasoned beef. "M-m-m, delicious."

Patrick tasted his meat. "Not bad at all. "

Relieved, she regained her composure. She took a swig of her wine and bravely resumed her line of inquiry. "Again, why aren't you going with your uncle?"

"Oh, he won't need me, at least not until he gets established down there. For now I want to start our life together. I have no desire to pack up and move away. Besides, I need to make sure my parents have someone to replace you and me. If Mike has some work for us in the meantime, I can still do it from here."

She gazed at the treasured new possession on her finger, admired it and took a deep breath. "Right, let's enjoy this fabulous meal."

They chattered merrily, savoring each bite, pausing now and then to gaze into each other's eyes. They talked about their future home. Patrick said he had explored building lots in St. Louis, particularly one located beside a wooded creek, which seemed to suit Kitty's description of her ideal home.

When they were done, they rinsed and stacked the plates and started the dishwasher.

"What about dessert?" Patrick said. "I have ice cream—we can make sundaes—with chocolate sauce and raspberries."

Kitty held a finger to his lips, put her arms around him and said. "I want you."

"Sounds good to me."

"How much do you love me?" she asked.

"There are no words for it."

"Then show me."

He wrapped both his arms around her and held her tightly to

his body. She could feel his urgent need. They found the way to his bed. Heavy languor and inertia replaced her ingrained instinct to resist. Her body clung to his, awakening electric heat in all her soft and secret places. With his heart beating hard against her breast, she lost all remaining will to fight. He lowered her gently to his queen bed. Her head propped up on his pillow, she half closed her eyes. When he disappeared into the bathroom, she slipped out of her clothes and slid beneath the satin top sheet. A moment later he loomed above her naked, his rippled chest, strong arms and muscular thighs, so pale in the fading glow of twilight were beautiful. She stared deep into his intense and piercing eyes, which were riveted on the object of his reverence. Breathless, afraid to break the spell, her own eyes widened as she saw he was ready, perhaps even more so than her casual Parisian lover had been, throbbing with each beat of his racing heart.

Almost, it seemed. He reached in his bedside table drawer, removed a foil wrapper and applied a condom. "We 're ready for each other, but the rest will take some time."

He placed a knee upon the bed, lifted the sheet and eased to her side. Now nothing shielded her naked flesh. He stroked one breast and then the other. "So sweet, so soft," he whispered. As he kissed their rosy tips, they stiffened. He brushed the flatness of her belly with his lips, kissed her Venus mound and buried his face in her rosy cloud of angel hair. Her burning thighs returned the warmth of his face, until she could bear it no longer Now trembling too, she drew his head to her face and kissed him on the lips.

A shudder of pleasure rolled deeply though her, tingling in the heart of her womanhood. When he entered her, gently, ever so slowly, she inhaled sharply. Her heart hammered in her chest. Her smooth cheek rested on his scratchy one, her breast crushed against his. His rhythm sparked little waves of pleasure inside her womb, increasing with each thrust. At last he exploded into her, sending his body, his soul and his future forth into the unknown. White-hot with his desire, she melted into him and grasped his giver of life with her powerful sheath. With a joy she never knew existed she cried, "Oh, Patrick, don't ever leave me!"

"Never—now you have my promise." He relaxed and lay inert at her side.

Afterward, Patrick regarded her coolly, with a sigh of relief from his urgent need.

"A penny for your thoughts, my love," she said.

"This is where it is, right here and now," he said. "Scrambling for gain, posing in society, showing off with the tallest, most stylish building — all vanity, as the prophet said."

"Why, Patrick, you're beginning to see things my way."

"The supreme perfection to be sought is right here — in your perfect breasts, your sloping hips and your pretty little ass."

"You really think it's pretty?"

"Best I've ever seen."

She wondered if this meant he would stop seeking. But she would have to take that chance. They lay back on the pillows, content, gazing at the setting sun as it peeked beneath the clouds.

Yet when she stroked his tenderest part, like watering a sweetly wilted flower, it woke up again. She addressed it like an old friend. "Paddy, do you want Little Kitty again?"

"Oh yes we do!" Patrick whispered thickly. When he embraced her, again she had no power to refuse. She answered with a yearning from her deepest recesses, which so craved him that she must give him anything, everything he desired. He took her tenderly, exploring, kissing and caressing each part of her from the most exposed to the most hidden places, until she had given him all of her. His trembling released in another climax and then ceased. They lay exhausted, he nuzzling her breast, she stroking his face and tousled hair.

"You've been too good to me. I don't deserve it. Don't you hate me now?"

"Why would I?" she said.

"Most girls do."

"No, I rather like you," she teased.

"That means more to me than any other woman's claim of undying love."

Kitty was proud she'd given her most precious gift, to the person who most deserved it.

Again, he smothered her with kisses, rose and left the room.

When he returned, he opened the blinds to the multi hued glory of the sky. A last ray of sun set her copper hair ablaze, and lit her where she lay, a golden odalisque.

He kissed her again. "It's a sign—Hestia, Greek goddess of domestic fires—hearth, home and architecture."

FORTY-NINE

The following Tuesday Patrick answered the phone at 9:15 a.m.

"Mr. MacKenna, it's Gertrude Simms. I'm back in Chicago to settle my affairs and arrange the move to my sister's home in California."

"Yes, Ms. Simms. When would you like to meet?"

"Mr. Angionomo's lawyer will read the will tomorrow at 10 a.m. You are welcome to attend if you wish — at our office, our last official function there."

"Have you informed Angela Atkins?"

"Naturally. She will be there."

"I'll see you then."

At the scheduled time, Patrick rode the elevator, walked the corridor and found Angela Atkins in her office.

"Patrick MacKenna, how good to see you. I'm so grateful to you for putting me in touch with Nicholas McGurk. This is not just a new job—it's a whole new business opportunity."

"You'll have to tell me more about that later. Are you going to join Gertrude?"

"Yes, let's walk over together."

"How's your mother doing?"

"She needs help every day. I've hired her a day nurse. Mother is already feeling a little better."

"Great, but isn't that expensive?"

"Yes, I'm glad to start this job with Mr. McGurk. I can use the extra funds."

They entered the lawyer's suite and then his private office. Ruined books had been removed and all surfaces scoured. Gertrude Simms stood and introduced herself and another man who sat behind Fabrizio's desk. "This is Melvin Steinberg, who wrote the will."

"Good to meet you, Mr. MacKenna. Fabrizio and I were classmates at John Marshall Law School," he explained. "We often consulted each other and became close friends."

"It's so good to see you, Gert," Angela said. "I guess I'll be losing you soon enough."

"My sister needs me," she said.

Steinberg got right down to business. "Fabrizio has no living relatives. The only business he did with the late Walter McDougal Howe was to search for his missing Clarion Company bonds. Per his agreement, he found them. There were twenty certificates, each with a face value of one hundred thousand dollars. Today, each of these bonds is worth two hundred twenty thousand dollars. In the agreement with Fabrizio Angionomo and Walter McDougal Howe, Fabrizio was to retain fifteen percent, or three of these certificates."

Steinberg opened the will and began reading the bequests:

> To Melvin Steinberg, in consideration of Executor services, good advice and our friendship, I bequeath one third of my estate,

> To Gertrude Simms, for loyal service over two decades, I bequeath one third of my estate, and

> To Angela Atkins, professional colleague, confidant and loyal friend, I bequeath one third of my estate.

"As it happens," Steinberg explained, "Fabrizio's cash on hand and in a small checking and savings accounts will cover his funeral expenses, burial costs and disposition of his few possessions and the contents of this office. I will settle this estate by redeeming each of these three bonds, providing each of the three of us a check for approximately two-hundred twenty thousand dollars, and later issue a second check to each to distribute the cash remainder from all other sources. I will deliver the remaining seventeen bonds, to the executor for the estate of the late Walter McDougal Howe, for distribution in accordance with the terms of his will. His parents are his only living immediate family, but his executor tells me his dogs will be well provided for, with lifetime care and an ample supply of dog biscuits. The rest will be up to the executor and the terms of his will.

"Mr. MacKenna," he continued, "I would appreciate it if you would witness our signatures on these receipts."

Patrick obliged. "Angela, I hope this will help you care for your mother."

"Oh, it will. Fabrizio, my guardian angel, is still looking after us!"

"This will certainly help with moving costs," Gertrude said, "and my sister can use help paying the bills."

"What about you, Mr. Steinberg?" Patrick asked.

"I'll spend whatever it takes to solve Fabrizio's senseless murder."

"What about a motive?"

"Could be high values on the bonds, but I think there's more to it."

"How so?"

"Fabrizio told me before he died, he thought that it's mob business. He was caught in the cross-fire of a a turf war."

"With Detroit?"

"He left me a phone message the day before he died, ending with a cryptic question: 'What do you know about Jimmy Roma?'"

"Well, what *do* you know?"

"He and his thugs threatened Fabrizio. Gertrude confirmed that."

"About what?"

"A promissory note for half a million dollars signed by Scott: a juice loan. We found a copy in the recovered safety deposit box of Walter Howe. They were into poor old Walter, counting the vig, two years' extortionate interest, for one-and-a-half million dollars."

"Wow," Patrick said, "that certainly explains a lot. Can you find that document, Ms. Simms?"

"Why yes, I think so. I recall it was filed under 'H' for Howe, or perhaps 'D' for Disputes – Howe estate."

Patrick looked at Steinberg with amusement, as Gertrude opened the top drawer of the file cabinet, labeled A – F. "Here it is, under 'D', signed by Jimmy Roma and Walter McDougal Howe."

"Is this negotiable?" Patrick asked.

"Doubtful, but it will certainly serve as good evidence of extortion. I'll turned it over to Detective O'Malley and Piotr Radwinski for their indictment." He turned to face Ms. Simms, still rooting in her file cabinet. "While you're in there, Gertrude, will you please get out the remaining seventeen bonds, so I can hold them in the estate?"

"Of course, that would be in a different folder She dug for a moment. "Ah, here they are, all except the three I separated out." She laid the folder on her desk.

"Where are the other three missing bond certificates?" Steinberg said, "his legacy to us."

"No problem," she said, "I forgot, I gave them to Mr. Angionomo, so he could redeem them and claim his fee." She unlocked and opened the top center drawer of his desk and removed a large envelope marked, in her own handwriting, "Take these to the McDougal Estate on Monday and redeem them for a cashier's check."

"Why did you write that note on there?" Patrick said.

"So Mr. Angionomo wouldn't forget to cash them in. Then I left to go visit my sister."

"Saved by Gertrude's unique but efficient filing system!" Steinberg gave her a chaste hug.

"There's your motive, Mr. Steinberg," Patrick said. "The bonds seemed fair payment to the Detroit mob for their juice loan."

"Gertrude, what was Walter Howe's reason for borrowing on such unfavorable terms?" Steinberg asked.

"Mr. Angionomo asked that very question, and that horrible man told him it was because he was a frequent patron of their Las Vegas casino. They extended him easy credit, and he liked to double down on his bets, in hopes of winning big."

"Sounds like he had some of founder McDougal's grand vision, but none of his business skill in hedging bets," Patrick said.

"After Mr. Howe's demise, I did a little research myself. Steineberg said. "I tracked down his parents in Washington. His mother,

Tippy McDougal Howe, a wealthy socialite, told me her son was very depressed lately but wouldn't tell her why. It was my duty to tell her about his gambling debts to the mob. She said she thought he had reformed, but it made her very sad. After I got her calmed down, she said that explained why he had tried to kill himself with an overdose of heroin on his recent trip home to see them.

"Excuse me, while I fill Radi in on this development." Patrick punched Radwinksi's number into his cell phone and tapped the desk impatiently until he got him on the line.

"Good news, Radi. I'm here with Angionomo's secretary, his lawyer and his office neighbor, the court reporter, to read his will." He put the phone on speaker. He reported what he had just learned from Gertrude about the juice loan, the Detroit mob's pressure on Howe and the demands on Angionomo for the bonds, leading up to his murder.

"The lawyer's last gift to us was the bonds," Steinberg said. "They're right here in his office."

"There's his motive—good." Radwinski said. That wraps up one aspect of the case. You'll be happy to know, Patrick, that we captured Candicci when he returned to the house you pointed us to in Irving Park. The forensics proved the bullets in Angionomo, the crane operator and Howe's body all came from the same gun, the one we found on Candicci. You've been dropped as a suspect."

"Sounds like you and O'Malley have been busy," Patrick said. "Thanks for the nailing our hit man."

He hung up, and Steinberg resumed the wrap-up of estate details.

"All Howe's proceeds, not including Mr. Angionomo's fees, must go through probate," the lawyer said. "But if the note is ruled an illegal loan, as I suspect, his executor's duty, even if he has to deduct the amount in question for the mob note, will be to distribute the principal and interest from the other seventeen bonds, worth over three million dollars, to Howe's estate. Moreover, his wealthy parents will spend whatever it takes on lawyers to disqualify that note. "His parents will most likely recover his money."

"And he's going to have some lucky dogs," Patrick said.

It sounds to me," Angela observed, "as if this case is closed."

FIFTY

Strolling to work on a crisp September day, Patrick climbed to the elevated platform and looked eastward. The sun shone cold and bright on his head, sheltered only by a thinning thatch of dark brown hair. Four-story fronts of taxpayer flats lined the street below. Their street-level storefronts faced walks swarming with workers, vagrants, runners, dope dealers, delivery men, tourists, and shop girls. People awoke to resume routines, prepare children for school or plunge into their tasks. Some mourned loved ones cut down by automatic weapons fire, killed in drive-bys while playing on front porches or stolen and sold into the sex trade. Workers scurried, drove and rode bug-like to jobs in cafés, industrial plants, building sites and office cubes — if they were lucky. Others were awakened by the dull roar of traffic under viaducts, in abandoned lofts, and under cardboard carton roofs on littered sidewalks. The plaint of far off sirens, thumping dumpsters, crunching metal, tinkling glass and grumbling engines sounded a prelude to the day. Through a distant slot beyond glinted the great inland sea that anchored the metropolis.

Patrick reflected on recent events and wondered what they meant for his future.

Mike MacKenna, always looking ahead, abandoned the hustle of the big city and entrusted his Chicago operations to his younger associates. He traded "the city of big shoulders, hog butcher to the world" and the city motto, "I Will," for the St. Louis metropolitan area's four hundred local government units, whose fractious politicians flaunted an unspoken attitude, "I Won't."

He slowed down to the pace and friendly yet surprisingly cosmopolitan atmosphere of the Gateway City, which many locals called a "big small town." He scarcely missed the furious, insistent pace of the larger metropolis and sought to expand his business into the great hinterland of Missouri, with its easy access to the seven Midwestern states on its borders—Illinois, Iowa, Kansas, Oklahoma, Arkansas, Kentucky and Tennessee. He saw opportunity in the fragmented urban governmental structure of St. Louis. The lack of coordination among the multiple governments further concealed the fact that this urban region of three million people was a potential economic powerhouse. Local politicians in the multiple governmental jurisdictions were too busy in fighting over crumbs to notice the huge opportunities that lay unexploited in the Bistate region.

In St. Louis Mike met the new mayor, served on the Visitor and Convention Bureau and volunteered for the City-Arch-River Board, planning and raising money for the St. Louis Bicentennial celebration in 2004. He formed a close relationship with a local old-line architectural firm, Childress & Marks. He helped them expand their job portfolio from wastewater collection and treatment systems, bridges, highways and airports to include buildings urban design and industrial parks.

Nick McGurk and Gloria became a "thing." She reigned like royalty in the casino, giving lessons to new gamblers and dancing to the rhythms of tribute bands to the big names of the 40s and 50s—The Glenn Miller Orchestra, Harry James, Tommy Dorsey, Michael Bublé and other Frank Sinatra imitators, and jazz combos reminiscent of Dave Brubeck. They entertained in a big new nightclub, based on Patrick's vision, built on a man-made island in the lake accessed by a covered bridge. The building, with glass side walls which could be opened in summer, formed an oversize gazebo in a modern, Frank-Lloyd-Wright-influenced Japanese teahouse style.

Gloria revolted against her mother's Miami Beach Moderne tastes. She undertook the restoration of the old farmhouse on the property in the Victorian theme, and furnished it with wing chairs, Victorian sofas, pie-crust tables and Tiffany lamps. She restored the parlor until it oozed 1890s charm. In a television interview, she treated her audience to a virtual tour saying, in the manner of Jackie Kennedy, "We decided to leave it exactly like it was."

Tom Buttafumo was convicted of aiding and abetting a kidnapper. Because he was young and it was his first offense, a kindly judge granted parole based on months served, on the condition that he would work at his former firm under Chet Neuzing's watchful eye and thumb. Chet kept Buttafumo busy, if not happy, checking and stamping the firm's approval on shop drawings, ordering supplies and helping out with the drafting chores.

Although they had solved the murders to the satisfaction of police, he lived with uncertainty. Sure, they had pinned them on Bulldog Dugan and Marco Candicci. But the rest of the story, about the increasing influence of Detroit, had been swept under the rug by the cops, with the willing help of Mona Strong, whose slanted news stories completed the whitewash job for the public. But that case hadn't yet gone to trial. What about Jimmy Roma? If the law really wanted to nail the mob, the key to the puzzle was really quite simple—follow the money. Was he really so fat and wealthy he wouldn't miss several million dollars? He gathered from what Ross Hunter said, Roma was already on the trail of his missing funds.

What about Joe Bohannon himself? Who had ever retired from the mob and lived to tell about it? He'd heard of Michael Franzese from the East Coast mob, who quit, got religion and lectured all over the country about it. He hadn't been whacked—yet. Maybe he could thank his lucky stars the law caught the hit man, Candicci.

Before Mike left town, he bid farewell to Joe. "Come on down some time and see what's going on in St. Louis," he said. "We'll have a great time."

"I'd love to, whenever I get back. Maybe in three years or so," Joe said with a sigh. "But it won't be *theasible* by then unless I get out early for good behavior. I cut a five-year deal with the feds. At least it includes release from all charges and will be served at the nice, new federal residential facility north of Phoenix."

"You put them off for ten years on that sports management deal that went sour," Mike said. "Too bad you got involved with those bad guys in sports and didn't stick to the music business. Look at all you've accomplished in the meantime—a proud legacy to return to."

"I have a lot of confidence in Nick McGurk," Joe said. "When I get back, everything should be running smoothly—a legitimate business at last."

Despite all McGurk's entrepreneurial talents, had he really forsaken the mob? Organized crime was a business, and McGurk had an innate flair for it, as demonstrated by his innovative laundry and security operations. He was also ruthless enough to stay on top. But he was only two steps ahead of a shakedown—with the Detroit Outfit breathing down his neck. They were lying in wait, prepared to settle scores and pull the rug out from under McGurk if he ever let down his guard.

Patrick had made some big mistakes—one of them almost fatal. He'd been spared by good luck and the miraculous arrival of Kitty during his deepest despair, like Clarence, the guardian angel who appeared to George Bailey on Christmas Eve, in the 1946 Frank Capra film, *It's a Wonderful Life*.

Patrick and Kitty moved in together in a larger apartment, this one located on Lake Shore Drive. They made plans to fly Kitty's parents and eleven siblings over from Ireland and scheduled the biggest, grandest wedding ever celebrated at MacKenna' Irish Pub.

Patrick sighed with relief. Like Joe Bohannon, he was bone tired—of the rackets, the hassles of the big city and the constant threat of revenge by La Cosa Nostra. What if he followed Uncle Mike to St. Louis? If he stayed, he would not be through with the mob, he was sure. If he left, they could still find him. He concluded it didn't matter where he went. He was placing his bets on staying out of their sight and out of mind.

But it was a beautiful day, in this city's finest season. A sense of well-being buoyed him up and put spring back in his step. True, it was a city about as good or bad as any other, full of striving souls, burgeoning life, screaming pain and lonely death. A place rich, vigorous and proud, a city besieged, run down and defeated. "It all depends on where you sit and how you score," Patrick used to tell Chet, his colleague and best friend. He had scored about even, with as many wins as losses.

But the glass, which he once thought half-empty, for once looked half full. Now he cared. He would soon have a wife and a family to love, support—and protect. Maybe he could try to improve his city, be a force for good.

Could he get a second chance? He would never know if he didn't try.

About Author Peter Green

PETER H. GREEN, writer, architect and city planner, found his father's 400 World War II letters, his humorous war stories, his mother's writings and his family's funny doings too good a tale to keep to himself, so he launched a second career as a writer. His first book recounted the often hilarious antics and serious achievements of his father's World War II adventure, *Dad's War with the United States Marines*, Seaboard

Press, 2005. re-issued as *Ben's War with the U. S. Marines* in 2014 by Greenskills Press. His first novel, *Crimes of Design*, a Patrick MacKenna mystery, an intrigue of murder and sabotage set in St. Louis during the highest flood of record, first appeared in 2012 from L&L Dreamspell. It was republished, along with the second in this series, *Fatal Designs*, by Greenskills Press in Spring, 2014. He lives in St. Louis with his wife Connie, has two married daughters and three very young grandchildren. The story of the last pet his family owned, "The Night We Ruined the Dog," can be found on his website: https://authorpetergreen.com

Facebook Page: AuthorPeterGreen

Twitter handle: www.twitter.com/writerpeter

LinkedIn ID: Peter H. Green

Before you go....

Authors depend on the approval and reactions of our readers. If you enjoyed this book, please leave a brief review, even just a few lines, at this book's Amazon detail page, accessible from Peter's author page:,

www.amazon.com/Peter-H.-Green/e/B008749FPC

or on Goodreads, accessible from his author page:

www.goodreads.com/author/show/5864519.Peter_H_Green

Thank you!

ACKNOWLEDGMENTS

I owe many thanks to my late parents, Alice and Ben Green, both writers, who insisted I read steadily and write well. Without the love, forbearance and support of my wife, Connie, I would not have achieved what I have in my life and career.

I'm also indebted to a host of classic and modern authors, including mystery writers Arthur Conan Doyle, Georges Simenon, Agatha Christie, Dorothy L. Sayers and especially noir pioneer, Raymond Chandler. Particularly influential for this story were Charles Belfoure's, *The Paris Architect*, S. J. Rozan's Lydia Chin and Bill Smith architectural mysteries and the ever dark, heartfelt and atmospheric crime novels of James Lee Burke.

I would never have had the courage to pursue a second career in writing without "a little help from my friends"—fellow authors at St. Louis Writers Guild, celebrating its 100th Anniversary in 2020, the Greater St. Louis Chapter of Sisters in Crime and St. Louis Publishers Association. They include: T. W. Fendley. Catherine Rankovic, Claire Applewhite, Jennifer Stolzer, Brad R. Cook, David Alan Lucas, Fedora Amis, John Frain, Warren Martin, David Margolis, Ed Protzel and the many experts who come to St. Louis to speak to our organizations every year. Thanks also to editor Meghan Pinson, of My Two Cents editing, who made many helpful suggestions on the manuscript. I am especially grateful to my devoted beta readers, who have provided many excellent tips to improve this work: Rob Postill, Cherie Postill, Scott Miller and Jessica Matthews.

While others have contributed much to this book, any errors are mine.

—Peter H. Green., St. Louis, August, 2019

Readers praise Fatal Designs

Suspenseful coming-of-age story

In this action-packed sequel to CRIMES OF DESIGN, architect nd sometime-detective Patrick MacKenna not only has to worry about the seedier elements trying to take over the city, but his rebellious daughter...Erin MacKenna thinks her father is overly protective when he refuses to let her go on a float trip she helped organize. She goes anyway, and a series of disasters greater than he ever predicted place Erin and another girl in grave danger. The trip intended to expose inner city girls to nature and a different way of life instead teaches Erin some streetwise survival skills. Erin wrestles with her feelings for her first lover as she takes the initial steps toward independence among drug-dealing strangers who exploit women and kill those who stand in their way. She learns to value her father's protectiveness, while facing the life-altering consequences of her own actions.

—T. W. Fendley, Author of *Zero Time* and *Solar Lullaby*

Mystery solves more than crime

Peter Green's new mystery, Fatal Designs, is not just a "good read," but an important one, in my professional opinion. It brings up a critical topic, human trafficking, that is far more common than most people realize. It also reveals the dynamic evolution of a father/daughter relationship. Thank you, Peter, for showing the reader what that looks like! I recommend that parents buy this book for their teenagers as a way of starting conversations about these two vital topics.

—Anne Redelfs, MD – retired psychiatrist, Author of *The Awakening Storm*

A cast of believable characters ...

Peter H, Green, the king of disaster, both real and man-made, has struck again. As usual, murder was involved and Patrick MacKenna is in the middle of it all.

A high school canoe trip, earthquake and seamy underworld characters blend to form a psychological thriller worthy of James Patterson or Patricia Cornwell. MacKenna is still battling the emotional wreckage from losing his wife in a tragic accident he feels responsible for causing. Now, will he lose the rest of his family to drug dealers and human traffickers?

Erin MacKenna has also not done well since losing her mother. Will dealing with her overly protective father, harboring her own troubling secret and the Stockholm syndrome combine causing her to bond with her captors?

Green provides a cast of believable characters who cover the spectrum from good to bad to worse. With Green's prompting, the characters create a book you can't put down until you reach the last page. —W. Slade, Amazon Reader

St. Louis Sizzles

This book has it all—violence, sex and gritty language. A brutal murder with a twist grabs the reader's attention. Patrick MacKenna is dragged into solving this murder as he searches for Erin, his seventeen-year-old daughter, while he struggles with his professional obligations.

The characters in this book are haunted by personal demons. One of my favorite characters...is teen-aged protagonist Erin's "little sis" Aliesha who lives in a disadvantaged area of St. Louis, similar to pockets of Ferguson. Her quick thinking and common sense force the reader to love her despite her foul mouth...the reader hurtles through situations that deal with "kidnapping, drug dealing, child endangerment, human trafficking, conspiracy to commit murder, racketeering and teenage pregnancy."...this book realistically portrays vice and greed. It portrays plausible challenges for concerned parents when two well-grounded teens are confronted with deadly peril. —Paula B., Amazon Reader.

To buy this book, please consult the links on the website, https://authorpetergreen.com

www.ingramcontent.com/pod-product-compliance
Lightning Source LLC
Chambersburg PA
CBHW071139180726
48291CB00007B/2253